STELLA
QUINN

ISLAND FLING

THE ISLAND ESCAPE SERIES

STELLA QUINN

Antonia pulled her new jaffa-red suitcase from the carousel, teetering on her heels as the full weight of the case nearly knocked her over.

"What have you packed in that thing, Toni?" said Charlotte.

She gave her friend a grin. "I was panic packing, so I can't really remember. Random outfits, umpteen pairs of shoes, a polka dot bikini. I've never been to a wedding on an isolated coral cay before. I wasn't sure what the dress code would be."

"Mmm. You sure you haven't tucked a few pounds of work in there too?"

Antonia turned for the customs gate, pushing away the thought of her problems at the office. She'd spent the flight out working, so now she was taking a break from worry until Monday when she flew back to London. "A girl's got to eat, Charlotte. You want a hand with anything?"

Her friend smiled and rested a hand on the barely-a-bump baby belly that curved the front of her dress. "I'm fine. Jack turned into an overprotective mother hen the day I told him we were expecting again. If we deny him the pleasure of carrying my bags, we'll ruin his day."

Antonia slung her hand through her friend's arm. "You're a lucky girl," she said, her eyes resting on Charlotte's husband as he expertly wrangled two suitcases, a tote bag of toys and a fractious toddler into an orderly line.

"It was good of you to organize a charter flight from Ballena to the wedding, Jack," she said. "Thanks for including me."

Jack perched his son on his shoulders and gathered his wife into his free arm. "No problem. The thought of two planes, an island taxi, and a wet speedboat ride with a toddler in tow was making me lose my hair. Chartering a sea plane to the Manatee Cays was an entirely selfish gesture on my behalf, I can assure you."

Antonia grinned. There was enough hair on Jack's handsome head to rethatch the British princes. "Your sacrifice is duly noted."

The Manatee Cays. Just the name of it sounded romantic. She sighed, just a little, and wondered why a reunion with her old schoolfriends, Charlotte and Sabrina, should feel so bittersweet.

She adored her friends, she did, but marriage had changed their friendship, even though they'd sworn a pact it wouldn't. She could accept it, because she could see how happy they were. Charlotte had been the first to leave the sisterhood, and this afternoon, after Sabrina tied the knot with Ben on a scrap of sand in the Caribbean ocean, she'd be the only one still single.

Antonia Da Silva, spinster. *Spinster!* Whoever invented that hideous-sounding word should be sent into a dungeon and cursed.

She sighed. Her friends hadn't even been looking for love, and they'd stumbled across it. Not like her: she'd devoted her adult life—and much of her adolescent life, too, if she was honest—to the pursuit of romance and adventure, and where had it got her?

As a teenager, she'd dreamed of being swept off her feet, carried away to exotic locations, being feted and adored by some tough-jawed, soft-eyed prince charming. She'd long ago abandoned those silly notions. Mostly. And she didn't need to be swept off her feet to be carried away: she could run on her own two feet towards adventure. In stilettos, if she had to.

But for some reason, romance and adventure had proved elusive. All of the princes she'd found had developed warts, like a wife, or an on-again, off-again ex-girlfriend, or commitment issues.

She handed her passport over to the customs official and followed the Diamond family out into the glare of the airfield.

Ballena. She breathed in the salt and humidity. Her plane from London had arrived over three hours ago, but she'd not stepped outside the terminal yet. Waiting for Charlotte and her family to arrive from Hawaii, typing out a few urgent emails for work, spritzing her way through the perfumes for sale in duty-free—she'd been too busy to take stock of the view through the airport windows.

But here outside the airport terminal, it all came flooding back. Perhaps that was why she was feeling a little blue. It had been in Ballena, after all, that she'd had one of her failed romances.

She still bore the scars from that one—they were crisscrossed over her heart, the way she'd crisscross a manuscript when she was editing it. Only, when she was at work, editing the articles published in *Bella Magazine*, her marks improved the article. She was yet to work out how the marks left on her heart had improved her. On the contrary: some of the wounds to her heart felt like they'd never heal.

"Auntie Toto."

She felt a fat little hand tugging at her skirt,

smiled, and swung Charlotte's little boy up into her arms.

"Yes, my precious pumpkin?" She'd long since given up trying to teach Charlie how to say Auntie Antonia. She was fine with Auntie Toto.

"Charlie likes planes."

She smacked a kiss into his plump cheek, making him squeal. "Do you, Charlie? What about sea planes?"

The little boy looked around. "I see lots of planes, Auntie Toto."

She chuckled. "No, my lamb. We're going on a special sort of plane today, called a seaplane. Look, there it is, can you see it?" She pointed across the glaring concrete of the runway towards a neat little blue-and-yellow plane.

"I can see it."

"It's called a seaplane because it can land on water. That's what's taking us to Manatee Cays today."

The little boy slung his arms around her neck. "Charlie likes seaplanes," he said.

"Me too."

At least, she hoped she did. She'd never actually been on a seaplane before.

A baggage attendant had pulled ahead of them in a vehicle that looked a bit like a golf buggy and was towing their luggage in a metal cage. Charlie was entertaining himself admiring his reflection in the mirrored lenses of her sunglasses, so she didn't take much notice of the man in the pilot's uniform until she'd reached the airplane's tiny staircase.

But she noticed his voice.

"Jack Diamond," she heard Jack say, as he reached out a hand to shake the pilot's. "Thanks for meeting us here."

"You're very welcome. Four passengers, the booking says; so we're all here?"

That voice. Antonia peeled one of Charlie's hands away from her face so she could see for herself what her ears were refusing to believe.

The pilot wore whites: white shorts, a white short-sleeved shirt with epaulettes and stars that she barely processed because her eyes were skittering up to his face.

A pilot's cap was pulled low over his forehead, and his eyes were shielded by sunglasses. But that hint of dark hair shadowing his jaw...that flash of grin as he welcomed Jack and held Charlotte's arm to assist her up the narrow stairway into the tiny confines of the seaplane's cabin...

And then it was her turn.

Music was playing from the inside of the plane, a tinny little waft of Caribbean reggae that drifted down the stairwell alongside the smells of air conditioning and musty carpet. She had a sudden vision of herself, a flashback, looking up as she was looking up now, into the same face. But the time she remembered was three years ago, when her heart was still free of scars and she'd felt as happy and carefree as this music.

The pilot hadn't recognized her yet. His attention was still directed towards Jack and Charlotte as he pointed them to the tiny seats that furnished the interior of the plane.

But then his hand found the crook of her arm, and he was smiling as he turned to help her up the stairway.

"Watch your head as you step into the plane, ma'am, it's a low—"

She watched the smile drop from his face, and felt a teensy—okay, massive—amount of satisfaction as his jaw dropped slightly.

So. Maybe the rat hadn't totally forgotten her.

She hoisted Charlie around to her other hip and removed his fingers from her bottom lip, where he was busy trying to smudge her lipstick all over her face. "Captain Cooper. We meet again."

"Antonia."

He didn't sound overly thrilled to see her. Well, that made two of them; she wasn't overly thrilled to see him, despite the giddy somersaults her heart was flipping in her chest. She wouldn't have thought it possible to find a better-looking guy than the Tyler

Cooper of three years ago, but the living proof of it was standing before her. Three years had barely touched him; if anything, his jawline was more chiseled, his mouth even more delectable than—

She dragged her thoughts off his mouth and reminded herself that this was the guy who'd brought to a smashing end the most intense two weeks of her life. She'd been blissfully surfing the wild wave of romance and adventure she'd found in his company, and he'd wrecked it all.

She decided to swan past him as though she'd moved so far beyond him he was barely a recollection and mounted the stairs into the plane.

Jack took Charlie from her and buckled him into his seat, and Antonia moved through the tiny aisle. Charlotte gave her the googly-eyed look of interrogation.

"Captain Cooper? Were you reading his name tag, or do you know the guy?"

Antonia frowned at her. *Later*, she mouthed. She kept frowning as the captain entered the plane, pulled up the stairway after him, and made his way to the cockpit. What had he called their relationship, when he'd carved those scars into her heart?

Just an island fling.

TYLER FLICKED through the start-up procedure of his Cessna and tried to concentrate on the voice from the control tower talking in his ear. Every second word seemed to be Antonia.

Flight Alpha Yankee Antonia, you are cleared for Antonia...

He was losing it. "Control tower, this is Alpha Yankee 6446. Repeat clearance, over."

"Flight Alpha Yankee 6446, you are cleared for takeoff."

"Copy that."

Tyler took a second to shut down his emotions. He was good at that—he needed to be. Flying needed a cool head, and no one's head was cooler than his.

He flipped the switch on the intercom in the passenger cabin. "We've been cleared for takeoff. Please make sure your seatbelts are fastened. If you've not been in an amphibious plane before, you might find the takeoff a little steep. Nothing to worry about; we'll level out pretty quickly, and you'll be able to enjoy the journey over to the Manatee Cays."

There. The social part of the charter flight was over. He flicked a glance into the mirror that gave him a wide-angle view down through the cabin, then wished he hadn't. The copper-bright hair of the little boy shone in a shaft of sunlight coming in through the cabin window, and in the seat behind him, gazing over the airstrip, was Antonia. Those eyes—like honey melted through dark, sweet rum and her smile—as warm as it was generous. He felt a stab of pain, deep in the part of his soul that he'd locked firmly shut. His Antonia: the English girl he'd lost his heart to, back when he'd thought his heart was his to give.

Mind on the job, Tyler.

He grimaced. Even he was referring to himself by that name now. He couldn't remember the last time he'd been called by his real name. Shoving the thought aside, he pressed his finger to the ignition and watched the propeller sputter and then catch, its revolutions causing the body of the plane to judder against the brakes.

He used the flaps to guide the plane out through the apron markers and onto the runway, before clamping the brakes on. His hand tightened over the throttle—a hand that had once held the woman sitting barely eight feet behind him—and the plane's propellers ripped through the resolutions, faster and faster, until the fuselage rocked with leashed power. He felt the same urgent desire to yield, to release the brakes he'd had to clamp down over his own life the day he'd had to run.

He swore under his breath. He could never yield. Never.

Slipping the brake, he allowed the plane to surge

forward on the runway, feeling that release of tension he always felt with a joystick under his hand, and wings spread out to either side of him. The world below fell away, and the seaplane climbed, a push of power and ingenuity and cold-molded steel, up into the sky.

God, he loved flying.

He banked sharply to clear the congested airspace above Ballena International Airport, not unhappy to be leaving. Ballena served as a transport hub in the Caribbean. International flights serviced it daily, and tourists used it as a gateway port for the many smaller islands in the Caribbean—too many tourists.

He'd made money there, sure, back before he was spotted three years ago. Recognized by a dumbass minion from the drug cartel in the States, who knew his real name and his former occupation. He'd had to switch his base of operations to St Novia after that near miss. Kept his visits there short.

He could never rest easy, because one day, someone else would recognize him. He could never get involved with a woman, because they'd get caught up in the shitstorm that was his past life. He found his eyes traveling to the mirror once more— and his gaze locked with Antonia's.

Her hair was longer, its golden-brown curls clustering about her head like an angel's. A fallen angel, he thought, as a memory pierced him: wild days and wilder nights, from that crazy, idealistic, foolish two weeks they'd spent together back...when? When he'd been on the run so long, he'd forgotten how to be cautious.

Well, he'd learned his lesson.

There'd be no more trysts for him with beautiful women whose skin skimmed like parachute silk under his work-roughened hands. whose laugh could cut through his worries into the warmth he'd forgotten he possessed. The risk for the women was too great.

His eyes dropped to the little boy again. He'd made the right decision. Antonia had clearly moved on with her life. The two-foot-tall living proof of it was sitting in his wing-side seat and galloping a plastic dinosaur along the arm rest.

He hoped she was happy, even while a little part of him hoped she could never be as happy as she'd been when she was with him.

An accented woman's voice began speaking in his ear, and he acknowledged the message from the control tower. He was out of Ballena air space. Next stop, the Manatee Cays in Anguilla.

He switched the plane over to autopilot and pulled his clipboard out of his flight case. Paperwork was a necessary evil for any pilot, and his more than most, seeing as he was the boss and owner of this plane and half a dozen others. Island Escape Aviation was the only thing he cared about. The only thing he *could* care about.

A sqwark from his watch some time later let him know it was time to start paying attention. The whale-shaped mass of Anguilla was looming below them through the light cloud. He switched on the microphone that connected him to the cabin.

"Hi, everyone. We're just traveling up the east coast of Anguilla. Soon we'll be able to see the Manatee Cays come into view. There are two of them; we'll be landing in the lagoon of the larger cay, where we'll be able to motor over to the jetty and see everybody and their luggage disembarked without having to get their feet wet."

He dropped his eyes to the clipboard as he spoke, checking his flight plans for the next day. "I'll be returning to the cay tomorrow morning in time to collect you all at ten o'clock."

He flicked the microphone into the off position and checked his watch. About thirty minutes from now he'd be back in the air, making the short hop over to Saint Martin for a cargo flight. He nodded; two birds with one stone. He'd earn money from a charter to help him pay down his big-as-hell business bank loan, and he'd put a few hundred sea miles between him and the girl currently sitting in seat 2A on his plane.

It was a win-win.

His plan went belly-up on landing. Well, not quite belly-up, but it was enough to turn a few hairs grey, even on a seasoned pilot like him.

The problem was that Manatee Cays wasn't a designated seaplane port. It was barely a designated boat port. Why anyone would plan a wedding there, and expect guests to be able to make it, was more than Tyler could comprehend.

The only people who lived on the island were the staff and volunteers of a turtle conservation project, and they didn't fly in—they came over from the big island in a speed boat. None of them had thought to do a sweep of the lagoon for floating debris.

Tyler brought the plane down in a low swoop over the lagoon, angling his wings so he had the longest stretch of protected water for landing. He eased back on the throttle, skimming just feet above the waves pounding on the outer fringing reef. He felt the skids kiss the water and bounce, just a little. He eased the joystick back a fraction more, and the skids bit into the water, slowing them down into a nice easy glide.

"Piece of cake," he muttered, then bit off an oath as the bleached white back of a submerged log rolled under his port float. His hands tightened on the controls, and he hauled on the joystick, willing his speed to be enough to lift them clear of the danger. *A log!* Heaven only knew what other obstacles had slipped over the reef edge on a high tide.

They could have skimmed over it. They would have skimmed over it, but for a swell of wave moving across the lagoon which brought the end of the log up just as his port float passed over it, and then all hell broke loose.

The sea plane canted into a hard turn to left, and the crash and bang from behind him let him know his passengers' luggage and toys and handbags had just scattered from one end of the cabin to the other. He fought with the controls to keep the nose up, revving the engine to keep enough lift so the port wing didn't stab into the water.

That would be a disaster, and Tyler wasn't having a disaster today.

"Come on, girl," he muttered, and suddenly, the wing lifted and he was clear. He brought the sea plane to a sharp and shuddering stop in the calm of the lagoon, but rather than risk sinking at the jetty, he decided to motor in to the sand. Until he'd been out there and seen for himself, he didn't want to guess at what damage the log may have done to his float.

He pulled off his earphones and the cacophony from the cabin nearly ruptured his eardrums. The kid was crying, and three adult voices were making a valiant effort to calm him down.

"Charlie doesn't like sea planes," he heard the little man wail.

Tyler blew out a breath. If he was wailing like that, he hadn't been injured in the rough landing. He flicked the switch on the microphone.

"Rough landing, sorry, folks. The plane float hit a submerged log. I'm going to bring us up onto the beach in case the float's taking in water. There's nothing to be alarmed about." Nothing for the passengers, at least. A ruptured float was going to seriously stuff up his own plan to take off before he could fall under Antonia's spell again.

When he'd nudged the nose in to the beach, Tyler let the plane stairs flop open and made his way down them to where cool sea water lapped over his leather loafers. He sighed. They'd been wet before; they'd be wet again. He glanced at the float, at the gash running along the length behind the wheel hub. Wet shoes weren't the biggest problem he'd be facing today.

The lady with the auburn hair was the first to the door, with Jack's face peering round behind her. "My wife's pregnant. I'm sure she's fine—she assures me she's as tough as old boots—but if you could help her to the shore?"

Tyler swept her into his arms and carried her the few steps necessary to find dry sand. He set her on her feet. "You sure you're okay?"

She smiled at him. "I'm fine, Captain. Great job on a tricky landing."

The little boy was next, wide-eyed and wail-free. "We're at the beach, Daddy," he was saying, as Jack passed him to Tyler, who stood, arms outstretched, ready to receive the toddler.

Daddy? But that meant—

He shook his head. It didn't matter what it meant. He was the charter pilot today, nothing more. A pilot who had no business wondering whether his ex-lover did or did not have a copper-haired son.

Jack had made his own way down the stairs by the time Tyler made it back to the plane, and he lifted the luggage hatch for him.

"Thanks, pal."

"No problem."

Which just left Antonia. She stood on the sea plane steps, her silver heels slung in one hand, her sunglasses back on her face. The breeze over the water whipped at her dress, billowing it about her lean curves in ways that made him forget his promises to himself, the restrictions under which he had to live his life.

He held out his hand, and she raised her eyebrow at him. Then, after a second, she took it. Her warm fingers clasped his own, and it was as though the years between them vanished.

He could have let her wade to shore. Hell, her

shoes were already off. But the devil in him made him cast caution to the sea breeze. He tugged her hand, swept his arm beneath her knees so she fell on his chest, her body bumping warmly into his.

It took just four strides to walk her to the beach, but it was four strides too long. He felt his heart break one more time.

2

Oh god. Antonia squeezed down the sentimental balloon of want that had inflated when Tyler had scooped her up in his arms.

She *wanted* to be swept away, damn it. A strong man, clasping her to his chest, wading through shark-infested waters to carry her to safety on a palm-fringed shore. It was the stuff her dreams were made of—and destined to be just as short-lived.

And Tyler to be the one carrying her!

Before she'd had time to do more than sniff at Tyler's neck or feel the hard curve of bicep beneath his no-nonsense white shirt, she was being dumped on sand and he was striding back to the death trap which had just flown them here to the Manatee Cays.

Antonia sighed. Another day, another doomed romance. So what else was new?

Romance wasn't entirely missing from the day, however. Even her wistful—okay, jealous—eyes could see that. The crowd of onlookers waving and smiling at her from farther up the beach must have been the entire staff of the turtle project. College boys wearing frivolous board shorts carried scuba tanks and crates of gear. A magnificent yacht was moored at the farthest end of the jetty, where jewel-cool water deepened into cobalt.

Her eyes traveled to the happy couple welcoming the Diamond family farther along the beach, and her man-angst dissolved. Oh, how she'd missed her friends. She took two steps toward them, but she needn't have bothered. Sabrina, the bride-to-be, was flying towards her.

She squealed as Sabrina wrapped her into a fierce hug.

"Darling girl. I can't believe you're here."

Antonia held her away so she could look her over. "You look amazing. Engaged life agrees with you."

Sabrina dimpled. "You are so right. You remember Ben, of course?"

She snorted. She was human, wasn't she? With blood running through her veins and a pulse? Who could forget Ben?

He ignored the hand she held out to him and

wrapped her in a bear hug. "You put a gallop in our hearts when we saw that sea plane stumble, Toni."

"You know me. I love a dramatic entrance."

Sabrina was staring over her shoulder. "And, hang on a second. Isn't that—?"

"Don't ask."

This was the wrong thing to say in Ben's hearing. The man was a data processor on two fine-looking legs. "No way," he said. "Pilot uniform. Dark hair. Brooding attitude. Don't tell me that's the guy I promised to flatten on your behalf?"

"The one and the same. However, no need to get into that now. We've got a wedding to plan, and he's about to fly off into the big blue sky and break some other sucker's heart. Where's the champagne?"

Sabrina slung an arm over her shoulder. "Come on, then. Let's go up to the house and meet everyone properly. You can fill us in on the way."

She joined in with the gaggle of wedding guests making their way along a narrow sandy track. Charlie had found his feet and was walking hand in hand with a girl who must be Little Bess. Antonia had heard all about the island dwellers from Sabrina: Pablo, the Puerto Rican who ran the turtle project, and his Irish wife Maggie. Little Bess was their daughter. She couldn't be more than three, Antonia thought, as she watched the little girl in the frilly pink dress guide the toddler up the path. She'd been born about the time that Sabrina had first met Ben, by accident on his yacht. He had been volunteering on the project, and it was here, on this island, that they'd fallen in love.

Antonia ran her palm over lichen growing up a tree to the side of the path. Chilly London and the even chillier atmosphere that had overtaken her office seemed a long way away.

"We've put you in a tent, Toni," said Sabrina.

She laughed, enjoying the joke. "Of course you have."

"No, seriously, Toni. You're in a tent."

She frowned. "Have you met me, Sabrina? I don't do tents. I need an electric socket. A hair straightener. Hot and cold running water."

"Sorry, my love. The spare room in the house is for Jack and Charlotte, since she's the one who's carrying an extra passenger at the moment. Charlie's bunking in with Little Bess."

"Wow. It just doesn't pay to be single anymore, does it?"

Ben stopped outside a drab canvas lean-to in the clearing before the house. "Here's your stop."

He dropped Antonia's suitcase onto the grass. "The wedding's at three, so you've got about"—he looked at his watch—"four hours to have a swim, drink champagne, and cry over Sabrina while she buttons herself into her wedding dress."

"I so will not cry," she said. Which was rubbish; of course she would cry. Hadn't she packed waterproof mascara just for that eventuality?

Sabrina was grinning at her betrothed. "How do you know there'll be buttons?"

He pulled her in and smacked a kiss on her cheek. "Is this where I confess I snuck a look in the garment bag?"

Sabrina waved him off. "Go. I don't want to see you again until one minute past three. It's girl time."

They both watched him head back in the direction of the beach. Antonia found herself wielding her clutch purse like it was a fan. Ben was so calm and smiley. So besotted with his girl. So absolutely unlike Tyler Cooper.

"Does he have a brother?" she said. Clearly, she needed to rethink the type of guy she was attracted to. "I can't believe I've not thought to ask you that before."

Sabrina smirked. "Only child."

"Figures. The blows just keep coming, don't they?"

"Come on, Toni. Let's go find the others in the kitchen and crack a bottle of the good stuff."

"Okay. But I'm warning you, since Charlotte's got the bedroom, I'm having her share of the champers."

"It's a deal."

Linking fingers with her friend, she headed into the house.

THE KITCHEN LOOKED like a laboratory that had just blown up as a result of an over-ambitious experiment. A huge man with a head full of braided dreadlocks was icing a cake with the precision of a nanophysicist. Behind him, on counters and windowsills, lay test tubes filled with different colors of icing, measuring jugs and scales. A laptop had been wedged open on top of the fridge, and it was blaring an online tutorial on making icing rosettes.

Calmly ignoring the mess and noise was a tiny woman with a carrot top of red hair.

"Pablo, Maggie, this is Antonia."

"Our little friend! We have heard so much about you." Pablo dropped his icing bag and wrapped her in a cloud of powdered sugar and vanilla.

"Hello, Antonia." Maggie's welcome was just as warm, if not as sticky. "Bumpy landing, I hear?"

Antonia nodded. "Mmm. Some floating log started our day with a bang. What can I do to help?" She eyed the half-finished cake with mild alarm. She could follow an instruction video as well as the next person, but the cake was already buried in enough icing to make it seem more like an igloo than a dessert.

"You just got here, relax. Anyway, Pablo has it all under control. I hope."

"I've promised Antonia champagne," interrupted Sabrina.

"What a marvelous idea. Let's go into my bedroom," said Maggie. "I have all the wedding finery laid out in there. We can drink a glass to friendship and trade secrets about our menfolk."

"I heard that," said Pablo, his attention once more on the silver-spangled growth poking upward from the cake that may or may not have been a miniature version of a yacht.

"Why are you decorating the cake with spiders?" Antonia couldn't help asking, her eyes on the green-legged critters circling the base of the cake.

Sabrina chuckled. "They're turtles," she said. "Baby ones."

Pablo fixed them all with an intimidating stare and flapped his hands in a shooing motion. "Be gone, women. You are messing with my creative energies. Leave the kitchen to me."

Maggie collected a bottle of champagne from the fridge while Sabrina plucked glasses from an over-head cupboard. They left Pablo to his work of art, and Antonia found herself settled in a rattan chair under the fan in Maggie's brightly furnished bedroom.

A gown hung in a garment bag from a hook by the dresser, and the bed was littered with shoe boxes, parcels wrapped in silver paper, and florist boxes of bougainvillea and hibiscus.

"The flowers have arrived. How lovely," said Sabrina. The college kids must have collected them in the dinghy from Hawk Bay.

"Oh, forget all that for a minute," said Maggie. "There's time and plenty for fuss later. Let's put our feet up and catch up."

"Not without me," said a voice from the open doorway out to the veranda.

"Charlotte! I was wondering where you'd disappeared to."

"Charlie was keen to have a swim with his new bestie, so I've been holding him down while Jack greased him with sunscreen. They've gone to the beach. I suggested to Jack he might try and make it a long play—if he can wear Charlie out, he'll have a nap."

"Amen to that," said Maggie, as she popped the cork with a celebratory flourish.

"Budge over, will you, Toni?" said Charlotte, as she wedged her bottom into the space next to her on the chair. "Champagne already, girls?"

"We're debriefing," said Sabrina, as she gave Antonia a glass and a meaningful look.

Uh oh. This didn't sound good.

"About the pilot?" said Charlotte? "I *knew* there was something going on. Spill the beans, Toni."

Crap. These girls didn't miss a thing.

Maggie was looking from face to face. "Hey, come on. Don't leave me in suspense. The sea plane pilot? What are we debriefing about?"

Sabrina fixed Antonia with a stare that would have stopped a London bus in rush hour traffic. "Will you tell this story, or will I?"

She sighed. There was no getting out of this one. "Okay. Do you all remember when Sabrina and I first came on holiday to the Caribbean? It was about three years ago."

Maggie was nodding. "And Sabrina stowed away on Ben's boat."

Sabrina grinned. "Well. Not literally, but yes, that trip."

"Well," Antonia continued, "before Sabrina went galivanting about the open ocean in search of love and lust on the high seas, she and I were in Ballena. I met a guy."

Charlotte rolled her eyes. "When do you not meet a guy? Hang on a—" Her pregnant friend paused, her mouth comically agape. "Captain

Cooper, who just flew us here, is *your* Caribbean pilot? Tyler? The one you mooned over for months?"

Antonia took a sip from her glass, holding it for a second in her mouth while the dry pop and snap of French bubbles distracted her from her memory of those long, lonely months. There was always something to enjoy in the moment, even if she was being forced to recount a hideous memory from her doomed love life. And right now, it was champagne.

She nodded to Charlotte. "The one and only. Captain Tyler Cooper. When I met him...oh, he was divine. More than divine. Intense, focused, brooding—and totally into me. Or so I thought."

"What happened?" said Maggie.

"We spent two weeks together. I thought I'd found my forever man."

"Prince Charming," murmured Sabrina.

Antonia smiled at her old school friends, and they each leaned forward and held her hands. They all knew what a romantic sap she had been her whole life. She cleared her throat, and shook off the little ray of melancholy. They knew how affected she'd been by Tyler.

She turned to fill Maggie in on the unhappy-ever-after of her story. "But my forever man turned out to be more of a thirteen-day-and-six-hour man. Because that's how long we'd been together when he dumped me."

"The rat," said Maggie.

"Yes, that's what I thought. And I flew home to London with a deep tan and an even deeper wound slashed through my heart." Sniveling into her airline blanket the whole way, but her friends didn't need to know quite that much detail. "But then I did what any modern-day Cinderella would do when she finds herself at the ball with no handsome prince in sight."

Charlotte frowned. "I don't remember you doing anything besides mooching about your flat like a cloistered nun. It was most unlike you."

She sent her friend a huffy look. "I would never be so lame."

Maggie leaned forward. "Let me guess. You got drunk? You ate ice cream? You swore off men? You threw yourself into your career?"

"All of the above clichés, yes. But then I bought myself a nice shiny pair of new shoes, because who needs to be given a glass pair anyway? Although, they did give my credit card company a nasty fright. I'm probably still paying them off. Where was I? Oh, yes. And I decided who needs Prince Charming when you've got a great job and great friends, like I do."

Sabrina smiled. "I can drink to that."

"To friends," they all echoed.

Antonia polished off her glass. "And besides, it doesn't have to be too weird. Captain Cold-Heart will be gone by now. He's flying in to pick us up tomorrow morning at ten. Forty-five minutes later, when we land back in Ballena, I'll never have to see him again."

"Umm, Toni?"

"Yep?"

"I don't mean to burst your sunny bubble of optimism, but—"

"What?"

"Isn't that Captain Cold-Heart sitting out there by the firepit having a beer with Ben?"

3

Antonia stood on the white sand at the end of the beach track and gave the view a moment to etch itself into her memory.

To the right, the beach curved into a rocky break-wall, and perched above the rocks was a bleached timber jetty. Ben's yacht sat, serene and blindingly white in the noon sun.

To her left, the sand ran a hundred yards or more before a headland of palm trees and coastal scrub blocked the wider ocean from view. Anchored into the shallows was Tyler's plane.

She didn't see the man-camp set up at the beach until it was too late. She'd ditched her hat and sarong, and was ankle deep in the limpid aqua water of the lagoon before she noticed the huddle of experts crowded round the far side of the sea plane.

Beer time by the firepit had clearly been replaced by tool time.

She slid her sunglasses down her nose and looked under the belly of the plane to the shallow water on the far side. A flurry of squealing could be heard, where two little helpers, Charlie and Bess, splashed about in the shallows.

Hell. Well, she wasn't going to run away like Brave Sir Robin in a Monty Python skit. She was on a three-day holiday she didn't have time for, half a world away from the London winter and the career she was hanging on to by the skin of her teeth, and she was having a pre-wedding swim. It might be months before she got the chance again.

Voices carried across the calm water, and she heard the ripping sound of adhesive tape being peeled off a roll. "I've got epoxy resin on board, and fiberglass cloth. We could patch it like new if we had time for it to cure," Ben was saying.

"Too long. And the structure of the float hasn't been damaged, just the outer skin. If we can make it watertight, I can take off. I'll be landing on land, so I won't need to worry about water gaining entry then."

That was Tyler. She hoped he knew more about plane repairs than he did about relationships, or tomorrow's takeoff was going to be pretty darned hairy.

"It's all about the angles. On takeoff, the front

edge of the float is above the waterline, so if we use this gaffer tape it should be enough to keep the float from splitting further, and that's all we need."

Antonia rolled over onto her back in the warm water and tried to ignore the man talk. The sun was a golden orb high in the sky, and she squeezed her eyes shut beneath her glasses. Her hair flowed about her as fairy-sized waves eddied through the lagoon.

"What about a thin coat of epoxy over the tape? It'll dry by tomorrow, and double the strength of the patch. What do you reckon, Jack?" That was Ben again. Always thinking. He was a keeper all right; Sabrina was a lucky woman.

Jack sounded as though he was preoccupied with minding his non-swimming toddler. "Hey, don't ask me. I'm just here to wear out the youngsters. If you needed a cost-benefit analysis done on patch versus repair, I'd be your man, but all this epoxy and gaffer talk is above my pay grade."

"You got tools on board, Tyler?"

"Only a basic kit; they're too heavy to keep on board a light aircraft like this one."

"I'll grab you some tools from the *Silver Girl* and find that epoxy resin."

"Ben, I appreciate your help. But don't you have a wedding to attend in an hour or so?"

"Relax, Tyler. We run on island time out here. Who's in a hurry? Hey, kids, who wants a chocolate chip cookie? I think my boat has a secret cookie jar with some secret cookies in it."

Antonia rolled over onto her front and began a lazy breaststroke through the water. She wished she'd thought to bring a mask and snorkel down with her; the outer reef beckoned. The salt of the lagoon kept her so buoyant she barely had to move her arms and legs. She smiled as she heard the eager voice of young Master Diamond.

"Charlie likes cookies."

Her smile vanished as the trio of men rounded the nose of the plane, with their two little apprentices in tow. Three fine looking men: two of them taken, and the third a heartbreaker. She had so come to the wrong island.

"Auntie Toto! Do you like cookies?"

At least Charlie was thrilled to see her. Tyler stood by the propeller of the plane, his bare feet planted in the white sand, and for some reason known only to the cruel gods of fate, he'd taken off his shirt. She blamed the giddy rush she felt on the champagne. Drinking before she'd eaten lunch—what had she been thinking?

She certainly wasn't thinking now. But she was looking. The sun was stroking golden shadows over Tyler's arms and chest, and dark hair arrowed low across his muscled stomach. Heaven help her, he'd not grown less attractive over the three years since she'd last laid eyes on all that burly man flesh. He'd taken his sunglasses off, and his dark stare settled on her.

She cleared her throat. "No thanks, Charlie. I'm having a swim." She noticed Pablo and Maggie's little girl peering out at her from behind Ben's leg.

"You must be Little Bess," she said. "Hello." She waded out of the water and leaned down to shake the little girl's sandy hand. "I'm Antonia. But you can call me Toto too, if you like."

The youngsters seemed way more interested in raiding the cookie jar on Ben's boat than making small talk with her, and they proceeded to drag Ben up the beach, with Jack following behind carrying towels and sunscreen and a rainbow floaty unicorn.

Which left her. With Tyler. Alone. The silence lengthened between them, and Tyler was the first to break it. "So. How have you been?"

"Fine," she said brightly. Fine and lonely. Fine and single. Fine and dumped.

"And work going well? Still a...magazine editor, was that it?"

"I'm surprised you remember."

"Antonia." He reached out and grabbed her arms, above the elbow, and turned her so she faced him. "Don't be like that."

"Like what? Hurt?"

He rubbed his hand through his hair. "Hell." He

paused and opened his mouth to speak, but whatever he had been about to say stayed unsaid.

She pushed her sunglasses up into her hair so she could look at him properly. They were standing close. Too close, and they each had way too little on. Her polka dot bikini was dripping seawater down her skin, and every nerve ending felt like it had just woken up after a three-year hibernation in an ice cave.

And Tyler. Heat radiated off him like a plane engine after a long-haul flight. Her nose was level with his chest, and she could smell him, the salt and soap and sunshine of him.

A gull soared to a landing on the sand near them, but its harsh caw was less than a whisper in Antonia's ears, the vivid red of its feet barely a color. Tyler was all she could see. A shadow grew over his jawline, the promise of bristles to come—the scratch of which she well remembered.

The years had marked him, she realized now. Worry lines splintered out from the corners of his eyes, paler than the tan of his face. From long hours in the sky, she supposed, flying into a sun that was always bright, up there above the clouds.

Because what would Tyler have to worry about? When the going got tough, he got the hell out. She should know. When their island fling had been overshadowed by her looming departure—her life in

London, his life in the Caribbean—he'd not stuck around long enough to see what change could bring. He'd just thrown his hands in the air and pulled up his drawbridge—okay, airplane stairs—and flown off.

But even with the memory of being dumped percolating through her thoughts, she could not drag her eyes away. A connection sizzled between them, hotter even than the sun's rays beaming down on them on this isolated beach.

If he truly was the Prince Charming she'd been dreaming about ever since her hormones kicked in at age thirteen, music would be playing: something fluid and formal like a Viennese waltz. Woodland creatures would be tidying her hair, slipping a jeweled gown over her trembling shoulders. He'd be offering her a rose, or a slipper, or a claret-velvet ring box.

But he did none of these things. Instead, he swore, the rough language barely leaving his lips before his mouth landed, firmly, on hers.

The woodland creatures she had imagined trilling brightly about her head clamped shocked hands to their mouths, shrieked, and disappeared in puffs of smoke.

This was no fairy-tale kiss. This was no happy ending. This was the grit of out-of-control desire. This was racing hearts and jet-fueled pulses. This was a dark, intense man who'd ripped open his safety cord and plunged recklessly into the void.

Antonia didn't bother trying to catch her breath; she plunged equally recklessly with him.

Her hands reached up to grip his skull, her fingers sinking into his dark hair. She felt she could never be close enough. Her feet sank into the swirl of water over sand even as she arched upwards. The rough fabric of his tailored shorts bumped her salt-damp hips. His arm reached behind her, settled in the sway of her back and brought her in tight against him.

His lips moved on hers, and she moaned. In the months and years that had passed, she'd wondered if she'd misremembered the heat between them, exaggerated it, the way she might exaggerate a story to entertain her girlfriends over drinks.

But, no. Her memory was a pale ghost compared with this flesh-and-blood kiss. She could never have enough.

A small voice and the flap of something wet and plastic against the back of her leg broke her concentration, and she pulled her head back, startled.

Tyler's dark gaze was on hers. Shock. Lust. Regret. She recognized the emotions in his eyes because she felt them herself, only hers were overlaid with confusion. Why? Why would Tyler turn his back on this? Why had he done so before?

The wet plastic tapped into the back of her leg again, and she looked down. A rainbow unicorn floaty was tapping its horn into her leg, helped by its owner, Little Bess.

"Hello, Toto."

Antonia tried to get a grip on her flustered emotions. Tyler's arms had fallen away, and he'd stepped back from her.

"Bess! Umm, hello."

"Uncle Jack says it's time to stop kissing the pilot and get ready for the wedding."

She felt a flush rise from her collarbone up through her cheeks. She shot a glance over to the *Silver Girl*, but no one was in sight. Her gaze traveled over to the track which led away from the beach up to the house, and Jack stood there, a sleepy Charlie perched on his shoulder, grinning.

"Crap."

"What's crap, Toto?"

Antonia raised eyes to the heavens, even as she heard a snuffle of laughter from Tyler. Really. This was not how she had imagined her day was going to unfold.

"Crack," she said brightly. "I said crack. Let's crack on, shall we? That's what we say in London when it's time to get busy."

Little Bess held out her hand, and Antonia took it. She stopped to gather her sarong and hat from the beach where she'd left them, and turned to take a last look at Tyler as she left the beach.

He stood by the water's edge, tall, remote, staring back at her.

He looked very alone.

4

Tyler dunked the brush in the foul-smelling bucket of epoxy and applied a thick coat over the patchwork of tape holding his plane together. He didn't mind the maintenance work that came with the job when you earned your living flying between the remote ports of the Caribbean.

It was honest work. And he valued honesty, especially now that his whole life was one damned lie.

Although, he'd not been honest with Antonia, but how could he be? She had a life, a career, dreams—and all of those could be snuffed out in an instant if she was with him and he was recognized.

He dropped the brush into the jar of cleaning solvent and hammered the lid back on the tin of epoxy, sealing off the noxious smell within. He wished he could seal his emotions off as effectively.

Five years. That's how long he had been living the lie that was Tyler Cooper. He snorted. It was a name he'd written on a beer coaster in a crack den the day his life ended.

He didn't dwell on it, much, because what was the point? He could never go back to that time, and he got satisfaction out of his planes, running his business, turning a profit.

And he sure as hell didn't miss being shot at and tortured. The drug cartel had broken three of his fingers before the Baltimore police arrived. Beaten the living crap out of him until he was more dead than alive. To this day, he still didn't know how the drug lord, Pavlov, had found out he was an undercover narcotics cop.

He shoved his toolbox into the open hatch of the plane and slammed the door shut, letting the double-riveted skin of aluminum take some of the frustration that simmered in his veins.

He'd been careful. And he'd been good at his job. Four years undercover, six years before that in uniform. And about ten years before that as a foster kid running amuck in the big city. Oh yeah, he could blend in with crooks, all right—he'd not been the reason his cover had been blown.

The sound of music drifted above the rustling

gray-brown leaves of the mauby bark trees, and he lifted his head. The wedding must have started. The groom, Ben, had urged him to join in the festivities, and a little red-haired woman with an Irish brogue and a name he couldn't remember had brought him down a bacon-and-egg sandwich and an open invitation.

Hell. He had nothing to do here at the plane besides watching epoxy dry, and he was about ready to sell his shirt for a cold drink. Dropping his pants onto the dry sand, he threw himself into the lagoon to wash off the grime. The water was warm, like lemonade with not enough ice in the glass. The tide had dropped over the course of the day, and the afternoon sunlight beat through the shallow depths.

He hung suspended in the balmy salt and let the sea soothe his ragged edges. He'd been mad to kiss Antonia, but there was something about her that had snuck in under his defenses and left him feeling raw. Vulnerable.

Waves lapped at his shoulders, cooling him so he could think. He knew why she had power over him; he just didn't like to admit the truth of it. She'd cared for him, and he'd had little enough of that in his life for it to hurt like a boot to the ribs when he had to turn his back on it.

His mother hadn't cared. She'd been too nose deep in drugs to think twice about her son. Left to her, he may well have ended up working for Pavlov for real. No, the first woman who'd cared about him had been a snarky schoolteacher, who'd given him detention and mothering in equal measure, both of which he'd been in sore need of.

Drums and brass instruments clamoring some hot Caribbean track shimmered over the water, carried to his ears by the breeze. He smiled, just a little. Whatever was going on up there with this lively crew of people sounded nothing like any wedding he'd ever attended.

Who knows, maybe he'd even like these people, if he wasn't what he was. He had a fondness for music. When he made cop, then detective, then got poached by the Narcotics division and finally had enough money in the bank to buy himself a home, he'd filled it with music. Bought a piano, just because he could. He might even have gotten around to taking lessons if he'd stayed in Baltimore.

He'd had a fondness for flying, too, which was why he'd spent his days off earning himself a pilot's license. Luck or fate, he wondered? Flying was the only thing he'd had left when his cover was blown and he'd had to get out of the States.

They'd offered him witness protection, but by the time the police made it to the crack den where he was being held, the drug cartel had fled and there was no one left to arrest, which meant there was no way to find out the ugly truth: who had ratted him out? He couldn't trust anyone, not even the cops on his own squad.

He'd accepted the new ID the witness protection officers had offered. He'd accepted a few IDs, but Tyler Cooper was the one that had stuck. He'd let them spin their bullshit story to the press about the bleed in the brain that took him, so that when his body arrived at the hospital he was pronounced D.O.A.

Then he'd made his own escape plan. He'd lived undercover long enough to know how to move around off the grid. He headed south, and he kept on going, not looking over his shoulder, not stopping until his healing fingers had stopped throbbing, his battered ribs had eased up bitching.

He didn't stop until he reached the Caribbean.

Then he'd drunk himself stupid for a while—he missed his life, his cat, his damn piano that he couldn't even play—but when his lawyer came through with the money from the sale of his town-house, he bought himself a beat-up Cessna. Island Escape Aviation was born the same day.

Ducking under the water until the need for oxygen felt like a kick to the chest, he made his decision. He'd go to the damn wedding, but he'd be keeping a wary eye on his long-ago lover. She couldn't be allowed to breach his defenses again.

SHE WAS WEARING RED. Not some washed-out, half-assed version of the color, but eye-smacking, burning-down-the-house red. There were other guests gathered under an arbor twined with palm fronds and flowery things—there may even have been a bride and groom there exchanging vows—but he didn't notice. His eyes were locked on to Antonia like iron filings to a compass.

Her skin was burnished gold in the late afternoon light. He wondered what lucky blend of genes had managed to meld in the making of her: that wild crown of hair, the amber gleam to her skin. She looked at home on this island that skirted so close to the tropics.

He tried to imagine her in London. He'd been there years ago, before he made detective, on a holiday with a long-forgotten girlfriend. Tracy? Stacy? Bleak streets, and rain so constant he'd had a hard time working out where the streets ended and the muddy river that cut through the city began.

Antonia sitting at a desk in an office in a glass-sheathed high rise, mouth pursed and prissy as she dragged lines of red pen through pages of double-spaced type...nope. He couldn't imagine it. She'd be a hothouse flower trapped in a cold glass conservatory.

"They always know when you're looking."

Tyler frowned at the kid who'd stopped beside him and accepted the beer he was offered.

He took a long swig. "Who always knows?"

"Chicks."

Chicks? The kid didn't look old enough to shave, let alone be handing out relationship advice to strangers over bottles of beer. "Who are you?"

"Mickey. I'm a volunteer here at the sanctuary, third time. Marine biology major."

"Tyler," he said, and forced himself to concentrate on the kid rather than risk his gaze locking back on to Antonia. But the kid was looking over his shoulder, a grin on his face like he was a young dog who'd just spotted an unguarded sausage.

"What's so funny?"

Mickey chuckled. "I told you, they always know."

Tyler turned so he could see what Mickey was looking at. Antonia was staring at him from across the grass, a glass of champagne in her hand and a militant sparkle in her eye.

Crap.

Antonia had known the instant Tyler had walked into the clearing. The bittersweet rush of longing nearly brought her to her knees.

She pushed back at the feeling. She spent a moment trying to pull herself together, then decided to hell with it. What were weddings for, if not an occasion for its guests to get a little emotional?

"Our little Sabrina, look at her now, Toni."

She linked her fingers into Charlotte's, who stood beside her, and dragged her attention back to the bride and groom. "Who would have thought? Do you remember when she locked herself in the bathroom at school because she didn't get an A on her biology test?"

"Mmm. And how she always had to have her socks turned over just exactly right."

She laughed. "I'd forgotten that. I gave her a broken cookie once, and it was like I'd handed her a dead hedgehog. And here she is, getting married barefoot to a free spirit like Ben."

"A handsome free spirit," said Charlotte.

"Oh, yes." Antonia fanned herself with the bouquet of frangipani Little Bess had made for her. "Speaking of handsome..." She let her words trail off dramatically.

"What? Antonia! Wait, is that a twinkle in your eye? You know I don't trust that twinkle. How much champagne have you had?"

She couldn't stop the secretive little smile from emerging. "So, the Captain kissed me."

Charlotte reared back like a comic book hero

evading a villain's wild punch. "Hang on a second. I thought he was a heartbreaker. A rat. Captain Cold-Heart."

"Oh yeah. But he can kiss. And I didn't have time to think about the pros and cons of it. He just grabbed me by my arms and hauled me into him and pressed all that manly man-ness into me, and I swear we were kissing like the world was about to end."

Charlotte's mouth dropped open. "Tell. Me. Every. Detail."

Antonia sighed. "But then Little Bess interrupted us, and the mood switched from awesome to awkward in about a nanosecond."

"Little Bess?"

"Yep. On the beach, she was with Jack and Charlie. Where is the little man, anyway?"

"Fast asleep in Bess's old cot, I hope. Jack and I are taking turns checking on him. But now I've heard your manly man-ness kissing story, I might have to drag Jack up to the house with me for the next check."

"Really, Charlotte. You're a mother now. Tidy away those naughty thoughts."

Her friend grinned. "Oh, Toni, it's so good to see you. I miss you terribly, now we're all living so far apart. They were fun days working on *Bella* magazine, weren't they? When we were young and full of ourselves and thought the world was ours."

Antonia grimaced. "Certainly more fun then than now."

Charlotte narrowed her eyes. "What do you mean? Is something going on at *Bella*?"

She shook her head. "Nothing I can talk about. Sorry," she added, as she saw her friend start to speak. "There's change afoot, and we've all been sworn to secrecy. The magazine business has taken a big hit since online news content became king. I'll know more after the meeting with the owners of *Bella* next week. Until then, I'm a closed book."

Charlotte gave her hand a squeeze. "I could worm it out of you," she warned.

Antonia grinned. "You could try. This meeting's going to be the start of a huge shakeup, that much I can say. It's the reason I couldn't make this trip more of a holiday. I need to be at that meeting."

Her friend frowned. "You're not worried about your job, are you?"

She shrugged. "No. Yes. Maybe a little. But if I am, I'm not worrying about it today. Today is celebration day."

Charlotte gave her a hug. "It sure is. And you haven't even cried yet. I thought weddings turned you into a watering pot."

"They usually do. Why, I wonder?" She shot a quick glance to the far side of the clearing, where a tall, dark-haired figure stood on the edge of the party. Someone had switched on fairy lights as the afternoon shadows slipped into dusk, and the coastal scrub was dark behind Tyler's white uniform. "I used to think I cried because I was happy for the couple. Then I wondered if I cried because I was sad the day wasn't all about me."

She felt an upwelling of optimism and hoped it wasn't a side effect of the champagne she'd been helping herself to with abandon. "But today I don't feel at all weepy. I feel like seizing the day."

"Oh oh," murmured Charlotte, whose eyes had followed the direction of hers. "Toni, be careful. Do you really want to get hurt again?"

"I'll tell you what I don't want. I don't want to be a cynic." She didn't want to give up on love, that was the truth of it—and she didn't want to go back to London wondering about what could have been.

She spied Jack coming down the front stairs of the house with a ball of toddler energy clinging to his back. "I think your menfolk are looking for you," she said, and made her escape. She had plans on the other side of the clearing.

"I think we should talk."

Tyler's eyes met hers but they held no expression.

This Tyler held little resemblance to the man she remembered. "I've got nothing to say."

"You were saying plenty on the beach with your hands and your mouth."

He shrugged. "I was scratching an itch."

She heaved in a breath. If her dress wasn't so damned tight, she'd have passed out from the influx of oxygen to her brain. "An itch," she murmured, keeping her voice low so as not to attract attention.

She saw Charlotte in a huddle with Sabrina out of the corner of her eye, both of them looking at her with suspicion. She sent them a bland smile. Let them wonder, her two smug married friends. She was single, damn it, and if she wanted to dangle herself in front of a high-risk-of-heartbreak pilot, she'd do it. Even if he was calling her an itch.

Besides, maybe it meant she was getting under his skin. He was sure getting under hers.

"Perhaps I've got an itch of my own," she said.

He drank the last of the beer from his bottle and tossed it into the cardboard box that was doing duty as a trash can. "Don't push me, Antonia."

"Why?" She'd had just enough wine to read his statement as a challenge. She stepped in closer to the fray. "Maybe you need a bit of a push."

"Not from you. Not from anyone."

"No one kisses like that and walks away, Tyler. What's really the problem?"

She eased in another step, so the ruffle of her dress nudged his shirt. The balmy climate, the scent of bridal flowers sweetening the sea breeze—her senses were in overload, and she wanted more. "What about a dance? For old time's sake?"

"I don't dance."

"Umm—yes. You do. You taught me to salsa, remember?"

His lips twitched. At last, the wooden-faced man was waking up. She felt like reaching out and pulling his nose, to remind him he wasn't Pinocchio. He *was* a real boy.

"Just one dance," she said. "I want to salsa in my new frock under the Caribbean sky."

He didn't want to. Or did he? She was having a hard time reading the expression on his face. She raised her arms, clicked imaginary castanets, swished her hips in a flirtatious manner that made her skirts rise and fall.

Faster than her champagne brain could compute, she found a warm hand placed in the small of her back, bringing her in close to six feet of brooding, pulse-fueled male. Her own pulse went from zero to sixty in less than a breath. Tyler's hands found hers, lifting them high and wide, as though the two of them were paused on the threshold of a lover's embrace. Her eyes locked on his, but then they were moving, and she had no time to think about the heat that linked them. The dance had begun.

Knees whispered together, then fell apart. Hips bumped and shifted.

"Three steps to every four beats," said Tyler, as he applied pressure to her arm to remind her where to step.

She laughed, tossed her head, worked a stamp and swivel into her next turn. "It's coming back to me."

The music coming out of speakers tied into the trees paused, allowing the hubbub of voices and laughter to fill the clearing, but then a giddy mix of congas and horns blared through the air; someone had put on a salsa track and cranked the volume up to party level.

Antonia spied Pablo coaxing his wife Maggie up from her chair. His beaded dreadlocks shook almost as much as his, err, bon-bons. Was that the term? She grinned as a surge of dancing couples found the rhythm and bumped them to the side of the grassy clearing.

Tyler let go of one hand, and she spun out, breathless, her skirts a flurry of red beneath, her heart a flurry of joy above, before returning to land against his chest. The rasp of hair on his jaw grazed her temple, and she shut her eyes for a second, wanting to hold on to the moment.

If a second was all she could have, she was taking it. But if she could have longer, she was taking that too.

She stretched up onto her toes and whispered into Tyler's ear.

"You see that tent pitched over near the jalopy?"

Tyler's eyes flicked to the tent, but he said nothing.

"It's mine, and I'll share it with you. Tonight."

The sway of hips and limbs ceased. Tyler looked down at her, his expression shuttered. He pulled his hands from hers, and she read the *no* on his face before he said the words.

The bubble of joy she'd been flying on popped, and she took a step backwards, suddenly feeling very alone amid the throng of dancing, laughing, buoyant couples.

"Don't wait up," said Tyler. And he turned and walked off into the darkness.

Something snapped in Antonia's brain. Why was he always walking away from her? She knew he felt something for her, he had to. The chemistry between them would have been obvious from a jumbo jet flying overhead at thirty thousand feet. Why was he so set on denying it?

She pursed her lips and set off after him down the dark sandy track. "Wait. Tyler, wait!"

His shadow paused, ghostlike beneath the spread

of branches, the white of his uniform picking up the faint light from the moon.

She stood before him, waited until his eyes were on hers. "Please, Tyler. It's the not knowing that I can't stand. Why do you keep turning away from me? Can't you see how much it hurts me?"

His dark eyes were unreadable, the grim set of his face chiseled like axe marks into granite. "There are worse hurts than this, Antonia," he said, and resumed his walk to the beach.

5

The waves reminded Antonia of horseshoes from up here in the sky, as though a string of wild horses had galloped across the deep blue ocean, kicking up crescents of white seafoam. She gazed down at the sea through the tiny oval window while the propeller droned on and on, its noise pummeling through her head. Her brain felt filled with rocks, which were all grumbling about in her headspace, unable to settle.

Someone should have told her: small planes and headaches don't mix. Apparently, neither did champagne followed by Jamaican rum followed by throwing yourself at sad-eyed loners at island weddings.

She sighed. She'd made a fool of herself, and now as punishment, she had to spend forty-five minutes trapped in a flying metal tube with the man she'd made a fool of herself for.

She kept her eyes away from the cockpit. The romantic comedy she'd tried to read lay open on her lap, its characters too happy for her current state of mind. Who were these vivacious women whose dialogue sparkled like diamonds and who managed to turn a no-win drama with a shirtless hero into a happily ever after by page three hundred?

She was fun, wasn't she? She'd been known to crack a joke, and she could ogle well-honed abs as well as the next person. Only, her happily ever after was always just a distant dream.

She stroked a finger down the page, the words blurring into a black-and-white river as her eyes filled. She was a fool for love. Tyler had no interest in her, he'd made that abundantly clear. Over and over. And she'd been carrying on like her wants and needs were more important than his.

He wasn't interested. How many times did he have to tell her? How many times was she going to allow her foolish heart to break?

She felt a hand on her knee. Charlotte was looking at her, squeezing her hand.

"Toni? Are you okay, my love?"

How she adored her friends. Even the smug married ones, like Charlotte and Sabrina. In the takeoff, they'd circled low over the lagoon of the

Manatee Cays. *Silver Girl* had left its mooring in the early hour of dawn, Ben and Sabrina on their honeymoon, sailing where the winds took them. They'd flown over the yacht, its sails set, its hull a white streak pointed to a distant horizon.

Tyler had waggled the plane's wing tips at them, then turned for Ballena.

Tyler. Just thinking his name brought a rash of color creeping up her cheeks. After her bold offer and his curt refusal, she'd struggled to keep a smile on her face. Not wanting to spoil the festive mood for Sabrina and Ben, she'd hidden in the kitchen for a while and dried dishes with the volunteers manning the sink. Their college banter had filled the small space, and she'd not needed to pretend to be happy there.

She'd crawled into her tent after the groom had thrown Sabrina over his shoulder and manhandled her back to the boat, and she'd lain there, brooding —okay, crying—until the music faded and the wind rose and she'd drifted off to sleep, alone.

The thump-squeak of rubber tires biting into the runway tarmac snapped her out of the doze she'd fallen into.

At last, Ballena. Saying goodbye to Jack and Charlotte and Charlie so they could rush off to their connecting flight would be gut-wrenching, but then? Coffee. A vat of it, big enough to drown in, black and strong and mind-numbing, while she sat in an impersonal chair in an even more impersonal café and tried to blot out the last sixteen hours of humiliation.

TYLER PUNCHED through the post-flight checks on the instrument panel and listened to the propeller's whine thin, then cease. For once, the silence was unwelcome. As long as the drone of the engine and the buck of the joystick had claimed his attention, he'd been able to keep thoughts of Antonia at bay. Just barely.

He passed a hand through his hair, wincing as his fingers caught in the salt-tangled mess. He'd swum at dawn to shake off one of the shittiest night's sleep he'd had in years. It wasn't the first time he'd bunked with his plane overnight on a remote island atoll, and he kept a yoga mat rolled up in the cargo hold for just such an occasion—and no pilot flew without a kitbag to get them through an unscheduled layover. But it was the first night he'd camped out on an atoll knowing he was about three hundred yards away from a mattress and a woman...and not just any woman but *the* woman. Antonia.

What a disaster. And now she looked like

someone had taken a sledgehammer and bashed all the fun and bubble of her personality into oblivion.

He looked down at his hands, hands that could remember every curve and lean plane of her body, every beating pulse, every tangled curl. That was the trouble, he could remember everything, including the way he'd turned her down last night. What choice did he have, damn it?

Guilt ate away at him like rust on a poorly painted strut, but he forced it aside. Guilt was nothing compared to the misery Antonia would endure if he allowed her into his life.

He blew out a breath. Enough procrastination; it was time to lead his passengers into customs to clear their arrival. He pulled a passport down from the clip where it habitually lived and flipped it open to the photo page. It was him all right. The photo was an old one, taken on that crazy night when his world imploded and he became Tyler Cooper. The witness protection detail assigned to getting him out of Pavlov's reach had taken excellent photographs, then exercised their considerable talents doctoring them to make them as crap as an ID photo could be. Black hair, pushed back from his face so it could have been short or long, wavy or straight. Eyes open but shuttered, jawline shadowed and unkempt. He could be anyone or no one—which was how he'd felt ever since.

"You poor schmuck," he said to the picture of his younger self. Punching numbers into his phone, he sent a message to Aviation Fuel Supplies to bring a fuel truck over to his plane, then climbed out of his seat. It was time to bring this unhappy reunion to a close.

Door. Stairs. Thank you for flying with Island Escape Aviation. Cargo hold. It was a four-step process, and Tyler had managed it hundreds of times without faltering. Why would today be any different?

His passengers all made it out of the plane and onto the painted path leading to the customs door at the terminal. Antonia stood apart, hat low, sunglasses on, her face unreadable beneath. Just as he was returning the flip out stairs into their lock position, the wailing began.

"Bongo, Bongo, Bongo, Bongo. Where's my Bongo?"

The kid's mother dropped her bags and started rifling through them. The father, Jack, patted his pockets, then frisked his son's pockets.

"Jack, when did you last see it?" said Charlotte. "I've got pregnancy brain this morning. I can barely remember what I had for breakfast."

Jack frowned. "Bongo was in his cot this morning. Then he came for a swim with us—sorry, it's a blank after that."

"Perhaps you have pregnancy brain too, my love," said his wife, her hand on her husband's arm.

"You know me. Mr. Empathetic."

Tyler looked at his watch without trying to make it obvious. He had to clear customs, see the maintenance crew about the tear in his float, contact his booking agent to check they'd found a replacement pilot for the cargo job he'd not been able to do the day before...and all that had to be done before he could attend to the real business of the day, which was numbing his bruised heart with a well-earned shot of whiskey followed by a cold-as-hell beer.

Charlie had opened his mouth to cry, and his desperate wail of "Boooooonnnggggooo" broke the mood of his parents, who seemed to have gotten lost staring into each other's eyes. Tyler rolled his own eyes. Hurry up, he implored them silently.

Antonia cleared her throat. "He had it on the plane. When we flew over *Silver Girl*, Bongo was waving to the boat through the window."

"Bongo drums can wave?" he asked, before he could stop himself.

Antonia shot him a withering look that even her hat and sunglasses couldn't disguise. "Bongo is a dinosaur, Captain. Of course he can wave."

She knelt down beside the sobbing toddler. "I bet he can jump too, can't he, Charlie? Shall we see if he jumped down off your seat in the airplane? Maybe Bongo's gone exploring."

The kid seemed quite struck by this idea.

Tyler sighed and pulled the keys back out of his pocket. He could see the fuel truck approaching, at least, so maybe the whole day wasn't going to be a disaster. Just this bit.

"Make it snappy, will you, Captain?" said Antonia, her tone inferring he was some inept servant she'd been saddled with. "We don't want Bongo starting up the engine and flying off back to the cretaceous era."

He frowned at her over his shoulder, then flipped the stairs back down. A stampede of toddler and parent feet sounded behind him, so he held up a hand. "I'll look. You relax."

"Two big hind legs," he heard Antonia murmur. "Little grasping hands. A head like a brick with heartless black eyes. I think you'll recognize Bongo when you see him."

He spied a flash of red under a seat in the cabin and fished out the recalcitrant toy. So Antonia was feeling a little waspish, was she?

Finally. The toy safely delivered to its owner, Tyler locked the plane again and directed his group to follow the painted lines leading to the customs door. The Diamond family had a tight connection to the mainland, and hurried ahead, leaving him walking in Antonia's wake.

She was wearing an outfit wholly unsuited to traveling across the globe from a tropical island to London's Heathrow airport. Her shoes had to be, what, three inches high? And strappy. Thin bands of leather wrapped her ankle in crisscrosses of bold orange. His eyes lingered on the tanned length of leg above, before settling on her dress. Silk? Was that what that floral and ivory stuff was called? Whatever it was, it had a mind of its own, clinging and releasing her curves as she walked. Its hemline shivered with every step.

"Antonia."

She paused mid-stride, the rumble of her suitcase wheels coming to an abrupt halt.

He'd spoken her name without knowing what he would say next. In a few moments, he and she would clear the customs counter and he'd never see her again. Which was for the best, he reminded himself. For her, if not for him.

This was his chance to say goodbye.

A warm breeze smelling of ocean and spices and aviation fuel wafted over them, snagging at Antonia's hat. She took it off and stuffed it into her hand luggage. She raised her sunglasses and popped them into her hair, her eyes resting expectantly on his.

"So this is it," she said.

He nodded. She was right. This *was* it. "I hope you have a good life, Antonia. I really hope that for you."

"Yeah. Me too, Tyler."

She looked as though she wanted him to say something, anything—but what was there to say? There was no way to make this more bearable. There was no way to make this cut clean.

Her lips tightened, then she turned to the airport building, dragging her luggage behind her. The automated door opened with a whoosh, and she walked over to the counter with him following. Their moment alone was over.

Whoever was in charge of servicing the air-conditioner that cooled the customs shed had done a mighty poor job of it. Two strands of electrical tape tied to the vents barely lifted the thin stream of air; the room, when he followed Antonia into it, was a sauna.

She slapped her passport on the counter, and he moved in beside her. To stop himself from saying anything foolish, like *Don't leave*, or *I love you*, or *I don't care where you are in the world, you'll always be mine*, he filled the void with something banal.

"The best coffee in the terminal is at a place called Hasta Luego, if you still like coffee as much as you did three years ago."

Antonia turned, then almost smiled at him.

"Tyler, the promise of a coffee is all that's getting me through this day."

"I hear you." He smiled back at her, letting the warmth of the moment soothe his heart. It was a happier parting memory than their tense conversation on the beach track last night, and he could be grateful for that, if for nothing else. He cleared his throat, then moved his glance across to the customs official seated behind the counter.

Tyler's eyes met the startled gaze of the customs guy, and in the millisecond of time it took him to work out he'd seen the guy before, in his old cop life in Baltimore, he realized he had just made a catastrophic error.

Three things snapped into Tyler's brain.

The first was that the official behind the counter wasn't Junita or Miguel or Sam or any of the others he'd come to know over the years he'd been flying safely out of this airport.

The second was that he knew exactly who this guy was: Consuelo Garcia, otherwise known as Flaco. The Latino man seated at the counter, staring at him as though he'd just been handed a parcel and didn't know quite whether it held a lotto ticket or a bomb, was the skinny lowlife who'd run the street sellers for the Baltimore drug boss Pavlov.

The third was the kicker, the enormous, life-changing firecracker of a fact. He, Captain Idiot

Cooper, had just smiled at Antonia like some addled, lovestruck teenager. He'd just handed Flaco the leverage he needed to drag him in, like a dog, to face Pavlov's justice. They'd take Antonia, they'd use her as bait to catch him, then they'd kill her.

It was what they did.

He reached his hand out to snag back Antonia's passport but Flaco was faster and grabbed it off the bench. Tyler breathed out, hard, like a bull about to charge. Instincts honed by a life on the street, on the job, on the run kicked in.

He scanned the room for cameras, found plenty of them twinkling down on the drama playing out around him. He couldn't rip the passport out of Flaco's hands. He couldn't walk into the terminal. The second he left the customs shed, Flaco would be on his phone to his boss.

There was no chance Flaco was no longer connected to Pavlov. Zero. Once you were in, you were in for life. The only way you got out of your apprenticeship with Pavlov was in a six-foot-long pine box.

He might make it through the terminal, but as soon as he was in the streets, he'd be a dead man. A bullet to the spine. A knife to the heart. And if they missed him, they'd take Antonia.

He swore. There was only one escape route, so he took it.

Antonia was standing patiently at the counter, her burnt-orange fingernails doing a little tap dance on the scratched formica, oblivious to the storm headed her way. She jumped when he grabbed her arm.

"Run," he said. "Run now." And he didn't give her a choice. His hand above her elbow, gripping like a vice so she couldn't get away, he turned and sprinted in the direction from which they'd arrived.

"Tyler! What—?"

He ignored Antonia's shriek. Behind her, Flaco was on a walkie-talkie, a fluent stream of Spanish alerting airport security to get the hell here, *muy rapido.*

"If you want to live, run," Tyler roared, and then they were outside, in the harsh light of the midday sun, racing for his plane.

The fuel truck had unhooked, thank heaven. A siren screeched through the air behind them as the airport went into lockdown; Flaco was pulling out all the stops. The fact that Flaco had the benefit of law enforcement on his side was an irony that he'd think about later—if there was a later.

Antonia staggered and nearly fell, and he hauled her back up. Fear for her safety spiked his adrenaline to a level it hadn't reached in five long years.

"Run, run, run!" he urged, and they reached the plane just as he heard the fire engine klaxons whine to life and the squeal of speeding tires as security cars approached.

His keys were in his hand, and he stabbed them into the door of the seaplane, reefing it open so he could lift Antonia off her silly freaking sandals and throw her bodily in.

Her hat was lost. Her glasses hung crazily in her wild corkscrew hair. Her shocked eyes held his, but he had no time. *No time.*

He vaulted in after her, slamming the lock home, and had the propeller at full revs in seconds.

"Strap in," he ordered.

"What the bloody hell!" Antonia shouted back.

"I'm taking off right this fucking second, so strap the hell in."

An airport security truck slewed in front of his plane, but he had the brakes off now, and he skimmed past them and hurtled down the runway.

Fire trucks barricaded the strip—he'd never take off in the short length of concrete between him and them. Shit shit *shit*. His brain went into overdrive. Fight or flight—he felt like cornered prey, but he was damned if he was letting Flaco get him, not now.

Tyler could fight. In fact, he'd have loved nothing more than to plant his fist squarely into Flaco's thin little rat face. The frustrations of five years could have used the release.

But not with Antonia there, which left flight as

his only option. Literally. And the fire trucks thought they'd blocked that option.

He bared his teeth. He still had a few tricks up his sleeve. He spun the Cessna through 180 degrees, the flash of smooth silk and smoother limbs distracting him midway through the turn, and the plane juddered as he positioned it to face the wrong end of the airstrip.

"What are you doing?" he snapped.

Antonia climbed into the co-pilot seat, her hands shaking as she wrestled with the shoulder straps. "What am *I* doing? I'm not the one who's just gone stark raving bonkers. What the hell, Tyler?"

"I've got to concentrate. Stop talking, please. I'll explain later." And he put her out of his mind as far as he could—which wasn't, admittedly, far. He pushed the joystick down and floored his little amphibious plane.

"Um. That's a very short runway, Tyler."

"Yep."

"Can we take off in one hundred feet of concrete?"

"Nope."

"Well, I hope you've got a plan," she said, her voice rising. He could see her fingers from the corner of his eye, their knuckles white, gripping the cloth-and-metal rim of the co-pilot's seat.

"We're not taking off on land."

She shook her head, and opened her mouth to speak, but he tuned it all out then: Antonia, the security vehicle roaring alongside, the guard bellowing out the window through a loud hailer, the three fire trucks blazing up the runway behind them, their lights and sirens blasting, because as the airstrip came to an end, he reefed back on the joystick and felt the wings and struts and floats of his plane shudder as the torsion and twist of a too-sudden lift from a too-slow plane fought against the laws of physics.

Grass flew by beneath them, then gravel—he was clearing it by two feet, four feet. An airport perimeter fence flashed by, cleared by perhaps inches, then a break wall, and he relaxed the joystick, bringing his floats down to kiss the water.

"Oh, thank Christ," breathed Antonia beside him.

"Don't thank him yet," he said, and hauled the plane around so he was facing into the breeze, with a smooth stretch of water ahead of him long enough to effect a safe takeoff. Let's see if your fire trucks can drive on water, he thought, and gunned the little plane forward.

6

_____

For once, Antonia had nothing to say. Not one word. But high at the top of the things she wasn't saying was: who the hell was this man flying her off to who knew where?

He looked like the Tyler she had once known—strong arms curving up to flick switches, dark hair curling over his collar, a jawline shadowed with stubble kept ruthlessly at bay—but this man's face was remote behind the aviator glasses, so she couldn't guess at his thoughts.

A rogue thought cut through her adrenaline. She'd dreamed of being swept away like a heroine in a fairy tale. Only, this sea plane was no white stallion, and she wasn't being clasped against a muscled male chest with her hair streaming in the motion of the stallion's gallop and her suitor's warm hands gripping her thighs.

She sniffed. No wonder those clueless heroines existed only in stories. Being swept away wasn't all it was cracked up to be, and unlike a horse—which any girl worth her salt would be able to jump off and so rescue herself—being swept away in a plane made for a mighty risky jump.

She pressed her fingers into her forehead, willing the addled thoughts running through her brain to calm themselves down. Idealism was not going to be able to put a positive spin on this particular adventure. Nor was flippancy.

It was time this new Tyler, the one who was clearly off his rocker, realized the Antonia he thought he knew was only part of the picture. She was a London editor at the top of her game who could make hardened journalists cry with the sweep of her pen through their redundancies and dangling modifiers. She needed to know what the heck was going on, and he was going to tell her. Or else.

"Okay, Tyler. Can I talk now? Or are you about to perform some new kamikaze routine that involves me being put in mortal danger and you breaking a host of international laws?"

He reached a hand over and rested it on her arm, his fingers squeezing. He rubbed his thumb over her skin for a moment before speaking. "I'm sorry, Antonia. I wish you hadn't been caught up in all this."

"In all what, Tyler? What is going on?"

She saw his jaw clench and unclench and wondered what he was finding so hard to say.

"I'm taking us to St Novia. I live there. When we've arrived, I'll tell you everything, I promise. We'll be landing soon."

Antonia peered down through the narrow window of the cockpit. Twin islands gleamed like giant turtle backs in the blue sea below, their shorelines studded with clusters of pastel-painted houses: The Federation of St Novia and Brisa. So this was where he had been living all these years. Glancing at her watch, she winced as she saw that her flight out of Ballena was due to depart in four hours' time. How in hell was she going to make her plane?

She flicked a glance back into the body of the Cessna, thinking about phone reception, whether or not she could google later flights, and suffered a bolt of horror. Her bags! They were all sitting at the customs counter in Ballena Airport's light aircraft terminal. Along with her passport, her phone, and every stitch of clothing she'd brought with her for her three-day mini break to the islands of the Caribbean.

Bloody hell. The enormity of the drama Tyler had dragged her into hit home when she remembered the meeting she was due to attend in—she checked her watch—a little over forty-eight hours.

She closed her eyes and shuddered. Her notes. Her pages and pages of notes justifying the changes she was proposing to keep the journalists of *Bella Magazine* secure in their jobs were all packed haphazardly into her bag. She'd rested it on the floor next to her suitcase, she recalled, which meant she'd not been carrying it when Tyler gripped her by the arm like she was a sack of potatoes and run her off to his plane.

She had to get back to London. Which meant she had to get her passport, her wallet, and herself to an international airport, and soon. She couldn't miss that meeting. She'd played down the seriousness of the matter to Charlotte and Sabrina, but her job, and the jobs of everyone who worked on her team at *Bella*, were on the line. She didn't know if the board would listen to her plan, but she knew she had to try, and she wouldn't be able to do diddly-squat from an island called St Novia in the middle of who-knew-where.

Tyler brought the seaplane to land in water as smooth as glass in a tiny little cove. At any other time, Antonia would have been delighted with the crescent-moon-shaped stretch of white sand, the flowering shrubs, the trimmed green lawn abutting a white-timbered house.

But not today. Not with her plans awry and her head a-spin.

The propeller's whine took on a deeper pitch as Tyler nosed the seaplane into a work shed looming over a wide-planked jetty, and as they nudged forward under the overhanging roof, the glare of the heat died away. He turned the ignition off and silence stretched between them, just the ticking of hot metal breaking the quiet.

Tyler sighed beside her. "Come on, then," he said, and squeezed out through the narrow aisle between the seats and maneuvered the door open. He reached a hand to help Antonia through the plane and out into the jetty, but she ignored it and made her own way off the plane. She'd had about enough of heroes and stallions for one day. From now on, she'd be having a say in where she went and with whom.

Emerald-green grass glimmered to her right, and she headed for it, emerging from the shade of the old tin roof to find a frayed rope tied between two palms just beyond the jetty and a row of colorful tea towels waving in the mild sea breeze. A kayak lay against one of the palms, its orange bottom scuffed and crusted with dried white sand, and tucked under its shade lay a sleepy, pink-and-black-speckled piglet.

She stood on the last jetty plank, feeling a little like Dorothy must have felt when she'd landed in Oz, only the house she could see beyond the palm trees wasn't a tumble-down Kansas farm house, it was a spic and span weatherboard cottage, its white walls and aqua shutters gleaming in the bright sunlight.

Her eyes fastened on movement at the rear of the house. She took a breath. What next? Would it really surprise her now if a green witch in striped socks flew out from behind the house on a broom? Good witch or bad, she mused. Considering the day she'd been having, the arrival of a scary green witch would be a welcome improvement.

Her fanciful thoughts petered out as a woman came into view. Fifty-ish, wearing a cotton print apron over a violently aqua muumuu, she looked as plump and pretty as an exotic bird.

The woman waved a hand at her, and she lifted her own, then glanced down at the lush grass before her. No way was she going to ruin the only pair of shoes she now owned, so she slipped off her heeled sandals, held them in her hand, and stepped off the jetty.

She needed plans. She needed answers. She needed a seat on a long-haul flight to London, but for the moment, she'd just take a minute.

"Hello," said the woman, who was bearing down on her like a smiling hurricane, if hurricanes wore coral lipstick. "I heard the plane land."

"Er, hi. I'm Antonia."

"And aren't you the loveliest thing." The woman came forward and embraced her, which was slightly discomfiting as Antonia had no idea who the woman was. Hell, she had no ideas about anything at the moment. She made a half-hearted attempt to respond to the friendly hug.

"Now where's that dratted boy? If he's tinkering with his plane instead of coming to hug me like is proper, I'll be swatting his behind."

A deep voice sounded from behind Antonia. "Missy Jane, you know I only have eyes for you." Tyler put his arm around the woman and kissed her forehead. Despite the lightness of his tone, his eyes were serious as they rested on Antonia's. "This is my friend."

"Antonia. Yes, we've met," said Missy Jane, imbuing the short statement with a hefty dose of speculation.

She decided to nip the older woman's obvious interest in Tyler's love life in the bud. "I'm not staying."

Tyler frowned. "She might be staying, Missy Jane. Do you mind?"

Why did it matter if Missy Jane minded? The woman answered the question for her. "Mind? Of course not. I'm your landlady, not your prison warden. You be sure to let me know if you need anything."

So saying, she gave Tyler another squeeze, stroked Antonia's arm, then ambled away through the shrubs, out of sight.

Antonia looked at Tyler, who shrugged and spread his arms. "Okay. It's time for answers. Let's get a cold drink, and I'll tell you everything."

She followed him to the door of the cottage.

"Missy Jane lives in the big house up the road. She rents me this cottage and throws in the mothering for free."

Antonia took a last glance around outside before following him in. The beach was just feet away, and beyond it a quiet bay. A few houses nestled in the trees by the water, their tin roofs shining in the sun. There were no people, now that Missy Jane had left. No sounds, but for the gentle shushing of water on sand and the tick-tick-tock of some insect busy in the flowering shrubs. Tyler's home was an isolated one.

She hung her sandals from a hook by the door. She didn't have much experience with wildlife and wasn't sure if the diet of spotted piglets included Italian leather. Perching her sunglasses in her hair, she stepped over the threshold.

The cottage was one room. Floorboards gleamed with lacquer, and brightly colored rugs dotted the floor. A dining table sat in front of a large window, whose shutters framed the view of beach and sea beyond. No part of the table's surface was bare—

logbooks, files, a laptop, printer, cables and maps covered it. So they weren't totally isolated here. Tyler must have an internet connection; she just needed a clear head and an opportunity to get online and make some sense of this dratted mess she'd landed in.

A kitchen filled one corner of the cottage, a seating area another, and a narrow bed with a patchwork quilt completed the comforts of the space. Functional, but pretty. And not the home of someone who'd intended to kidnap an unwilling London editor and drag her here against her will.

"If you need the bathroom, it's through that door," Tyler said, pointing. "Iced tea okay?"

"Coffee. Paracetamol. Explanation. In that order."

His lips twitched. "Yes, ma'am."

She left him to it and made for the bathroom. She opened the door with some trepidation, experience having taught her that bachelors living alone often had bathrooms that resembled a scene out of a horror movie, but her fears were unfounded.

Sunlight and sea breeze moved freely through the white tiled space, and fresh towels hung plump and fluffy from the rails. She stood for a long moment in front of the mirror, studying herself as she washed her hands.

She didn't look any different. She looked like the same Antonia who went to work each day from her townhouse in Wimbledon to her office in the City of London. She looked like the same Antonia who'd woken that morning with a hefty hangover in a canvas tent after the wedding of one of her best friends.

But who was she now? A fugitive? A kidnap victim? A fool?

Coffee, and a damn good explanation, that's what she needed. Maybe then she'd remember who she was supposed to be.

7

Tyler had never told his whole story to anyone. Rob Cheng, the witness protection officer who'd created his ID, knew the middle of it: his career as a detective, his life undercover, and the disaster that had ensued when his cover was blown and he was exposed as a cop to the drug cartel. But Cheng hadn't known what his life as a detective had meant to him, and he'd not seen his struggle to start again.

His lawyer knew the bare bones. When Tyler had left Baltimore on the run, he'd needed someone to sell up his estate—his deceased estate, as the world thought it.

Antonia deserved more than the bare bones of who he'd been, what he'd been, but where to start?

He didn't want to lose any more of his life than he

already had—and revealing himself would put everything he'd achieved in the last five years at risk. He acknowledged the fear and put it aside. He was worried for Antonia, desperately so. Worry for himself could wait.

Coffee brewed as he gathered mugs, sugar, teaspoons, checked his fridge on the off chance a miracle had occurred and the fridge fairy had paid him a visit. Nope. Still bare. A packet of bacon sat next to a shriveled tomato and root vegetables in the crisper, and two brown bottles of beer stood guard in the fridge door. Long life milk from the pantry would have to do.

He took the coffee and a packet of cookies out to the shaded veranda. There was a table there, and chairs, ordinary furniture for ordinary activities like eating and chatting and laughing like ordinary people might do, people who didn't have to explain why they'd just fled an international airport like an escaped inmate from a federal prison.

While he waited for Antonia, he went back inside, stripping his pilot whites off and finding a clean T-shirt and shorts in the closet beside his bed. He'd swim later—a dozen hard laps of the bay—and burn off some of his tension.

He heard the bathroom door click and turned his head. Antonia's eyes were fixed on his, the trouble in them striking a blow to his chest. What a mess.

"Come on," he said. "Coffee's ready."

He led the way to the veranda and poured her a cup. "You want milk?"

"No."

"Sugar?"

"I want an explanation, Tyler."

He took a sip of coffee, letting the black heat clear a path to the words he needed to find, and finally realized where he had to start his story: with her.

"You remember when we met, three years ago."

She nodded, her hands wrapped about her mug. "I remember."

"That last day. We went to lunch in a café in St Johns, then you went into a bookstore and I waited outside in the street for you."

"Yes. I recall. I was happily browsing book covers, and you were outside rehearsing the words you were going to use to give me the brush off." She shrugged. "Is this really relevant? I really don't have time to be rehashing past wounds, Tyler. I have to get back to London."

He waited until she'd finished. "I wasn't rehearsing lines. A man came out of a bank and saw me, a man I recognized. A bit like I recognized Flaco today."

"I don't understand anything you're saying. Is Flaco the name of the customs officer?"

Tyler nodded, impatient to get the words said. "The difference between today and three years ago is that Flaco saw you. The man back then didn't."

Antonia frowned. "What does it matter that he saw me? He's a customs official. I'm a tourist. And I need to clear customs and get back to London so I don't lose my job, and the jobs of all the people I supervise. You're going to have to give me a bit more, Tyler, because so far, I'm not understanding anything."

Tyler swore. This was harder than he'd thought possible. "Okay. My name's not Tyler Cooper."

"What?" Antonia's mug hit the wooden table with a thunk.

"I'm not a criminal, if that's what you're thinking," he said, as alarm spread across her face. "I used to be a cop in the States. An undercover detective in Baltimore."

"Holy hell."

"Yep. My cover was blown; how, I don't know. But I was undercover at the top end of a drug cartel run by a psychopath named Pavlov. Back in the day, he was responsible for the shipment of millions of dollars' worth of drugs hitting the East Coast of the States. He probably still is."

"Good grief. What happened when he found out you were a cop?"

Tyler flexed his hand, his brain recalling the

fierce pain of having his fingers broken, of being tied to a chair and having the crap beaten out of him. "Nothing good. And they would have killed me if the cops hadn't chosen that moment to run a bust on the joint I was being held in. It was dumb luck that I survived, but that was the end of my career. Pavlov doesn't leave loose ends—it's part of his code, part of the power play he uses to keep his troops in line. You mess with Pavlov, you die. And you don't die pretty."

Antonia's face was pale as she helped herself to more coffee. "So how did you get away? Was Pavlov arrested?"

"Pavlov?" Tyler almost laughed. He'd been close, so close, to getting enough evidence on the kingpin himself to take him down. But being ratted out had taken away that chance. "No one can touch Pavlov. He's too clever and too well connected. No, I was offered a spot in the witness protection program so that if Pavlov ever *was* charged, my testimony would be an asset to the prosecution."

"I can't believe it. You're in witness protection? Wait, I would have thought they'd have kept you in the States."

"They wanted to." They'd wanted to tuck him into some suburban three-bedroom brick bungalow and leave him there, twiddling his thumbs and mowing his lawn while the rest of the world spun on without him.

No. He'd not wanted that. Besides, someone on his team, one of the good guys, had ratted him out to Pavlov. He wasn't safe in the States; he wasn't safe anywhere. The last thing he'd needed was a team of unknowns knowing where he was. "I didn't take them up on their offer because I didn't trust them. I took a bunch of fake IDs, they cooked up my fake death, and I left."

"What about your family? Do they know you're alive?"

"I don't have family."

"What, you just popped up in a pumpkin patch? You must have some family."

"Orphan. Foster care. Juvenile detention. That was my family growing up—a system, not people. And the system didn't give a shit about me when I was a kid, so I doubt it shed a tear when it read my obituary in the Baltimore Sun."

Antonia leaned forward and placed her hand on his. It felt good. Too good, and he paused. Where had that bitterness sprung from? He wasn't in the habit of feeling sorry for himself. He sighed. He wasn't in the habit of raking up the past, either. Perhaps the two came hand in hand.

"So three years ago, outside the book shop, was it one of the drug cartel who recognized you?"

He snapped back to the story he was supposed to be telling. "Yeah. Kuzman. A high-ranking member of Pavlov's inner circle. He saw me all right, but he wasn't alone, so he didn't act, but he was on his phone and leaping into a taxi within seconds. He drove right by me and made a sign with his hand as he drove past, like a handgun aimed at my head. The fake funeral, the obituary, all of it exposed as false. Pavlov has known I'm alive from that moment."

"So what did you do?"

"I cut ties. With you. With my flight office in Ballena. I moved my base over to St Novia, where there's a lot less people, a lot less chance of running into a drug lord on holiday. I fly the remoter routes, which don't attract the splashy spenders."

She looked bewildered. She still wasn't getting it. "But why cut ties with me? We had something, Tyler. Something special."

"Kuzman didn't know my new identity, he'd just seen me in the street. But he'd be asking around, showing my photo, and if he'd gotten lucky, someone might have connected the dots. Kuzman would earn a million brownie points if he could deliver my head on a platter to Pavlov, and he'd do anything, *anything*, to achieve that."

"I don't like the sound of that *anything*."

He nodded. "If he found me, he'd take me out. If he found I had someone in my life, he'd take them out. But these guys aren't assassins or snipers. They're predators, and they like to play with their prey. If you got caught up in their cat-and-mouse game with me—"

He broke off. He couldn't do it. He couldn't articulate the words of what they would do to Antonia if they caught her with him.

She was nodding her head. "So that's why you ran today."

He rubbed his hand over his face. "Flaco's a real lowlife. Mean. I don't know why he's working in customs, but I've got an idea. Light aircraft, poor supervision, thousands of sea miles unguarded by a customs fleet: I'd say he's been placed there to facilitate shipments of drugs up through the Caribbean and onwards to the States."

"There's got to be someone we can tell. The FBI, the CIA, someone. International Rescue."

A chuckle forced its way out, dissipating some of his tension better than any swim would. "You do know the Thunderbirds are only real on television, right?"

Antonia snapped a shortbread cookie in half, scattering crumbs over the table. "Pity. All these palm trees had me hoping. But speaking of what's real and what's not real, what about you?"

He frowned. "Me?"

"Tyler Cooper isn't your real name, so what is?"

He shifted in his chair and took a long moment to look out over the water, at the endless sea rolling quietly into the shore. He'd turned his back on his old life—on the idealist he'd been, the young cop who'd thought the good guys could actually win. "I'm not that person anymore. It's better if you don't know."

8

He could keep his secret name, for now, while she figured out the more immediate problem of her about-to-depart flight to the other side of the world. "But what now, Tyler? My bags, my passport, everything I brought with me is back in Ballena, and I'm due back in London. I have to get back to work."

"Flaco took your passport. He knows your name."

"Well, then, I need an embassy. A British one."

Tyler shook his head. "You can't use your name. I agree, we've got to get you to London, but until you get to the other side of the world, you can't use your name."

Antonia pressed the palms of her hands to her face. "Surely an embassy can protect me? Pavlov and his crew can't be more powerful than the British Government."

"Pavlov's drug empire is big business. His annual turnover would exceed the gross domestic product of most of the Caribbean nations. He offers a few grand to a taxi driver? A courier? The bloke who makes the embassy officials their tea and cakes? The embassy can't protect you."

"So what, then? How do I get home?"

"I'm going to message my contact in the States. If the United States Marshals Service can organize fake papers to get you through customs and have them delivered to a center near us, that might work. But we need to move quickly."

Antonia stared out across the bay. "My head feels like it's about to explode, I hardly know where to start with the questions. Okay—why would the US government drop everything to bring me fake documents in the Caribbean? That sounds a little too James Bond to be true."

Good question, and he didn't know for sure that they would. It would depend on how badly they wanted to take Pavlov down and on whether or not they'd amassed more evidence on him in the years since Tyler had been undercover in the gang. Five years was a long time. "If they want my cooperation on the happy day when Pavlov is finally on the wrong side of an arrest warrant, they'll find a way."

He hoped. Problem was, Pavlov was probably more invested in hunting him down than the US Government was in keeping him alive. Probably willing to devote a whole lot more resources, too.

"Okay. Next question. When you say we need to get out of here quickly...do you mean they could find us here?"

"Flaco has access to flight plans. It won't take him long to trace Island Escape Aviation and get a list of its pilots. As soon as a photo of Tyler Cooper pops up on his screen, he'll have my identity."

"And your address?"

"Not here. I pay cash to Missy Jane. But my amphibious plane is covered in identification numbers. Sooner or later they're going to find out about the Island Escape Aviation Cessna with call sign Alpha Yankee 6446 that tucks itself up in the sea plane shed at Esmeralda Bay most nights."

"So you'll make contact with the US Marshal Service?"

Tyler nodded. "Rob Cheng. He's an officer for witness protection."

"And then we get me to my new documents, and I fly to London, where presumably I can return to life as Antonia De Silva without fear of retribution."

His stomach clenched, but yeah. He thought so. London was a long way off Pavlov's home patch. "Yes," he said, with more conviction than he felt.

Antonia's nails clicked against her empty mug. "And what about you? What do you do?"

He had no answer to that, not on the back of a poor night's sleep and a morning of high adrenaline. "Let's get you figured out first. I'll worry about me later." And he'd have to worry about his business, too, and his bank loan, the other pilots he employed, the big-as-Texas investigation he was no doubt facing after breaking every aviation rule in the books this morning at Ballena Airport.

"I'm going to make some calls," he said.

Antonia looked at her watch. "Can I use your computer? I need to cancel my flights and alert my boss I'm behind schedule."

"Give me the details. I'll give them to Rob and ask him to do it. Let's not use your name on the internet just yet. We don't want to give intel away to any rogue search engines that might be looking for you."

Antonia raised her eyebrows. "Tyler, I don't think hearing from some random guy in the States is going to cut it with my boss when I don't turn up to work. We've got a board meeting coming up, and the future of the magazine is going to be tabled. It is critical that I am there. My boss is going to need a solid gold reason for me not calling in person to explain where the hell I am."

He cracked the knuckles in his hands while he worked it through. "Your passport's been stolen, your phone, all your ID. The US Embassy is doing what it can to assist you. Trust me, Rob is one officious agent. Your boss will believe him."

Antonia let out a sigh. "I'm really going to miss my plane, aren't I?"

He nudged her hand with his. "I'm sorry."

"You look sorry. You also look absolutely beat, which is why I'm going to stop pushing. For now." She snagged the box of paracetamol he'd placed on the coffee tray. "You mind if I lie down on your bed? I need to shut my eyes and re-group. Just for a bit."

He nodded and felt a little of the weight on his chest ease. "Sure. Help yourself. I'll make my calls, then head over to the Cessna and see what I can do about that rip in the float."

"Wait a minute. How is you making calls any safer than me using your computer? How does that work?"

He pulled his phone out of his pocket. "Black-berry. Military grade encryption on a closed loop— the phone of choice for crooks worldwide and witnesses on the run. Don't worry. I'll make sure Rob contacts your boss at *Bella*."

She wasn't convinced, he could see, but she let it go. As she walked back into the cool interior of his house, he flipped open the contacts file on his phone and scrolled down to the one number he'd hoped he'd never have to call again.

9
____

Antonia emerged from a deep sleep, her senses swimming. Half-remembered dreams skittered away, dreams of happiness and sunshine.

The bed she lay on was soft, its quilt a smooth, clean cotton. She stretched, and her hands reached out along the mattress to find the man who'd been beside her in her dreams, the man whose scent lingered in the bed clothes.

Her eyes snapped open, and reality crashed through the sleep haze. A cottage. On an island, alone in the bed of a man who wasn't the person she thought she'd known. One dress, crumpled, to her name.

She sighed. All of that paled into a papercut when she compared it with the great slashing drama that could unfold at the board meeting in London that she was due to attend in—she glanced at her watch, tried to account for time zones and plane journeys and Daylight Savings Time—who-knew-when but soon.

Perhaps Tyler—should she still call him that?—had heard from his contact. Perhaps even now the United States government had been in touch with the British Government, and a dull-looking public servant had slipped off his dull-looking shoe and used the old-fashioned rotary telephone dial buried in its heel to dial Her Majesty's Secret Service. And a dishy, steel-jawed agent was in the air right this second, careering from helicopter skids like a kid on monkey bars, with her new passport clenched between his teeth.

Or none of that had happened, and she'd have to find some way to contact her boss and let him know she was delayed.

Maybe she was worrying unnecessarily, and the board would agree to a one-week deferral? Or maybe they would charge on without her, and the whole of the international news coverage team would be made redundant.

Acknowledging it made her feel sick. And frustrated. For heaven's sake, she *needed* to be in London. She knew her team thought she was a heavy-handed boss, always micro-managing them and nosing her way into their work projects, but that was her style. Pushy but caring.

She threw back the light quilt on the bed and rose; lying there feeling aggravated would achieve precisely nothing. The cottage was empty. Two coffee cups sat, clean and upended, in the rack next to the sink, and a hibiscus swam in a jam jar on the counter. Beneath it lay a note: *Gone swimming. Come find me on the beach—I have news. Didn't want to wake you after such a rough morning. Help yourself to my clothes. T.*

What news?

There was only one way to find out. Grimacing at the state of her dress, Antonia turned to the closet. Pilot uniforms filled the hanging space along with piles of T-shirts—all massive—and shorts, also massive. But up high, in with a jumble of ball caps and swimsuits and epaulettes, was a sarong.

She shook it out. It was navy and wide enough to wrap around two people, let alone just her. It would do.

Doing a quick scan through the window to check Missy Jane wasn't gardening in view of the cottage, she stripped out of her clothes and fashioned the sarong into a wraparound dress. She took a moment to rinse her underwear out, then hung her dress on a hanger—because, really, she wasn't wrecking her silk frock even for an international crisis—then headed outside to pin her underwear to the clothesline.

Now to track down her host. Captor. Whatever.

The sun had lost some of its sting as she'd slept, and it slanted in over the mountains, chasing shadows of palm trees over the beach. A pile of clothes formed a small beacon, and Antonia made her way over to them, taking a seat on the sand. Tyler couldn't be far away.

The sea heaved in soft surges, its lagoon blue turning clear with white surf as it rolled up the length of beach. An idyllic spot—too idyllic for the story she'd been flown here to hear. She sifted sand through her fingertips as she thought through all she'd learned.

A criminal empire as powerful as it was vast, and Tyler with a target on his back. As she thought his name, a dark head and sun-bronzed torso emerged through the waves. She placed a hand over her heart, wondering at the thrill the sight of him invoked.

She sighed. London and her problems, Tyler and his ex-cop, drug-boss revenge problems...as urgent as they were, they still seemed less urgent than the churning tide of emotion seeing him again had caused.

He walked up the beach, lean and tall, a brief pair of swimmers hugging his hips. He looked tired, but something else lingered in the look he levelled at her. Something she couldn't define.

"Hey."

"Hey," she replied, and he swung into the sand next to her, blotting the water from his face and chest with his towel.

"Feeling okay?" he asked.

"When I figure it out, I'll let you know. So what's this news? Did you get in touch with your contact?"

"Yep. Rob's been updated. He's alerting your boss that you've had your passport and handbag stolen and may be late."

Antonia nodded. It was as good an excuse as any.

"And he's going to pull some strings with the State Department to create temporary documents to get you back on British soil. When he calls with a rendezvous point, we'll need to be ready to fly."

Antonia drew a circle in the sand with her finger. "And what about you? What about the man known as Tyler Cooper?"

"Yeah. That's gonna be a problem."

"How do you mean?"

"That name's no longer safe."

"What will you do?"

"I've had a few thoughts." He stared out over the bay, his face grim. "The business should be fine. It's mine, but my lawyer set its ownership structure up with more legs than an octopus, and none of those legs uses the name Tyler Cooper. The hangar and workspace I lease is over the hill in Verdeterre, the main town on St Novia. The office manager knows

I'm the one who makes the decisions, but the other pilots don't. So when Tyler Cooper, pilot, doesn't show up for work, or loses his flight registration for an illegal take-off from Ballena Airport, they'll be surprised—" He grinned suddenly and cut his eyes to her. "And that's the understatement of the year. They'll be downright amazed. But the business will be able to keep going."

"Surely they'll recognize you when you rock up to work next week with a fake moustache and a brand-new name?"

Tyler rubbed his thumb and forefinger over his top lip, as though he was seriously considering the idea. "I won't be able to fly, not for a while. I'll need to lay low." He looked back over his shoulder at the timber cottage on the foreshore, the chicken that pecked at grubs under the beach almond trees. "I'll need to find a new home."

Antonia reached out and grabbed his hand. "I'm sorry, Tyler." She gave it a squeeze. "I've been so caught up in how this has affected me; I haven't given much thought to how it's ripping apart your life."

He didn't brush her hand off as she'd expected him to, as he had every time she'd come near him since they'd been reunited. Instead, he turned his hand over, linked his fingers with hers, their hands at least a warm union. She supposed, in a way, Flaco had forced this proximity upon them the minute he recognized Tyler and seized her passport to make her a pawn in the drug cartel's sick game of revenge.

They sat together in silence, watching the shadows creep low over the sand, the wisps of cloud drift across the late afternoon sky. How lonely Tyler must have been, she thought. Too worried about consequences to seek company, eking out an existence on the far-flung islands and atolls of the Caribbean Sea.

She'd been lonely in London, sure. But never *alone*. She'd had Charlotte and Sabrina—even when they weren't in London, they emailed and flicked saucy messages to each other on social media. She had her family, her work colleagues, old friends from university. She could fill her London townhouse with enough people for a party any night of the week.

But Tyler? Who did he have for company? A piglet, some chickens, and a kind and possibly zany landlady who called herself Missy Jane.

She asked the question that had been gnawing at her subconscious even while she slept. "How long will we be safe here?"

He squeezed her fingers but didn't let them go. "A day or two? No longer."

Antonia realized the circle she'd been drawing on the sand had become a skull, with big gaping eyes and bones crisscrossed beneath, like a pirate flag of old. She grimaced at the darkness of it and rubbed it out with her foot. "And you really think Pavlov will put all this effort into finding you, after all these years?"

Tyler nodded. "Oh yeah. He wants me, because he knows I could identify any number of his associates in a police lineup and be believed. I was a detective, after all."

"What info?"

"Pavlov's a smart business operator, but even he can't manage an empire without help. He sells drugs: methamphetamines that are cooked up in out-of-town labs and old fashioned street drugs like cocaine and heroin that he brings in from South America and cuts down in houses and shopfronts all over the East Coast. But the problem with making all that money from selling drugs is that you have to do something with it, so he buys businesses. Courier vans that operate legally some days and as drug transports on others. Laundromats, panel beaters, shipping brokers. His empire is enormous, and the business side of it is where he's most vulnerable. He has help there, some shady character he kept out of sight, called the Moneyman."

"You don't know the Moneyman's name?"

"No. Or even if it's a guy. The Moneyman is the only term Pavlov ever used."

"So, if you have information, how did you get it, if you didn't have access to the Moneyman?"

"It's not what I've got, it's what I've seen. There was a steady stream of men and women networking with Pavlov, and I'm good with details. They tie Pavlov to a small-time crook, and I'm alive to testify that I saw that small-time crook in a meet-and-greet with Pavlov. And the real juice is this: it's probable that I've seen the Moneyman, I just didn't know it at the time. If I can help tie Pavlov to the money being laundered through dozens of businesses, it would be a fatal blow to the criminal empire currently flooding the East Coast of the States with street drugs. It would be enough to indict Pavlov, and that's why he needs me silenced."

Antonia turned this over in her head. "So, if the federal agencies in the States can identify the Moneyman, and you can attest that you've seen that person, whoever he or she is, in meetings with Pavlov —that would be enough to bring Pavlov down?"

"Not just Pavlov. His whole empire."

"And you'd be free to lead your life. Be the real you."

Tyler dropped her hand like she'd burned him. "There's no happy ending to this story, Antonia. There is no real me anymore."

"I don't believe that. You still have a real name, don't you?"

Tyler was silent.

"Don't you?"

10

No happy endings. The words went round and round in Antonia's head, in bold, in italics, underlined.

Tyler's words of warning were the polar opposite of the dreams she had for herself, the dreams she warmed herself with when she was feeling down or lonely or dispirited.

She rose to her feet, dusted off the sand, and looked down at Tyler. Tension streamed off him in waves. No wonder. How did he warm himself in the lonely hours of the night if he'd given up on dreams? What bastards those crooks were, to wield their power over him with such relentless malice.

Hunted. That's what Tyler was—a lone wolf with a steel trap shackled around his leg.

"Why don't we fight back?" she said, surprising herself, unsure where the words had come from.

Tyler squinted up at her, holding a hand up to shield his eyes from the sun. "Fight back? Antonia." He put a hand around her ankle, rubbed his thumb over the clusters of sand that lingered there. "How? I'm not a cop anymore. I don't have access to law enforcement databases or backup. The only reason Rob's helping me stay alive is on the off chance Pavlov is arrested one day and they can use my evidence to help prosecute him."

"I could help you."

"You?" He grinned up at her, the flash of a smile easing the harsh set of his face. "You're an editor. What are you going to do, throw adverbs at the bad guys?"

"Tyler, you're thinking like a cop. It's time to start thinking like a journalist. What's the cliché? The pen is mightier than the sword. Well, the world's changed a little since that phrase was coined, but in my industry, we think news coverage is mightier than a crook with a shiv or a drug dealer with a gun-wielding henchman."

She reached down and smoothed his salt-wet hair back from his forehead. She ran her other hand down his arm, over a thick welt of scar high on his bicep. She rubbed it absently as she spoke, her eyes intent on his. "Words have power, Tyler. Journalists from the Washington Post brought down President Nixon in 1974. And look at the current President running the US. There are reporters circling the White House like sharks around a carcass as we speak. Maybe Pavlov isn't as untouchable as you think he is."

"Maybe." He didn't sound convinced.

"Tyler, dirt sticks. And journalists have more skills than ever before to share someone's dirty deeds with the world. If we can gather the proof, a journalist can get a story plastered over every TV screen and phone screen in the United States."

"Antonia."

"You don't believe me, do you? You think I'm being naive."

He frowned. "A little. You remind me of myself back in Baltimore, when I still believed I could make a difference. Before shit got real."

The bitterness in his voice cut at her. "Hey," she said, and held out a hand. "How about a walk?"

He let her haul him upright, until they were standing toe to toe in the sand, her hands in his. His face was more relaxed as he looked down at her. "How about a swim instead?"

She frowned. "No luggage, remember? No bathing suit."

He ran his eyes down her, in a long blaze of looking that sent heat down to her toes. "I don't think that's going to be a problem," he said, and took a step forward, his thighs nudging hers so she took an involuntary step backwards towards the water. She went to move her hand out of his so she could step away, but he tightened his grip, and took another step, crowding her down the beach.

She pursed her lips. "Are you trying to seduce me?"

"Yeah."

"Tyler—"

Her protest was cut off as he dropped her hands and moved his arms around her, gripping her about the hips and hauling her up against his body so she was no longer standing, but instead held against the length of him, her face looking down at his, her hands pushing at his shoulders.

Oh, who was she kidding. She loved this. She slid her arms around his head and thrust her fingers into his close-cropped hair. Happy endings could go hang themselves for the time being. She could feel a happy-right-now coming on.

She laughed breathlessly, her lungs struggling to draw breath. He began to move, walking forwards through the sand to the water. Her toes, ankles, calves felt the cool. Water shimmied up into the spaces between them, soaking her sarong, a cool contrast to the warm heat of his chest against hers.

She squealed as the water came up to her shoulders, then wrapped her legs about Tyler's hips. Small waves lapped at her, and she felt the currents push and pull at her sarong.

Antonia was a wordsmith. Words, the arranging of them, the salt-and-pepper seasoning of robust verbs, the abrupt cut of the em dash—words were how she earned her living, but they were more than that. She was one of the lucky few whose work was a vocation.

She loved language and its nuances, its ability to describe an event, an emotion, a connection in vivid neon using tools that were two dimensional and black and white. But words were failing her now.

Tyler was going to kiss her; his intent was written clear on his face. A string of synonyms waltzed through her thoughts; how many ways were there to describe anticipation? Prediction, forecast, want, longing...

His eyes blazed. Her heart leapt. Her waltz of words cut out as she thought, *To hell with waiting.* This was going to be one of those occasions where reality outweighed expectation, and she was going to take it for her own.

She ran her hand up the column of his neck and reached up to claim his mouth. She might be stranded on an island without a hair straightener. She might be a fugitive blackballed from airports for the term of her natural life. But she was alive, wasn't she? And in the arms of Tyler. Well, someone who called himself Tyler.

And he could kiss like the devil himself.

11

*S*mooth curves, that's what she was. And beneath the smoothness, an inferno.

This is what it must feel like to fly a plane too close to the sun, Tyler thought. Engines on fire, oxygen burned out, the joystick out of control, and the pilot free-falling in a fireball through a white-hot sky.

He slid his hand under Antonia's backside to hold her more firmly against him, abandoned himself to the heat.

Too damn long he'd been living the cautious life of a man on the run, and where had prudence and denial got him? Nowhere. Pavlov and Kuzman and Flaco had taken his old life from him, but they weren't taking this moment, no way. This was a moment he was taking for himself.

Antonia shifted against him, and he groaned. The wet sarong had thinned to tissue paper in the water, and his roaming fingers lingered on the grooves where underwear should be. He tore his mouth from hers. "Are you wearing...?"

"Nope. Don't talk. Only kiss."

He groaned. He wasn't sure the sun-aged fabric of his swimmers was going to cope. Care factor, zero, he thought, and lifted Antonia in the water so he could find more skin to taste. More woman. More, *more*.

He pressed his teeth to the curve of neck above her collarbone, tasted the salt that lingered there. The soft swell above the knotted sarong was next, and he ran a string of kisses across her breast.

"Undo it," she said. "I'm begging you."

He grinned.

SHE WAS GOING to drown in a tangle of need any second now, but Tyler's hands had stilled beneath the warm, blue water. She gave him a quick pinch. "Earth to Captain Cooper. There's a high-maintenance woman in seat 2A who requires all of your attention."

But then she followed his gaze to where two people were walking down the beach from the direction of the jetty. One wore an unmistakable aqua muumuu and had to be Missy Jane. The other looked—official. Tyler's bicep had tightened into steel under her hand.

"You recognize her?"

"Police. That's the uniform of The Royal St. Novia and Brisa Police Force."

The seawater that moments ago had bubbled about her like lava suddenly felt cold. "Any chance they're just enjoying an afternoon stroll? Missy Jane and her bestie police friend?"

"No chance. Come on." Tyler let her down, then strode from the water, reaching to snag his towel and wrap it firmly round his hips. He held his shirt out to her. "Here, put this on. Your sarong's a little..."

She looked down. See-through. That was the phrase Tyler had been searching for. She grabbed his shirt and quickly pulled it on, then turned to face the trouble bearing down on them.

The woman with Missy Jane was tiny and neat as a pin. Her uniform had creases in the sleeves that could chisel through ice. Her dark hair was scraped back into a massive bun, and her eyes were shielded from the slanting late-afternoon sun by dark glasses. Her belt bristled with gear—radio, gun, taser—and she exuded an air of coiled authority.

Antonia cast a glance up at Tyler, but his face was

impassive. Sure, this was her first gig as a fugitive, but she wasn't getting a bad vibe from this policewoman. She seemed like someone who valued her uniform and wouldn't be on the payroll of drug-running murderers.

Missy Jane's chatter carried down the beach. "Oh, yes, and it's such a pretty plane, too. Tyler took me for a spin in it once. We flew so low over the water I could see the stingrays sunning themselves in the shallows."

Stingrays? She'd been canoodling barefoot in stingray-infested water? She banished the errant thought. On the digital scale of her current problems, a lethal stingray barb to the foot barely registered as a blip.

Tyler rested a hand on her arm, and not so subtly shoved her behind him. She'd have shoved back if she hadn't realized he was protecting her. Her eyes flew to the weapon clipped to the police officer's belt. Did he really think they were in danger?

She caught her breath and pulled the soft folds of Tyler's T-shirt around her wet frame, for comfort more than for warmth. The four of them stood, an odd quartet, there on the beach: a stern-faced young woman bristling with symbols of officialdom, the garrulous Missy Jane, Tyler a coil of repressed tension beside her, and her. Antonia. The newcomer from foggy London who had finally discovered that adventure and excitement in the tropics weren't all she'd imagined they'd be.

The policewoman cut Missy Jane off mid-sentence. "Tyler Cooper?"

"Yep."

"I'm Detective Lalonde. You want to tell me why the switchboard in my police station's been lit up like a Christmas tree all day while the Ballena Police try and track you down?"

"A misunderstanding. I had some airplane trouble—had to make a tricky takeoff this morning. I'll be filing a full report with the authorities."

Antonia tried not to show her surprise. What, Tyler thought he could just brush off a major trans-gression of flight rules as a misunderstanding?

Detective Lalonde's face showed no expression, surprise or otherwise. "Misunderstanding? There's been a few terms bandied about in police traffic this afternoon. Lunatic. Arrest warrant. Act of terror. *Misunderstanding* wasn't one of them."

"I'd be happy to come in to your office in the morning and answer any questions."

Would he? Antonia moved so she could see his face; surely he wasn't serious?

"Would you?" Detective Lalonde's tone indicated she didn't think he was serious at all.

Tyler smiled, a broad flash of dimple and teeth that made Antonia dizzy for a second. Was he finding this funny? His next words made her realize he was playing a role, trying to schmooze the police officer with charm and misdirection.

"Only—" Tyler paused and ran a hand up Antonia's arm to curl a lock of her hair around his finger. "Now's not such a convenient time. If you get my drift." He pulled Antonia in close and kissed her temple. "We just got engaged."

Antonia couldn't tell who was more surprised: her, Missy Jane, or the rooster that chose that moment to cock-a-doodle-doo from the flowering vines crisscrossing the upper reaches of the beach.

Missy Jane leapt forward, enfolding them both in a talcum-and-gardenia embrace. "But this is fabulous! Now, Jozy," she coaxed, turning to the policewoman. "Tyler will be along in the morning to sort out all this airport business. It's not every day a young man gets engaged. You can wait until the morning, can't you?"

Detective Lalonde's eyes narrowed. She nodded. "I can wait. Briefly. If Captain Cooper can give me a few minutes now, alone."

Tyler was clearly still inhabiting the role of happy, magnanimous male. Antonia couldn't believe the transformation from the quiet, intense man she'd lost her heart to. No wonder he'd lasted undercover for so long in Baltimore—he had hidden acting talents, clearly. She wondered what else besides this nonsensical engagement had been an act.

"Honey? I'll see you up at the house." Tyler gave her arm a squeeze, then left her to the smiling chatter of his landlady.

"I had no idea Tyler was seeing anyone," Missy Jane said, looping her arm under Antonia's and walking up the beach in their wake.

"Mm. It was pretty sudden." Understatement of the year, she thought, frowning. She wasn't sure she liked being used in Tyler's ruse to delay the police officer. Another thought struck her: so far, Tyler had been making all the plans. Maybe it was time she did a little planning of her own. "Missy Jane. I hate to be a bother, but did you know I lost all my luggage in Ballena?"

"No! Cherie, what can I do to help?"

"It's just..." Antonia lowered her voice. If Tyler could role-play, so could she. And suddenly-engaged-heroine-on-holiday was a role she'd been preparing for her whole life. "It's all been so sudden—I just want to call my mum, you know? It doesn't feel right, her not knowing I'm engaged. But my phone is lost."

Missy Jane tutted and sighed. "Come with me to my house, this instant. You can call your mother, and

I can look in my closet and see if we can't pretty you up some for your evening of celebration."

"Oh, no, I couldn't accept your clothes," she said, barely suppressing a grin at the thought of Tyler's face if she returned to his cabin wearing one of the oversized multi-colored muumuus Missy Jane seemed to enjoy wearing.

"Nonsense. I've at least two dozen outfits in my wardrobe that I haven't fit into since the turn of the century. You'll be saving me a trip to the recycling store if you'll take some. And then we can have a glass of champagne while Jozy Lalonde gives that man of yours a talking to."

Antonia giggled. She was beginning to understand why Tyler seemed so fond of his landlady. "If you say so, Missy Jane."

THE OLDER WOMAN wasn't joking when she said she owned a lot of clothes. When they arrived at the ramshackle villa perched on an elevated piece of land overlooking the bay, Missy Jane led her along a wide veranda into a spectacularly messy bedroom. The woman seemed oblivious to the books and shoes and scarves and lipsticks fighting for supremacy over every surface. She zigzagged through the clutter until she stood before the open closet doors, and tapped her lip thoughtfully. "Now let me think. What era?"

Antonia raised her eyebrows. "Era?"

The older woman waved a hand airily. "I'm an historian. I order my clothes into eras: seventies retro, eighties shoulder pads and sequins…"

Heaven help her if she had to accept a sequin-encrusted big-shouldered pantsuit. She'd look like a seventies disco star on her way to a Berlin rave.

She needn't have worried. Missy Jane dug out a canvas duffle bag decorated with hot pink flamingos, and proceeded to fill it with a couple of T-shirts, a couple of pairs of shorts, and, hallelujah, a pair of glitzy beach sandals that were only half a size too small. She plucked a buttercup-yellow dress off a hanger and held it up against Antonia. "Oh, this is perfect. I love this dress on you."

Antonia smiled. "You've been generous enough already. I don't need this."

"No way am I letting you leave my house without this dress. Tyler's eyeballs are going to pop from his head when he sees you in this."

She grinned. "Mr. Impassive? I'd like to see that."

Missy Jane was still holding the dress up against her, but at these words she tossed the dress onto the bed and gathered Antonia's hands in hers.

"I adore that young man. And I've been wondering why he always looks—not impassive—

but withdrawn. Sad. As though he's watching the world from a distance, you know? But when he looks at you –" Missy Jane fluttered a hand over her heart and smiled. "You'll think I'm a silly, sentimental old watering pot when I say this. But now he looks like someone who's been given, oh, I don't know. A gift he didn't think he deserved."

On impulse, Antonia kissed Missy Jane's cheek. What a dear. Her words reminded her of her goal in coming up to the big house. Pretty frocks and a fake engagement were all fun in their own way, but they weren't going to be of much use rescuing her and Tyler from their predicament.

For that, she'd need a brainstorm, and luckily, she'd had one.

She was going to contact Ben—honeymooner, all around good guy, and computer geek so smart he'd built a billion-dollar empire from nothing more than a hard drive and a fine pair of hands rattling over a keyboard.

Tyler had said the key to bringing down Pavlov was finding the Moneyman, but no federal agency had ever succeeded in doing so.

But Ben could find anyone, Antonia was sure of it.

Tyler would never agree to letting her contact him. He'd lived like a lone wolf so long he'd forgotten that strength came when the pack worked together as a team. And Ben was part of Antonia's team.

She picked up the yellow dress from the bed and folded it into the duffle. "I'll have a shower before I put it on, wash some of the salt off. Do you mind if I use your phone? I'll be quick, I promise. I don't want to run up an international phone charge on your account."

"Take your time, my dear," said Missy Jane, gesturing for Antonia to follow her into the house and leading her into a book lined study. "When you're done, come find me on the veranda. We'll have that glass of bubbles before I send you off to go find your man."

Antonia smiled. Her man. She liked the sound of that. She didn't care what Tyler said about danger and risk and his inability to be free to be with her. If he thought she was going to blindly agree with every plan he made like it was an edict from above, he'd picked the wrong woman to have a fake engagement with.

She had plans of her owns, starting with now.

She looked down at the receiver, planning what she would say. Tyler's warnings about spies lingered, so she decided she'd need to be cryptic. She had to let Ben know she needed to talk to him—but how?

Oh. Of course. She thought back to an investigation she'd been involved in some years ago. *Bella* had sent a journalist into Russia to monitor the movement of weapons across the border to Ukraine, and they had used coded language to discuss the journalist's movements. That journalist had been none other than her long-term bestie Charlotte, before Charlotte had left the magazine to start up her wellness blog.

But would she remember the codes, now that her life was one long merry-go-round of nappies and teething toys and public displays of affection for her blue-eyed husband?

Antonia snorted. Of course Charlotte would remember them. The woman was fifty percent human, thirty percent sniffer dog, and twenty percent filing cabinet. She never forgot a detail.

She picked up the phone, thanking her lucky stars she knew Charlotte's number off the top of her head. The digital ring sounded in her ear, followed by clicks and electronic hums as the phone switched over to message bank: the Diamond family must still be in the air somewhere between Ballena and Oahu.

Leave a message after the beep.

She took a deep breath, then began. "Moscow is cold this time of year," she said. That was the code for caution. "But I need to meet Ben there. No hurry, next month will be fine." That meant urgently, with no delay. "Perhaps you could pass my gmail address to him? Ciao, darling."

She placed the handset gently back in its base. Okay. She'd made contact. Now it was up to Ben to find a way to contact her. And somehow, in the next twenty-four hours, she'd need to get to an internet café so she could access her gmail account.

Her plan was underway.

12

———

*L*ittle white polka dots speckled the yellow of her dress. Her long legs carried her swiftly over the grass towards him, and Tyler frowned as she paused, plucked a white hibiscus from a bush, and tucked it behind her ear.

He fought back the frown; how screwed up was his life when all he could think was that the woman he loved didn't have time to be plucking flowers and wearing pretty dresses?

He tamped down the bitterness since it got him nowhere. Planning and a cool head were what had kept him alive this long, and he needed to keep it together until Antonia was far, far away from him and his problems.

And then—well. He'd have to see.

He leaned against the post of his veranda and

waited for Antonia to join him. The thick, white business card Lalonde had given him was in his hand, and he tapped it against his palm as he thought.

He'd liked her. No nonsense. She hadn't believed a word he'd said, which meant she had good instincts, because he was a damn fine liar. In his old life, he would have been inclined to give her the benefit of his many doubts, but that was then. Gut instinct wasn't enough to weed out who could be trusted and who couldn't. He wasn't the only one capable of living a convincing lie. No, as tempting as it was to place his trust in Jozy Lalonde and have her help him extricate Antonia from his mess, he couldn't risk it.

Risk didn't bring reward, not when a megalomaniac drug lord was on your tail. Risk brought you a knife to the throat or a bullet to the spine.

He looked at his watch. Lalonde was expecting him to present himself at her office in Verdeterre at nine A.M. sharp the following morning. She'd taken the keys to his amphibious plane with her and made him give her his word that he would come—neither of which meant a thing to a man on the run. For all her smarts, the Detective clearly knew jackshit about planes. His keys locked the door which he could break into with a screwdriver and an allen key in a heartbeat, and the plane's ignition worked off a switch, not the turn of a key.

Rob Cheng needed to get back to him with a rendezvous point, and soon. He wasn't out of options, not totally, but he was feeling the squeeze.

Antonia came to a stop in front of him, smelling of sunshine and...wine?

"Missy Jane been leading you astray, has she? My landlady doesn't mind a sunset tipple."

She smiled at him, that knowing quirk that cut through all his carefully built up defenses and woke up the yearning for a normal life that he'd spent years trying to suppress. "No handcuffs? No house arrest?"

He shrugged. "Not today. I wouldn't be taking bets against it tomorrow, however, if I show up for my appointment. Lalonde indicated her superiors wouldn't have hesitated about arresting me."

"I liked her. She had an honest face."

"Yeah. But it's not her face that counts, it's the leverage. Who does she have in her life that Pavlov could mess with? That's the way Pavlov gets even the honest ones to do whatever the hell he wants them to."

Antonia gave his arm a brief rub. "Okay, I get it. We don't trust her. But what now?"

"Lalonde may be a step ahead of the rest because she's friends with Missy Jane, so she knew there was a pilot renting the cottage out here. But she'll be filing a report at St Novia Police HQ. Talking to Ballena Police. We're not safe here."

"But where will we go? Have you got money? Fuel for the plane? I've got nothing but a few hand-me-down clothes and a flamingo-patterned duffle bag. I don't think we'd get much of a trade-in for it at a pawn shop."

He linked his fingers into hers. "Let's eat, I'm starving. Then I'll call my contact again. But keep your bag close. Maybe grab your, erm—" he nodded in the direction of her underwear, waving like rose-colored flags on the washing line. "We need to be ready to move."

She nodded. "I'll gather my things."

Tyler let her fingers go so she could move away. How quickly things could change, he thought. Two days ago, he'd been quietly living his half-life. And now this: a roller-coaster of need and want with Antonia, and desperation as he wondered how he was going to stay one step ahead of Pavlov and his men and get Antonia away. He felt like he was flying through the Bermuda Triangle with storm clouds rolling in and not enough fuel to make it to land.

Dinner was a cobbled-together affair of root vegetables roasted while he seared a lamb fillet on the grill, and a salad of leaves he'd helped himself to from Missy Jane's vegetable plot. Antonia tore through her portion like she'd been marooned on a sandbank for days. "I can't believe I didn't know you could cook."

He shrugged. "I like to. I find it relaxing."

She speared a cherry tomato on her fork and dragged it through the balsamic puddle on her plate before popping it in her mouth. "Sensational. Do you do dessert, too?"

"With the right incentive, I might feel inclined to whip up a little chocolate something."

He felt her bare toes skim over his foot, and stroke up the length of his calf. He quirked an eyebrow at her. "Nice try, but I was thinking more along the lines of you doing the washing up."

Two warm female toes gave his leg a quick pinch. She smiled. "Sure," she said. "For a meal like that, I'll even take out the trash."

He almost laughed. His world was exploding in great jagged chunks, yet with Antonia by his side, there was always something, some spark of fun and love and laughter, that kept the feeling of doom at bay.

She gathered the plates and turned to the sink, but before she reached it the electronic trill of his ringtone cut through the banter like an axe. The ease that had built up around him like a hearth fire as they'd eaten snuffed out.

The words *Private Number Calling* scrolled insistently across his screen. Antonia's eyes met his. He took a second to stare blindly into those dark-brown depths, then brought the phone to his ear. "Cooper."

"It's Rob. Here's the setup. Brisa, the Chihuahua Café, corner of Isolde and the Esplanade, one o'clock tomorrow. Can you make it?"

"Why Brisa? There's a better airport here."

"I don't make the bookings, Cooper. Can you make it?"

"We'll make it. But I'm getting a little too much interest from the local police. Can't we make it earlier?"

"No can do. The courier's just left—he's traveling plane-to-plane to get to you. One o'clock is the soonest. If you were in Manhattan, it'd be a piece of cake."

"Understood. How will I know the courier?"

"Male. Late fifties. He'll find you."

"Okay, we'll be there."

"There's more. The State Department have made a new ID for your friend on the condition she hands it in to the American Embassy in London as soon as she arrives. There are plane tickets too. Your girlfriend will be back in London by 0800 the following day."

He squeezed his eyes shut. Thank heavens. But then a thought stuck him. "The State Department's being awfully chummy about this. What's the catch?"

There was a pause. "My boss wants you to come

in. The DEA and Narcotics down in Baltimore, none of them are making headway on Pavlov. They want you as an asset. Getting ID for your girlfriend is the leverage they're willing to use to make that happen."

"Are they crazy? The last time I worked in an official capacity for the United States Government I got all my fingers broken because someone on Uncle Sam's payroll couldn't keep their mouth shut."

"That's their condition. You get your girlfriend out of Pavlov's reach, and you come in. They want to talk about the growth in business. Flaco being down there has them pissing their black suits. Your old crew in Narcotics are in the loop too."

"Rob. What the hell?" Had he lost his mind? Tyler still didn't know who had betrayed him last time. The last thing he needed was his old crew learning he was alive and living *la vida loca* in the Caribbean, not turning to rot in a Baltimore graveyard.

"Cooper, you're the one who said this was urgent, so I needed some leverage to persuade Uncle Sam that your problems matter. The DEA couldn't spare an agent, and I couldn't do it myself, I'm needed here; you're not the only shitstorm I'm in charge of right now. So I put out some feelers, and Narcotics vouched for you; they reckon you're still enough of an asset for them to free up an agent to bring down the new ID. That's the only reason your girlfriend's getting our help."

Tyler closed his eyes. Bureaucracy, deals, favors. "Nothing ever changes, does it?"

"Not while Pavlov's on the loose."

Tyler thought of the business he'd built up. His planes. His employees. His bank loan. He firmed his jaw. He'd sworn he was finished with letting the US government agencies play roulette with his life; he couldn't trust them. But he needed to get Antonia out, and he'd run out of options. What was his freedom, compared with her life?

"Tyler? You there? Do we have a deal?"

"Yep. But I come in my time. My way."

He killed the connection, then turned to Antonia, who was standing in the kitchen, eyebrows raised.

"Well?"

He smiled, putting an effort into making it seem real so she could feel some relief. God knows she'd earned it. "Good news. Your new passport and plane tickets are on their way. We pick them up tomorrow at one, then get you to the airport. Once you're through to the departure lounge, you'll be safe." He hoped. He hoped it like he'd never hoped for anything before.

She nodded. "Where's the pick-up point? Here?"

"Not quite. Looks like we'll be doing a little break

and enter in the amphibious plane. We've got to fly over to Brisa."

"What about the detective?"

"Detective Lalonde's expecting us at nine tomorrow morning, and I wouldn't put it past her to come and collect me from here in person well before that."

"So we go early? At sun up?"

He took a deep breath. "We go now."

"Now? It's dark out there. Don't you need sunlight? A runway? Traffic control?"

"All of those things would be a bonus, yes. But we need to get to Brisa without anyone knowing where we're going, which means we don't want eyes watching. We go now. In the dark." *And we better hope the moon's not stuck behind a damn cloud when it's time to land,* he thought silently.

Antonia rubbed her hands up her arms. "I sure as hell hope you know what you're doing."

Yeah. He did too. But by leaving now, he was also minimizing the risk of any of Pavlov's men tracking him down to Missy Jane's, and that had to be a good thing. He felt a frisson of worry for his trusting landlady. Would she be safe if the goons came sniffing around Esmeralda Bay?

"You get together what you need. I'm going to send a few emails to my manager to make sure my business can keep going without me for a time. Be ready in…" he looked at his watch and saw it was already past eight o'clock. The moon would be up by now; no point delaying. "Thirty minutes."

"Okay. You going to let me check my emails too?"

He frowned. "Nope. I told you. No communication. Nothing out of the ordinary. And my home computer's ordinary doesn't include Antonia Da Silva logging on from my IP address."

She held her hands in the air. "My bad. Just checking."

He turned to his desk, trying to prioritize the long list of tasks his admin team would have to resolve for him tomorrow. One of them, he thought with a wry twist of his mouth, would be reporting the midnight theft of Island Escape Aviation's amphibious Cessna from Esmeralda Bay, destination unknown. That would put a spanner in Detective Lalonde's day.

Thinking of the detective made him remember the other task he needed to do to ensure he wasn't leaving a disaster in his wake. He pulled up his email account and tapped his way into the program that allowed him to schedule an email for a specific send time. Three hours would do it: long enough for him and Antonia to be safely tucked up in a bay over on the island of Brisa, but short enough he'd beat whatever thugs might be inbound to his bayside cottage.

He pulled the card from his shorts pocket and propped it up against his monitor.

To: Lalonde.J@snandbpolice.com

From: Tyler Cooper

Message:

He paused. What could he write, exactly? He'd write as much of the truth as he could, damn it. His days as an undercover cop were a long way behind him, and he was about done with artifice and bullshit and strategy.

He returned his fingers to the keyboard and started tapping.

Message: Detective. Missy Jane could be in grave danger. Police presence in Esmeralda Bay is highly desirable. Potential inbound criminals who shoot people without compunction when they don't get the information they want. Tyler Cooper.

She'd be getting the subtext, he was sure. She'd know he'd be a no-show for his nine A.M. meeting, but he'd be long gone before she read this.

Antonia settled herself on the couch behind him, her flamingo bag bulging with the clothes Missy Jane had given her and whatever she had left of her original belongings. Had it only been this morning that he'd flown her out of the Manatee Cays? His hours and days and months were blending into one long nightmare. "That was quick."

She shrugged. "It's certainly the least I've packed for a trip in living memory."

He stood up and held out his hand long enough

to bring her to her feet. "I'm sorry your stuff was lost. I know you treasure your belongings."

She frowned, just a little. "Maybe not as much as you think, Tyler. I treasure other things more. Let's go, hey? If it's all right with you, I'd like to get this madcap night flight over and done with. My nerves are still shot from this morning's kamikaze takeoff. May as well get all the crazy flying done in the one day."

He pulled one of her curls, still damp from the shower. "That's my girl."

She reached a hand to click lights off as they left the cottage, but he stayed her hand. "No. Leave them. Let's maintain the masquerade of being here as long as we can."

She shrugged. "Okay. But I'm pretty sure everyone in hearing distance is going to notice an aircraft taking off across the bay."

"Mmm. Let's just hope the bad guys aren't in hearing distance."

He led the way down to the jetty, using a flashlight to light the path. A frog, startled by the light, leapt in front of her, nearly landing on her foot, and she shrieked.

"Oh my god!"

"Relax. They're local to the island. They're way more scared of you than you are of them."

Antonia held her hand to her heart and moved a

step closer to Tyler. "I highly doubt that. My fear level for all slimy hoppy things is fairly high."

"Hold the flashlight, will you? Shine it on the plane door for me."

He'd brought tools with him from his kit and slid needle-nosed pliers into the seam between the door and the plane's frame. "Come on, sweetheart," he muttered, using the allen key to keep pressure on the handle. A soft click rewarded his efforts, and he swung the door open.

"Madam," he bowed. "Your chariot awaits."

She took his hand, and he clasped hers, feeling the vital warm pulse in the underside of her wrist. Their final adventure together was about to start. He'd get her safely to her flight out of Brisa if it killed him.

He passed her in to the plane, then unlashed the floats from the dock. "I'm going to paddle us out as far from the beach as I can," he said, keeping his voice low. Sound carried across the water, and while Esmeralda Bay was isolated, there was the odd cottage like his dotted among the palm-fringed shore. Other residents could be enjoying the moonlight on a late evening stroll along the beach.

Antonia's face was framed in the doorway, the flashlight she held lighting up her hair like a halo. "Aren't you coming in?"

He held up the paddle he'd collected. "I'm going

to stand on the forward float. Do me a favor, would you? Get in the cockpit and shine the flashlight forward through the front windows? Thanks."

She did as he asked, and he moved forward along the port float. It dipped under his weight, and he spent a moment wondering if the gaffer tape and resin patch he'd secured back at the Manatee Cays would be holding up to all the punishment he'd dished out to it and was about to dish out to it again.

The seawater was like ink beneath the plane. As he plunged the paddle into the still water, sparks of phosphorescence darted and foamed in the wake. He cast a look back at the shore. His cottage windows blazed with light, and beyond them, up the rise, he could see the fairy lights Missy Jane left up on her veranda all year round, twinkling like baubles on a Christmas tree.

He wondered if he'd ever be safe enough to come back.

At last, he'd paddled the plane out from the jetty, covering a hundred yards or more out to the center of the bay. He'd taken off from here hundreds of times. Never at night, but that didn't worry him—he could probably do it with his eyes closed. No, it wasn't the takeoff he was worried about, it was the landing. At Brisa. In the dark.

Lifting the paddle, he shuffled his way carefully back on board the plane, stowing the paddle away in its davits before making his way to the cockpit. It was time to go flying.

THE MOON SAVED THEM. Not quite full, by the time the little Cessna had cleared the few miles of ocean that separated St Novia from its sister island of Brisa, the moon had risen to its full height.

The cloud bank had miraculously moved farther out to sea, and as they skirted the shore looking for the bay Tyler knew of, the moon lay a carpet of silver shimmer ahead of them on which to land.

"Like following the yellow brick road," Antonia whispered.

She was tired. Her neck ached from peering through the plexiglass windows of the plane, helping Tyler spot landmarks and townships and road patterns. Finally, they found the bay he wanted, which was close enough to Jamestown to walk there, but far enough away from the populated areas of Brisa to avoid unwanted scrutiny.

The floats touched the water with more of a splash than she'd expected. Water kicked up over one float, spraying over the windscreen until Tyler managed to bring the Cessna back into a level position.

"What now?" she said, into the sudden quiet that fell when the engine was cut off.

"I'm going to paddle us in closer to the other boats. There's more than one seaplane moored here—it's a bay that services a popular tourist spot. We'll be less noticeable here than if we were moored on our own. Hiding in plain sight, if you'll excuse the pun."

She sighed. She was too tired to think, let alone force a laugh at Tyler's attempt at levity. "Do you have a sleeping plan? Because I'm dead on my feet."

"Let me get the anchor sorted, then I'll dig out the yoga mat. I took some seats out of the rear to increase the floorspace. It'll be a squeeze, but not uncomfortable."

An hour later, as she shifted for the thirtieth time on the thin neoprene length of Tyler's yoga mat, she decided his idea of what was uncomfortable and hers were planets apart. The doorway was open to allow a sea breeze to cool the interior of the plane, and Tyler sat in the doorway, his back and shoulders a dark shadow against the star-studded sky.

"Are you on watch, Tyler?" she said at last, giving up trying to sleep.

"Sort of. Not really. I'm just a bit wired."

She knew what he meant. She kept pressing the

dial on her watch, looking at the illuminated display of minutes ticking by. It was nearly midnight—thirteen hours until their meeting with the courier, perhaps another half day after that for her to get to London and all the pressure her arrival would entail. Never mind the fact that she'd be traveling into freezing temperatures wearing a sundress and sandals. If she was quick, and if London traffic was on her side for once, and she didn't freeze to death between the airport and her flat, she'd make the board meeting.

"Crap," she said.

"What?"

"I just realized I don't have any money to catch a cab from Heathrow to my flat."

He turned his head. "I've got a stash of US dollars in my kit. I'll give you as much as you need, and you can change it at the airport into sterling."

She sniffed. "Okay. Thanks."

There was a smile in his voice. "It's the least I can do."

Suddenly, the hilarity of his remark caught at her, and she laughed out loud. "It really is," she said, dissolving into giggles.

When quiet had reclaimed the cabin, Tyler's voice was barely a whisper above the breeze over the water. "I'm sorry, Antonia."

She rolled onto her side and held her arm out

until her fingers could reach his. "I know you are. I am, too. I'm sorry this has happened to you."

She had to get back to London; her team was counting on her. But once she'd had her say and done what she could to avert the dissolution of the *Bella Magazine* international news team, she was going to be devoting one hundred percent of her efforts into helping Tyler.

Because he was counting on her, too. He just didn't know it yet.

Antonia woke in a betwixt-between state that her tired brain struggled to make sense of. Half of her was cramped, with a great metal rib rammed up against her back, but the other half was nosed up to six foot of warm male.

She ran a hand up the navy T-shirt she was snuggled into, feeling the rise and fall of Tyler's breathing. His heart beat strongly beneath her hand.

He'd been *so* strong. She could see now, after her brief foray into the world of organized crime, just how strong Tyler had needed to be. He hadn't just survived, he'd prospered: built up a business, a life.

A large hand covered hers. "Good morning," he said, his voice rumbling through the quiet of the dawn.

She leaned forward, pressed her lips to the skin

showing above the cloth neckline of his shirt. "I hope it will be."

His arm was around her, her head pillowed on his shoulder. He ran his other arm up the rumpled cotton of the secondhand T-shirt she'd slept in. "Me too."

"I feel like I've slept in the cargo hold of a tiny plane," she said.

He let out a laugh. "Yeah. I'd give my virtue away for a mattress. Hot water. Room service."

She wondered, briefly, how on earth she was going to salvage her hair. No comb. No hair straightener. She thought longingly of her black-and-tan beauty case tucked snugly into her jaffa-red suitcase—probably Exhibit A in the court case *The People Vs Tyler Cooper and Witless Airborne Friend.*

"You'll be able to grab a shower at the airport. Buy some gear."

"Hallelujah." She was silent for a time. In a few hours, she'd be walking away from Tyler, away from this maelstrom of events. "I wish you could come with me," she said.

His hand tightened over hers. "I can't. To Pavlov, I'm more valuable dead than alive. And the only way to stay beneath his radar is to disappear again."

His words angered her. "To me, you're more valuable alive. Promise me you'll stay that way." She felt tears start and blinked them away. Today was not a day for weakness. Today was step one in outwitting the bad guys: getting her out of here and away so she could do what needed to be done back in London, then plan her own strategy to help Tyler out of his cage.

She refused to believe there was no way for him to be free. She took in a deep breath, making a memory of the smell and feel of him, lying there pressed against her in the tight confines of the cargo bay. She could be sad later. She could worry later. Now was the time for something else entirely. She tiptoed her fingers up the cords of his neck, skimming over the bristles she found there. "Speaking of your virtue…"

She felt his cheeks grin under her exploring fingers and sucked in a breath as his hand at her back slid under her T-shirt and pulled it off in one smooth move.

Beneath it, she wore the rose underwear she'd pulled out of her suitcase back in Manatee Cays. Was it only yesterday? She'd been savagely hungover after the wedding and dressing for her return flight to London. Silk and heels, knock-em-dead underwear and perfume: dressing to kill was her go-to method for soothing her wounded heart, and after the rejection Tyler had doled out to her on the beach, her heart had been crushed.

She knew why he had, now. She knew he'd

thought he had nothing to offer her but trouble and heartache.

Well. There'd been plenty of that, and that was just in the last twenty-four hours. But there'd been something else too: a something that soothed her scarred heart. The pull of chemistry between them had always been intense, but now, with a deadline of separation rushing towards them, its pull felt like a tidal rip.

This moment they shared in the cool of the morning with the air clear and the seas glimmering with promise and beauty wasn't about what he could offer her. Now was about what she could offer him: a moment of comfort, snatched in the lull before the storm. A body to cherish. A brief moment of togetherness that Tyler could hold on to as he stepped forward into a future he thought he needed to live alone.

The gentle curl of lust she'd woken with on finding herself in Tyler's arms kicked into a tsunami. "Clothes off," she ordered.

"Make me."

She grinned. Oh goody, a challenge. She slid a hand down between their bodies and found a metal button holding together a canvas pair of shorts. Flicking it open could have taken seconds, but she made it last a lot longer than that. Same with the zipper.

"Death by patience," murmured Tyler, his hot breath scalding her neck.

She smiled and half sat to wriggle his shorts and underwear down his legs. She crawled, slowly, up the length of him from his ankles to his face, relishing the feel of her sleep-warm body sliding against his. The satin of her bra made its own soft sigh as she moved along him.

She slid her hands under the rim of his navy T-shirt and inched them upwards, enjoying the slow reveal of smooth tanned flesh. She dropped a kiss into the groove between rib and stomach, and goose bumps jumped to life across his torso. She spread her hands wide, up over his chest, then tugged until he obliged by lifting his shoulders so she could fling his shirt away.

She eased back on her knees, and he lay still, his eyes on her face. He was drinking her in, she knew it, and it touched her. He thought this was his last chance at being with her, maybe with anyone. No way was she letting that happen, she thought, as she reached behind her and undid her bra. She lowered the rosy froth of lace and satin and tossed it in the direction of the cabin seating. She smiled down at him. "You going to touch me? Or are you just looking today, Captain?"

His eyes were serious. "I could look at you forever, Antonia. I hope you know that."

In answer, she pulled up his hand and held it over her breast, where beneath the warm flesh he found there he would feel the wild skittering of her heart. "Show me."

And on a groan, Tyler reached up and pulled her to him, fusing his lips to hers even as his hands began their wondrous journey over her body.

And boy oh boy, did he show her.

14

The café they needed to locate was in the heart of Brisa's main tourist hub, Jamestown. After an early morning skinny-dip between the plane floats, Tyler inflated the small raft that was stowed in the hold, and they paddled into shore.

A beachside shower was a welcome discovery, Tyler holding up a towel so Antonia could use it without wetting the only underwear she owned. She lashed out afterwards with the mascara Missy Jane had pressed on her so she could pretty herself up for her fake engagement celebration.

Between the landlady's hand-me-downs and the toiletries she'd cobbled together from the supplies at Tyler's cabin, she was beginning to feel less like a vagabond and more like a smart, detail-oriented professional. She allowed herself a moment of smug indulgence: a professional who'd spent the early hour of dawn having all the details driven right out of her brain.

She ran her fingers through her curls in the hope that they would dry in some sort of order, then picked up her duffle and slung it over her shoulder. She was as ready as she would ever be for what the day had in store.

Tyler had found a farmer willing to let them share the bed of his pickup truck with his trays of guava and lychees while she was daydreaming with her mascara wand, so she hopped up into it, determined to take what pleasure she could from these last few hours.

The tiny roads crisscrossing this part of Brisa were thin strips of asphalt that petered out at the road's edge into lush, green carpet grass. Their route snaked between hills and valleys, and everywhere, blue sea glimmered in the distance.

Yacht sails made white triangles out in the bays, and she wondered if Ben had read her message yet. She had no clue even where his honeymoon would take him—she doubted he did either. For a man with a brain like an abacus, he had the planning habits of a hippy.

He'd get it soon. And when he did, she'd be a step closer to freeing Tyler from his cage.

She looked over at the man she'd soon be saying goodbye to, sitting on the opposite wheel hub to hers in the back of the truck. He had a backpack strapped to his back, stuffed with she knew not what. He'd not shared his plans with her about what he was going to do after delivering her to the airport, but she didn't think it involved returning to his beloved Cessna.

She ran her fingers over the bulge in her pocket. One thousand dollars in US money. She'd been amazed when he pulled it out of his pack in the plane. "I don't need this much," she'd said.

"Antonia. You've got a long journey on fake papers ahead of you. You need enough to tide you over if a few wild eventualities get thrown your way, and I won't be there to help you."

She pursed her lips. There he'd gone again, assuming she was someone in need of man-help. Tyler had an issue with giving orders.

She'd ignored his lack of faith in her abilities. "I'll certainly be buying something to wear. I don't want to arrive in London looking as though I'm about to play in a beach volleyball tournament."

He'd grinned. "And, honey?"

She cocked her head. Hmm. She kind of liked being called honey, who would have thought?

"Yes?"

"You might want to buy yourself a brush."

But that had been the end of their banter. The

closer they came to Jamestown, the deeper the furrows in Tyler's forehead grew.

After a dusty half hour, the farmer pulled into a parking lot near a cluster of market stalls, and they jumped out. Tyler handed the man some money, but the old farmer refused to take it, instead presenting them with a handful of lychees each.

"Thank you," said Antonia, and sank her teeth into one as they turned to walk through the markets. Out in the bay, dwarfing the wharves and local fishing boats, a cruise ship was anchored, a monolith of portholes and balconies and deck upon deck of expensive white ship. Its passengers were clearly all ashore, because the market was crowded with middle-aged Americans taking pictures, posing among the colored banners and fabrics of the market stalls.

"This is a stroke of luck," said Tyler. "We'll blend in with the crowd." He paused at a stall selling raffia beach hats, which were being snapped up by the tourists. He spoke a rattle of creole to the stall holders, who smiled and handed over two hats.

He turned to her and placed one on her head, pulling it down low over her face and hair.

"How do I look?" she said.

"Like you just stepped off a cruise ship in Jamestown and bought a cheap hat." He put his own on his head. "I think we should go scope out the café where the ID drop's going to happen. Get our bearings."

"Good plan. Maybe we could scope out its coffee machine while we're there."

"Amen to that," Tyler said.

They joined a crowd of holidaymakers headed towards the main street of town, but Antonia paused when a couple in matching safari suits struck up a conversation.

"Our first trip out of the States, isn't it, Farley?" said the plump woman whose lips and nails were painted a fussy shade of peach.

"Yes, dear."

Farley's wife didn't give him much scope to say more. She launched into a torrent of chatter as Antonia obliged them by taking a photo of the holiday pair with the cruise ship in the background.

"I've always wanted to see foreign places, but Farley's never seen much point in it, have you, dear?"

"No, love."

"But Betty-Lou died, that's my cousin on my daddy's side, the one whose no-good husband cheated on her and she never did get the brood of children she was itching to get, did she, Farley?"

"No, she didn't."

"Well, she ups and leaves me a little something in her will. We were that tickled, weren't we?"

"Right tickled."

"And I said to Farley, that's it. We're booking ourselves on one of those fancy cruises I've been seeing in the magazines all these years, and here we are."

"Right here," said Farley.

Antonia could see Tyler was itching to move on, but the woman seemed so delighted with life she couldn't resist lingering. "And have you loved your cruise?"

"Oh goodness, yes. And today's our last day. We call into St Novia this afternoon, then by tomorrow night we'll be back in Miami, won't we, Farley?"

"Yes, love."

Antonia handed the phone back and smiled her farewell. She hurried to catch up with Tyler who was waiting on a turn in the path frowning over the bay. "What's up?"

He shook his head. "Just thinking. Come on, let's go find this café."

Antonia felt her stomach rumble. "Let's get some food while we're there. I could eat a tourist."

THE CHIHUAHUA CAFÉ stood on the corner of two busy streets. Outside, tables facing the water were filled with locals and tourists, with plates of scattered crumbs and folded napkins indicating whatever they had been eating had been deemed most satisfactory.

The interior was dim after the dizzy glare of morning sun outside. Tyler's eyes flicked over the essentials as he gave himself time to adapt to the change in lighting. Kitchen—back left—and it would have an exit to a back alley where the dumpsters lived and where the kitchen hands no doubt snuck in a smoke during breaks. An old-fashioned serving counter ran the length of the back wall, with soda stands and overhead racks of glassware picking up the reflection from the lights.

A young guy in a red bandanna was punching numbers into a till for a gaggle of tourists lined up at the bar, and waiters scurried from table to table, delivering coffees and sugar-cake and coconut shrimp.

Busy was good. Busy was distracting.

A back corner glimmered with computer screens and a row of spotty, techno-mad teenagers hunched there, their busy fingers clattering on keyboards. He turned away. The nook reserved for the internet café was shallow enough for him to see there was no threat there, no exits or entrances, certainly no one older than the age of sixteen.

Antonia's nose was twitching like an eighteenth-century beagle on the scent of a fox. "This place smells like heaven," she said. "Coffee. Bacon. And what are *those*?"

Her eyes were glued to a platter being delivered to a local couple seated by the large windows overlooking the street.

"Johnny cakes. They're a Caribbean favorite. Like a cornmeal pancake, only deep-fried and dusted with sugar and cinnamon, or you can have them savory stuffed with saltfish. They taste even better than they look."

"OMG. I hope our runaway budget has enough juice in it to cover a platter of them."

He ran his hand down her back, enjoying the rush of comfort it gave him. "See if you can snag a table at the back. I'll order us something."

"Make my coffee a big one. The biggest they've got."

"You got it."

He relaxed a little as they waited for their food to arrive. Coffee was doing a salsa step-ball-change through his veins, Antonia's hand was in his, and he'd satisfied himself the café for the drop had a back entrance. Later, closer to the one o'clock deadline, if he chose a table at the back, he'd have a wide view of anyone on the street who might be taking an overzealous interest in him.

He could take a moment. He picked up a johnny cake from the platter just delivered to the table and held it out to Antonia. "Take a bite. See what you think."

She sank her teeth into the warm puff. "Oh, this is heaven. Like if donuts and French crepes had a secret lovechild, this would be it." She snatched up another from the platter. "I can't believe I've not heard of these before. I've wasted my youth, Tyler."

He leaned over a dusted a speck of cinnamon from her top lip.

"Another coffee, señor? Señorita?"

Red bandanna guy was hovering over their table, a linen cloth draped over his arm and some sort of modern waiter's pad that looked like a smartphone pointed in their direction.

"Gosh, yes." Antonia beamed up at the young man.

Tyler shook his head. "Not for me."

He waited until the waiter had moved away. "While you're having that coffee, I'm going to walk around the block, see if I can find the alley that leads to the kitchens. I won't be long. You okay with that?"

"Sure. Take your time."

SHE WAS MORE than okay with that. The second Antonia had entered the Chihuahua Café—okay, not quite the first second, that was taken up by breathing in the exquisite smells of perfect little coffee beans being ground up and immersed in steaming hot water—she'd seen the internet café sign tucked away in a corner of the room.

Now was her chance to see if Ben had received her message. Tyler wouldn't like it, but Tyler had trust issues. He'd never believe her if she told him Ben was smarter than any IT goons Pavlov would have on his hit team.

A teenager moved out of a seat in the corner, and she jumped up and slid into it, the vinyl chair still warm. A box blinked onscreen asking for a code. Crap. She had a thousand US dollars stuffed in her bag, but no local currency. No coins. No credit card. A waitress brought over her second coffee, and she flashed a smile. "How much is this? For me to use the internet?"

The girl smiled, and pointed to a sticker mounted across the keyboard: *your access code is Chihuahua.* "Free for customers, madam." She set the coffee down next to her, and Antonia typed in the café's name, relaxing when the glorious six-letter word that was *google* flashed up on the screen.

Perfect. She tapped into her gmail account and watched the flood of emails scroll down the screen. Clothing sales, travel insurance offers, spam, Amazon book purchase receipts. One from her mother, her yoga club, more spam, and the regency romance title she'd ordered had arrived at her local book store. But nothing from Ben.

Wait. She ran her eye back over the inbox again, and re-read the subject lines of the spam. *Does your man need help with his limp Manatee? Viagra can help with that. Free trial.*

She snorted. Manatee Cays—the very spot where Ben had married her childhood friend Sabrina a handful of days ago. She clicked on to the email and read the terse message below.

Write down this link. Type it into a search box. Follow the prompts.

Bother! She didn't have a pen. The teenager next to her was glued to her facebook screen, and it took a couple of attempts for Antonia to break her concentration.

"Excuse me. Honey? Hello?" In the end, she waved her hand beneath the girl's nose. "Sorry to interrupt. Have you got a pen?" She mimicked writing with her hand in the air.

The girl pulled a pen from her bag and handed it over.

"Oh. And paper?"

The girl rolled her eyes, tore a strip from the bottom of what looked like an exercise book used for homework, and handed it over, too.

Antonia scribbled down the link, rechecking every letter and digit in the long sequence of code.

She had it. She was just switching screens back to the search engine when big male hands came down on her shoulders, pinning her to her seat.

"What the fuck are you doing, Antonia?"

Crap. She twisted in her seat, wincing as she saw the naked fury on Tyler's face. She held up a hand, trying to placate him. "I'm trying to help."

"Help? How can you help?"

"If you'd listen to me—"

"This isn't some bullshit game of hide-and-seek we're playing, Antonia. I can't believe you went behind my back after I ordered you to stay offline."

She reared back. "Ordered me? I've got news for you, Captain Alpha. I don't follow orders. I listen to advice and make my own damn decisions."

His eyes closed, and he appeared to be battling with himself. "Antonia. Okay, I'm not ordering you. I'm begging you, on my knees if I have to. You don't know this world. If you want to stay alive, you have to do as I say, and that means no communication, no phone, and definitely no damn chitchat on Facebook."

She pursed her lips. She tapped her foot. She spun the chewed-up pen that was in her hand and contemplated what she would be doing with it right this second if it was a sword, not a pen, and she was living in the Middle Ages. Severing Tyler's balls from his headless torso? Skewering his eyeballs to an ancient Yew tree, then dancing round his chilling corpse while drinking mead with a troupe of lusty young warriors?

But here she was, wielding a pen, in an upscale café in Jamestown, and none of those options were available to her. She'd have to use her big girl words instead.

"Tyler—"

He cut her off. "We're leaving."

She slapped his hand off her arm and held up a finger. "Not yet. I'll come with you when I'm ready. But I won't be ready until you've heard what I have to say. Are you listening?"

He ran his hands through his hair, and she heard the scrape of his fingers over his unshaven beard. He looked tired. And stressed. His controlled demeanor was beginning to fray at the edges.

He nodded. "I'm sorry. I'm listening."

"Point one. Just because I'm fun, just because I like to live life with a swing in my step, doesn't mean I'm not capable of thinking for myself."

"I know that, I just—"

It was her turn to cut him off. "Point two. You know nothing about my career, and mainly, can I point out, because you haven't asked. I get it, you're juggling a lot of tricky balls in that thick head of yours, but a friend—and I think we're rather more than that to each other by now, Tyler—a friend takes an interest. Asks questions. Supports. Finds out. And if you'd done any of those things, you'd know this isn't the first time in my life I've been involved with organized crime."

He frowned. "What do you mean?"

"I'm an editor. I run a team of journalists. We send some of those journalists into bloody dangerous territory, and we don't send them in blindly. We take precautions. We communicate cryptically. We don't advertise their presence in hostile territory by chitchatting about it on social media."

He had the grace to look foolish.

"I'm sorry—"

She cut him off again. He could grovel later. She felt like she was back in the newsroom at *Bella*, having to bring a line of noisy and unruly junior journalists into line. "Point three." She softened her tone. The rest of her points could all go hang, really, because this was the main point. "You're not alone, Tyler—even though you are doing your damnedest to be alone in this fight. Maybe I can help you. Maybe together, we *can* bring this bastard Pavlov down."

She held out a hand and he took it, linking his fingers into hers.

His words, when he finally spoke, were bleak. "We can't beat Pavlov. And as long as he's free, I will always have to be alone."

She decided she'd had just about enough of his proclamations of doom. Now was the moment. She could tell the truth about why she'd been on the internet, or she could lie.

Did she want to lie? No. Not at all. But Tyler on the run with his cop-face and his hackles up was a very different type of man to Tyler the lover. He wasn't relaxed. He wasn't receptive to any idea that relied on anyone but himself. And he was already under more pressure that any one man could be expected to deal with.

How much of his aversion to trust related to his time on the run and how much to the grim childhood he'd touched upon, she couldn't tell. Only time and some sneaky questioning would gain her those answers, so challenging his knee-jerk reaction to trust would have to wait for another day.

She searched her internal catalogue of synonyms for lying and found one. She'd prevaricate...just until she'd had a chance to get some concrete data from Ben. Maybe Ben couldn't help, in which case she didn't need to say anything at all about her Grand Plan. Or maybe, as she suspected, Ben could do more than help. Maybe Ben could find enough info to shine a spotlight on Pavlov's Moneyman—in which case, she would share her plan with Tyler and he would understand that there really were people on his side who he could trust.

Prevarication it was then, as ugly as it felt. "I'm looking up flights, hotshot."

"From Brisa?"

"This island's about the size of a football oval. There can't be that many flights out that connect me with London. I want to know how likely it is that I'll be making it home in time."

Tyler squeezed her shoulders. "I'm sorry. I overreacted. You'll make it. What have you found?"

She turned back to the computer and typed *international flights out of Brisa to London* into the search bar. Her eye fell on the strip of paper where she'd scribbled Ben's link. Crap. She'd not yet put that away. This lying business was trickier than she'd supposed. "From St Novia, there's a British Airways out to Gatwick via Ballena late afternoon. I've missed the ferry, so we might have to go in the Cessna."

Tyler reached over her shoulder and closed the screen. "We'll make it work. Now come on. We can lay about on the beach among the flocks of tourists until it's time to meet. I'll even buy you an ice cream, to make up for being a jerk earlier."

She stood, turning to face him. "Which you-being-a-jerk occasion are you referring to? Because it seems to me you owe me a whole lot more than one ice cream."

"You've got a smart mouth, Antonia. I like it."

She smiled, and linked her fingers with his. In

her other hand she held the scrap of paper with Ben's link scribbled across it, the link that might be the way to save Tyler's future. She folded it carefully, then surreptitiously snuck it under the underwire of her bra. She'd find a way to use it, somehow.

As she stepped over the threshold that led from the cool interior of the Chihuahua Café to the busy street, the strap securing her foot into Missy Jane's flowered sandal broke. Bloody hell. She stumbled forward, wondering as she did so just how long they'd sat rotting in the humid darkness of Missy Jane's closet.

The grit of cement against her knee had her wincing as she hit the pavement, but at the moment of impact, a whip-sharp bark sounded once, twice, above her head.

Glass shattered.

Tourists screamed.

Tyler's fingers clamped, hard, over hers, then slackened and pulled away.

Her brain reeled with all the information it needed to process: the noise that still echoed in her ears had been gunfire, and one of those bullets had shattered the café window directly where her head had been the second before she'd stumbled.

But there had been two shots fired.

She staggered to her feet, too shocked to breathe, too frightened to truly think. All she could see was Tyler, slumped against the doorway. He had been a half step ahead of her, his arm reaching backward and holding her hand. Now he was barely on his feet, but his eyes were on hers, and that was good, that was okay, he could look at her forever so long as those eyes just stayed open.

But that was the only thing that was okay. Glass had exploded over his face, salting it with dust that glittered in the harsh sun. Red streaks of blood flowed from his hairline, but that wasn't the worst not-okay. A sob broke from her as she processed what she was seeing: the creeping bloom of color soaking his shirt, the hand he held pressed against it.

"Oh Christ." She struggled to say the words. "You've been shot."

He tried to speak, and she kneeled beside him, holding his head in her hands. "Tyler?"

He spoke again, and this time she heard it.

"Run. You have to run. Now."

She shook her head and argued with him even as the tears started. "I'm not running anywhere, Tyler. You need a doctor. I'm going to get you some help."

A movement caught her eye. At last, she thought, someone had come to their aid.

"Call an ambulance," she shouted over her shoulder. "*Il dottore.*" Crap. Was that even Spanish? Creole?

Why weren't people helping? Why wasn't she hearing ambulance sirens? There was a man shot here for god's sake. Her man.

She looked up, and met the eyes of the young waiter with the red bandanna. "Oh, thank heaven. Please get hel—"

But then her words failed as the waiter brought up a hand holding a dull black gun and her head exploded with pain.

Her world spun through a spectrum where grays and blacks were the only colors. Pain so sharp it burned flared in her head, bodies scuffled, men cursed, Tyler's voice groaned in pain. Above it all was the shrill pitch of a woman's voice calling in fear. Was it her own voice she was hearing? An onlooker's?

The last thing she was aware of before the blackness took her was the screech of tires; of Tyler being bundled into the backseat of a sleek, dark car; of a dreadlocked young man leaping in after him; of a bright-red bandanna fluttering to the glass-strewn pavement.

She slumped, unconscious, to the ground.

15

Tyler woke with his legs tied to a chair and his hands lashed behind his back. He was in the corner of a basement—or maybe it was a parking garage—and someone had forgotten to turn the air conditioner on, because the temperature was sitting at about two-hundred-and-boil fahrenheit.

His chest was burning, but the pain was remote, like it was happening in a different dimension to the one he was currently inhabiting. Was he drugged? He shook his head from side to side, felt the dull blur of barbiturates. Morphine? He hoped like hell he'd not been pumped full of some street drug. A bandage was inexpertly strapped to his chest, the adhesive on the tape pulling at his chest hair. Who would have bandaged him? And why? Why not just put a bullet in his head and be done with it?

An odd rumbling noise sounded overhead: loud, then louder, then rumbled off with a screech of tires. Definitely a parking garage above him. Which was good, in that it meant he'd not been taken out to sea to be chopped up for shark bait or out into the jungle interior of the island to be forced to dig his own grave.

But it was also bad, because it meant that they wanted something from him. He flexed his fingers, remembering their efforts last time they'd tried to get information from him. The memory of hearing his bones crack still made him queasy all these years later.

Broken bones notwithstanding, what information was there that he could possibly provide? He'd been out of the police force for years. The only information he possessed that could hurt Pavlov was in his memory: he could identify people who he'd seen doing business with the big man himself. He was potentially an important part of the chain of evidence that could one day indict Pavlov, but without concrete evidence, like bank transactions and proof of money laundering and credible links between drug procurement and sales, he was just a witness. Sure, a witness that would sway a judge and jury, as he was an ex-cop and ex-undercover agent, but still just a witness.

Which brought him around again to his first question—why was he still alive?

He craned his head, searching the dim shadows for movement, light, anything. Nothing shifted. No doorways beckoned, no footsteps broke the silence.

He yelled, and the sound echoed off the water puddled on the cement floor, the dull grey of cinder-block walls. He yelled again and again and again, bucking at the restraints that kept him chained to the chair like a beast.

No one responded. No one came.

He slumped back in his chair and closed his eyes. Antonia's face swam before him, her eyes wet as she saw the bullet wound in his chest.

He flexed his shoulders and hauled at the ties binding his wrists until he felt his skin give. Antonia. Who would save her now?

"I'M GOING TO SAVE TYLER," said Antonia.

Detective Jozy Lalonde eyed her over the wide expanse of desk before continuing to write on her notepad. "Okay. So Tyler was shot in the region between chest and shoulder?"

"Yes." Hell. She needed to be moving, not sitting here answering the same questions over and over again. Tyler had been kidnapped, for heaven's sake! He'd been in the hands of criminals for nearly twenty-four hours! She needed helicopters, SWAT teams, action.

She bit back her impatience and tried to calm her thoughts. She'd been back on St Novia since dawn, and had nearly chewed off her arm in frustration waiting for the police station to open. She'd come here to seek out Jozy Lalonde because she'd thought, back on the beach at Esmeralda Bay, that anyone with creases in their uniform ironed so perfectly had to be trustworthy. It was time to put that assumption to the test.

"He was then dragged off by a young man who until that time you had thought was a barista who worked at Chihuahua Café and then loaded into a"—Lalonde referred to her notes for a second —"dark sedan and driven off."

"Yes, that's right. I must have blacked out for a second. When bandanna guy was passing me to get to Tyler, he clubbed me on the head with his gun. When I came to, there were sirens roaring in every direction, a crowd in the café and on the street. I didn't know what to do, so I ran."

The detective paused her notetaking and looked up. "Why not wait for the police? A man was shot; you were a witness. Why flee the scene?"

Had this woman not been listening before when

Antonia explained about Tyler's trust issues with law enforcement? She pulled at her hair in frustration. "I don't know, okay. My instincts tell me to go to the police when there's trouble, but guess what? Until a few days ago, I'd never been in trouble. But Tyler *was* the police, and he was let down by one of his own and it destroyed his life. He had good reason to be wary, and he was no longer there with me to give me advice, and when I say advice, I mean orders, so I did what he told me to do. I ran."

"Okay. So you ran away. Where did you go? How did you get back over here to St Novia?"

"I had money. Tyler gave me some, but no identification papers. We were supposed to meet a US government agent at the Chihuahua Café at one o'clock who would have new papers for me. Fake ones, but enough to get me back to London. I thought about waiting around to see if the courier would show, but..."

The lure of a plane ticket back to London had been tempting, but not with Tyler's life possibly bleeding out in the back of some crook's car while she swanned her way back to the other side of the world. It didn't matter how many passports and plane tickets the courier was willing to shower down upon her, she couldn't leave, not now. Her boss must be thinking she'd lost her mind...her colleagues too, for that matter. The meeting was probably over by now, decisions made without any input from her. They'd think she didn't care. She might not even have a job to go back to.

Not that any of that mattered. Tyler, bleeding and in the hands of hardened killers—saving him was the only thing that mattered.

"And this was to replace your passport that you left in Ballena Airport?"

"Correct."

"So you had money. You had no ID. You decided not to wait at the café to see if Tyler's contact showed."

"Yes, yes, all correct. Tyler is convinced it was someone in his old narcotics team who betrayed him five years ago. The only people who should have known we were going to be at the Chihuahua Café were me, Tyler, his contact Rob and the courier bringing the paperwork. When Tyler was taken, it had to be through Rob or the courier that his location was discovered, because red bandanna guy was there *before* us. Someone had placed him there."

"And how did you end up here?"

"There was a tourist ship in, one of those mammoth white things, like a floating multi-story building with funnels. We'd been chatting to some of its passengers earlier in the day, and they'd mentioned the next stop was St Novia and then back home to Miami. I thought about St Novia, I thought about you, and then I snuck on board."

The detective frowned. "How? Security's pretty tight on those things."

Antonia smiled, for what felt like the first time in a lifetime. "Luck, sass, and a really large sunhat. I flirted my way on board after waiting until the shore crew were inundated with a crowd of tourists. I spent the night on a lounger in a hidden corner of the pool deck, which would have seemed like purgatory if I hadn't spent the night before that sleeping on a yoga mat in the cargo hold of a plane the size of a Barbie campervan. And here I am."

Detective Lalonde was silent for a time, considering her notes. She picked up the phone on her desk and snapped out a few instructions in the local patois, which Antonia couldn't understand.

"What are you—" Antonia began, but the woman held up a hand.

"One moment."

A young policeman entered the room, dragging behind him, wonder of wonders, her jaffa-red suitcase! She clapped her hands, and would have exclaimed if the detective hadn't frowned at her and silenced her with a cut of her hand through the air. She held her amazement in while the young policeman wheeled the case into a corner and deposited it, along with her travel knapsack, by the desk.

The door snicked shut behind him, and Antonia looked at the detective questioningly. "I don't understand. How did you end up with my stuff?"

Lalonde pulled open her desk drawer and brought out a red leather passport. She passed it over to her. "Is this yours?"

Antonia flipped it open to the photo page, and there she was, spic and span, makeup, tidy hair, the works. She huffed out a breath. "Well, I can understand why you'd doubt it, comparing this photo to the me sitting here before you, but, yes, I am Antonia Da Silva. This is my passport. I can't tell you how pleased I am to have it back. But how did you..."

Her words trailed off as a cold hand of fear clutched at her. "Are you working with Flaco?"

Detective Lalonde frowned. "I'm asking the questions here. But, no, if you mean the customs official at Ballena Airport who kicked off this ruckus, then no."

The policewoman tapped her finger on the desk, then appeared to come to a conclusion. "I already knew of Tyler Cooper before this, er, incident."

Antonia stared at her, open-mouthed. "You *knew*?"

"One of my roles within the police force is liaison with Interpol. We knew we had a person of interest living at Esmeralda Bay. We didn't know the details —clearly, the US has kept a cloak over his file to protect him from the reprisals of the drug cartel. When the Ballena police contacted us about an illegal takeoff and we tracked the plane down to Island Escape Aviation, it was pretty clear Tyler's past had finally caught up with him."

Wow. "Why didn't you just tell Tyler when we saw you on the beach?"

Lalonde nodded. "I wish I had, now. I had reached out to my counterparts in Interpol based in the US. I was awaiting their feedback before proceeding. We had very little information—I needed to know more before I involved the local police."

Antonia felt a flood of relief. "So you believe me. About everything."

"I believe that Tyler has been hunted down by Pavlov's gang. But where have they taken him? Why have they taken him? Pardon my bluntness, Miss Da Silva, but why not kill him when they had their chance? These are questions to which I do not know the answers."

Antonia thought about Ben, about what he may or may not be able to find out. She pursed her lips, thinking about what she ought to reveal. "If I had a lead, a small one, would you feel compelled to report it to your superiors?"

Detective Lalonde steepled her fingers. "Where are you going with this?"

"Tyler trusts no one. Not you, and barely even me, and events yesterday morning have probably only reinforced the way he feels. But I may be able to help find incriminating information about Pavlov, only I'm not willing to share my information with you if you're going to repeat it to your superiors. Tyler believes Pavlov's tentacles are everywhere: in government, in law enforcement, maybe in the service team who empty your trash and restock your coffee and cookies. Some are on the payroll by choice, and some because they've been threatened. How can I know that your boss isn't one of those people? Or your receptionist? Your floor sweeper?"

The detective stared at her through eyes that had narrowed. Cop eyes, Antonia thought. Tyler had given her the exact same look when she'd asked to borrow his phone. She sighed. Her people skills seemed to have evaporated along with her orderly, humdrum, dreaming-of-adventure life.

Jozy spoke grudgingly. "It is too soon for me to judge what I will, or will not, be including in my reports. And you are no one to be telling me who I can trust in my own workplace, but I can make allowances for the hell day you've had and the worry you are feeling about Cooper. Just this once." The detective turned and gazed out the window of her office to the palms in the manicured forecourt, the brilliant sea beyond. "Here is my suggestion."

Antonia waited. At last, here was the moment she'd been waiting for through twenty-odd hours of worry about Tyler while she hid in the dark on a cruise ship devoted to pleasure. Surely, *surely*, her idea to come to Jozy Lalonde would pay off and Tyler would somehow be found.

"Three things." The detective held up a finger. "One. Until we know how Pavlov's gang discovered Tyler was to be in the Chihuahua Café, we keep information sharing to a minimum. Two. You will share your lead with me and I will consider what we can do with that information."

Antonia frowned. "But—"

Jozy rolled straight over her complaint. "Three. I will investigate where Tyler has been taken. I don't care how big or small the lead is you think you have, Brisa is my patch. Reports will have been filed by officers on scene after the shooting. I don't care how deep Pavlov's men think they may have wormed their way into my homeland, I know Brisa, I know the people. We'll find him."

The unspoken words lay over them both in the airconditioned cool of her office. *But when we find him, will he be alive? Or dead?* Impulsively, she reached across the table and grasped the detective's arm. "Thank you. Thank you so much. Now—I need a computer to see if my lead is going to pan out. I think I'd better use an internet café in town, to be more anonymous. I understand nothing about internet security, but Tyler is paranoid about Pavlov's reach, and I'd like to respect that. I need to book myself into a hotel, too, now that I have clothes again."

A thought struck her, and she stood to retrieve her knapsack, fiddling through it until she found her wallet. She snapped it open: credit cards, driver's license, oyster card, money; her old life winked up at her from within its zippered confines. "Hmm. Flaco clearly only indulges in top-end crime, like murder and extortion. Robbery from underpaid magazine executives is beneath him, because even my cash is still here."

Jozy stood. "I wouldn't get too excited about your credit cards just yet. Find a hotel. Use cash. Meet me on the beach below the cruise ship terminal at noon. It is a public place, always busy with tourists. We can decide then the next step forward. Okay?"

Antonia nodded, and reached out to shake the detective's outstretched hand. "Thank you, Detective."

The woman smiled. "I think you can call me Jozy. Now, let's get to work, and see if we can find where those men have taken your fiancé."

Her fiancé. Antonia felt a bridegroom-sized hand squeeze her heart. He wasn't her fiancé—but what was one more layer of pretense in Tyler's life? She'd cling to it for now. Without Tyler here, his warm body and brooding frown towering over her, their pretend relationship was all she had left. And she wasn't ready to give it up.

16

An internet café was easy to find. So was a beachside hotel happy to accept US dollars in exchange for a cheerful room with no questions asked. Antonia took a long sip of the latte that had come with a cocoa-tinted macaroon, then scrolled her way through the entry procedure on the computer screen.

She pushed her bag to the side of the table to bring the keyboard farther forward and the phone she'd so recently been reunited with slipped out. She picked it up, flicked the leather cover open. Dead, of course. She rifled deeper into the clutter of her knapsack to find the charger, then paused. 4G, internet pings, satellite coverage: these words were a foreign language to her, but she'd read enough news, seen enough re-runs of Mission Impossible movies to realize data *was* vulnerable.

Pavlov had Tyler now—would anyone really care where some possibly-unemployed rumple-clothed woman from London was?

She itched to charge her phone, check her messages, call her boss, her colleagues, and find out what had transpired at the board meeting, or whether they'd postponed it pending her return. Or had the board charged ahead and decided her fate, and the fate of her whole team, in her absence?

With a sigh, she dropped her phone back into her bag. Events were unfolding that were out of her skill set. As much as she might wish she could be in London to face the possible end of her job, her priority now was Tyler. Nothing mattered but helping him.

Against his wishes, she'd put her trust in Detective Lalonde and come to her for help. If her instincts were right, Jozy was the one person able to find Tyler and rescue him from whoever had taken him on Brisa.

And she'd deliberately ignored his wishes when she'd contacted Ben, but Tyler wasn't the only person capable of making a decision. She *knew* Ben could help—not today, perhaps, not for rescue and police work—but for tomorrow and the next day and all the days that came after. She was thinking long term, even though she knew Tyler wasn't. She wanted him out of Pavlov's clutches for good.

She flexed her fingers over the grubby keyboard and put her mind to the job at hand. Ben's link was propped in front of her, and she typed it in, biting her lip as she hit enter. Follow the prompts, he'd said. The screen went black, and a flurry of script started rolling up the screen. A cursor blinked, then a command: *type your nickname from school.*

Her nickname? Bloody hell. Next time she saw Sabrina and Charlotte, she was going to find out who of them had broken the unbreakable vow of sisterhood and told Ben her old nickname. Her hair *so* did not look like pasta.

Grimacing, the stabbed the sequence into the textbox, *Toni Macaroni*, then hit enter, sending the hated name into the void of the dark web, or wherever Ben had organized her answer to be sent.

The screen flickered and the mouse pointer started acting in a crazy way on screen, as though someone else was in charge of the computer.

Hmm. Someone else *was* in charge. And that someone was Ben. Text tapped itself out in front of her. *Hey Toni. You can type freely. We're secure. What's up?*

Oh, thank god. Antonia started typing, for once in her life careless of typos and grammar and sentence fragments. *Big problems. Turns out, Tyler is an ex-cop who is (sort of) a person in witness protection. He's been shot and kidnapped.*

Holy shit. Are you safe?

Yes. Safe but scared. I've put my trust in a local police-woman, name of Detective Jozy Lalonde. She's trying to locate the place they've taken him.

Where are you? I take it you're still in the Caribbean?

St Novia. But Tyler was taken on Brisa. I need a favor.

Anything. What can I do?"

That, she thought. That was what Tyler thought he didn't have—people who answered requests to help with the words *anything, what can I do.* Well, that changed today.

She hunched over the keypad and shot off a response. *I need you to find enough info to take down a drug cartel. No biggie.* She closed her eyes as she typed the last word. Of course it was a biggie. It was the biggest favor she'd ever asked, and even by asking it she could be putting Ben in danger. And Sabrina, his new wife, friend of her childhood.

There was no hesitation in Ben's response. He was there for her, as she knew he would be. *Tell me what you need to know.*

I need you to find me irrefutable proof to bring down the drug lord known as Pavlov and the upper echelons of his business. Short version: there is an offsider who lives in the shadows who Tyler thinks could be the key to unravelling the cartel if only his or her identity were known. The offsider is known as the Moneyman. Pavlov's operational base is Baltimore, that's where Tyler was an undercover cop and infiltrated the gang before his identity was leaked. Oh, and Tyler Cooper is not his real name.

What is?

She paused, as a small sob choked its way from her. She typed out the horrifying truth. *I don't know.*

She pressed her hand to her mouth before she made a fool of herself in the café and drew unwanted attention. "Get a grip, Macaroni," she muttered to herself fiercely.

Ben's answer was brief. *Use the same link and check back with me when you can. I'll see what I can do. If your cop friend can hook you up with a burner phone, use this number to contact me. It's encrypted.*

She scribbled out the sequence of numbers and then the screen went dark.

"Thank you," she whispered.

THE NEWS FROM JOZY, when Antonia rendezvoused with her at the beach, was equally as promising.

"The dark sedan has been located, abandoned by a churchyard in the business district off Antilles Road. Your description of the red bandanna guy was solid—it allowed the Brisa police to focus on the barista who you identified as the shooter. The owner of the Chihuahua Café has been questioned about his employee."

Jozy looked down at her phone screen, reading from her notes. "Tommy Fernando. Dual citizen of Haiti and the States. He has been a casual employee at the café for a few months. He turned up for work yesterday even though he was not on the roster—insisted he should stay and help with the tourists. The owner of the café said this was most unusual, Tommy was usually a...how did he put it?" She looked down at her screen again. "A lazy worker."

Antonia nodded. "Maybe he wasn't even part of the gang. Maybe Pavlov or his men threatened him."

"Maybe." Jozy sounded like she thought it was a remote possibility. "The guy had a rap sheet as long as my arm, mostly for possession. I'd guess he was in debt to his dealer. His debt must have been substantial for him to shoot someone in the main street of town."

"What else have the Brisa police uncovered?"

"Some leads have come in, many of them worthless. The most promising one is a report from a—"

Jozy broke off as her phone rang. She held a hand over the screen to read the caller ID in the strong sunlight, then answered the call. "Lalonde. Go ahead."

A flurry of terse dialogue ensued, Jozy snapping

out questions, the tinny voice emanating from her phone answering with equal brevity, then she jammed the phone back in her pocket and looked up at Antonia, a militant light in her eye. "Okay, that was the police on Brisa. Come, we will go to the police launch and I will fill you in on the way."

"What? What is it? Has Tyler been found?" She asked the question that she was almost too frightened to voice. "Is he alive?"

17

———

The woman had the balls of an uncut bull mastiff. Not literally—even a man with a gunshot wound to the shoulder and a black eye from a fist to the face could see that there was nothing interrupting the tight lines of her ivory pantsuit. But metaphorically? Yeah. He'd forgotten just how ballsy Irini Kostovic was. He wondered if she'd been born that way or if being Pavlov's mistress for a decade or more had turned her into the heartless psychopath she so clearly enjoyed being.

"It's good to see you, Ricky. Oh, wait. That was your fake name when you were pretending to be a naughty Baltimore gang member, wasn't it? Such a good citizen: one of the city's finest, living undercover infiltrating the big, bad world of crime."

Tyler stared at her. The light had changed since

he'd last woken; thin beams of sunlight cut dust-filled chinks of gold through the gloom. His chest ached like a bitch, he could only see out of one eye, and he didn't know what the hell was going on. He knew which one of those things pissed him off the most. "Why are you here, Irini? What do you want?"

She clapped her hands and squealed, in a childish way that may have seemed cute a decade prior, but now, with her beauty dissipated by too much decadent living, it grated.

"So direct. So fierce. You haven't lost your cop touch, Ricky. Or should I call you Tyler now? That's why I took such a shine to you. You have a way of looking at a girl that gives her a bit of a thrill."

She walked in a slow circle around him, her needle-thin stilettos leaving pin pricks of damp as she moved between the oily puddles of water dotting the basement. An acne scarred henchman picked his teeth in a chair by the stairwell, his silence-enhanced handgun lying across his lap like a pet cat. Had he been there last time he'd woken? Tyler's mind felt numb, like it was filled with sea fog.

There was another of Pavlov's goons behind him. He couldn't see him—he was too well tied up to turn his head—but he could hear the occasional scratch of a match against flint, smell the rough bite of tobacco being chain-smoked in his near-aft vicinity.

Irini finished her circle, and he watched as she

slid a hand into a back pocket of her pantsuit and brought out a thin, miniature switchblade.

"You taken on a new role, Irini? Pavlov should have given you the heads-up. Never wear white to a stabbing; it's just a chore to get all that blood out."

She pursed her lips, pressed the hidden switch that released the spring and a thin blade leapt out from the handle.

If he could distract her, get that blade in his hand, in his teeth..."You know they're illegal, right?"

He didn't know why he was making conversation with her. She was going to do whatever the hell she liked, and he couldn't do a damn thing about it, trussed like he was, with the tail end of some foul drug poisoning his veins. He'd stared death in the face before, plenty. There wouldn't be a kid from the westside of Baltimore who hadn't heard the gang-bangers cutting each other down in tower staircases over who got the rights to sell drugs from it. "Banned under the Switchblade Knife Act of 1958. That'd be a nice one for your rap sheet, Irini."

She rolled her eyes. "What, this little toy, officer? I thought it was a nail file. I bet it's not even sharp." She drew its razor fine tip down the skin of his arm, and he sucked in air as the fine line sent a bolt of pain through his nerves. "Oops. Guess it's sharper than it looks."

He blew out a breath. "Just get it over with. I'm

not in the mood to play mouse to your cat." He'd been overdue for this moment for five years, expecting it even. He thought he'd reconciled himself to it, but was surprised to feel an ache of regret settle deep in his bones. If only he hadn't dragged Antonia down into his own personal hell.

Something had happened to him that night back in Baltimore when Pavlov found out he was a cop and he'd realized one of his own had turned on him. He'd grown up rough—his mother dead of an overdose before he was nine, juvie, foster care, the streets—and he'd been young enough when he joined the police to think of it as family. The force had given him his first taste of belonging, and he'd believed it, more fool him. He'd had a good lieutenant, who was more mentor than boss, and he'd been young enough, and naive enough, to not see how the law enforcement in Baltimore kept stabbing itself in the back with its petty squabbles over funding, judge favoritism, pleasing the damn media.

He'd overlooked all those flaws because the police had become the family he'd waited his whole life to have.

Some family they'd turned out to be.

There'd been a sick side benefit to being ratted out by one of his own, though—not trusting anyone, relying only on himself had kept him alive on the run way longer than he'd expected. Too bad Antonia hadn't known about his lone wolf strategy; she'd just shimmied her way in through his well-honed defenses and lodged herself, all five foot six of her, into the heart he'd forgotten he had.

He felt vaguely sorry for that naïve young man he'd once been, as though he was thinking about a barely known acquaintance. Who he was now was far from naïve, and he was about fed up with being a pawn in someone else's game. He tested his restraints again, but there was no give in the cable ties. The chair was too solid to bust by tipping himself over. No, the switchblade Irini was carrying was his chance. And trussed like he was, it was a damn slim one.

He needed a distraction, and a whole lot of luck, if this wasn't to be the end of Tyler Cooper.

Jozy stood in the lee of a hardened plastic windshield, her tightly restrained hair immune to the wind buffeting through the sleek police launch.

Antonia wished she could say the same. Her pitstop in a three-star hotel in downtown St Novia would have done a race car driver proud. The hedonist in her had wanted to wallow in the luxury of endless hot water, fresh-laundered towels, the creams and perfumes she'd crammed into her luggage. Instead, she'd dumped her bags, washed her face, and spilled her suitcase out over the bed while she rummaged for something suitable to wear. Why did she own so much frivolous clothing? In the end, she'd settled for denim shorts and an orange blouse with a minimum of fuss. Fear for Tyler's well-being had been beating a tattoo into her skin; the morning had not been the time for lingering.

Three uniformed policemen and a policewoman were with them in the launch, their smiles and chitchat tapering off every time Jozy cast a glance in their direction. Antonia wondered if she'd underestimated Jozy's seniority within The Royal St Novia and Brisa Police Force. She'd tried to drag more information from the detective as they pulled out of the boat harbor, but the wind tore the words from her mouth before they could be heard.

The police on Brisa had a lead on where Tyler might be being held, that she did know. Harrowing images of racing into a grimy backstreet drug den, only to find Tyler's bloodstained body lying still and alone among the detritus of crime, had been flickering through her mind's eye like scenes from a horror movie. But the recovery operation wouldn't commence until Detective Lalonde arrived to lead it, and the holdup bothered her: Tyler might not have time on his side.

The rough chop of ocean rushing through the inter-island passage slapped up between the twin hulls of the police launch, the sound as harsh and repetitive as though they were running Tyler sleek motor cat over gravel rather than the deep indigo of the Leeward Channel. They traveled bone-jarringly fast all the way to a concrete and timber jetty on Brisa, and it wasn't fast enough. Two unmarked vans and a police car waited for them on the foreshore, and Antonia hurried to keep up, thanking her lucky stars she was no longer hampered by Missy Jane's broken sandals.

She positioned herself behind Jozy, torn between getting in the detective's face and demanding to know what the plan was versus keeping a low profile so that Jozy forgot she had an accidental tourist with her who should wait in the boat. She wasn't waiting.

Detective Lalonde conferred with the driver of the unmarked car, then turned to brief the group. "Okay, we believe the American known as Tyler Cooper is being held in a disused canning factory in the industrial precinct off Antilles Road. Using the information from our witness," Jozy locked eyes with her, "the police were able to identify the shooter as a part-time employee of the café. Tommy Fernando was not difficult to track. Fortunately, he appears to have been less than careful when concealing his movements after the shooting. The owner of the Chihuahua Café was able to give us his residential address, which proved to be false, but the mobile phone number he provided was not."

Jozy smiled at the group, but her smile showed

no humor. It was the smile a cobra might give a rat as it decided whether to maul it with one strike or two. "A call was made from that number just before midnight last night, which our investigative team have confirmed was made in the Antilles Road district. Plainclothes officers have canvassed the area in the hours since. Unusual activity has been reported at the old canning factory in that district. Let's saddle up, team, we're moving out. Everyone clear?"

"Yes, ma'am." The agreements came thick and fast.

"Antonia, you will travel in the marked car. Alonzo? You will see to it our witness remains with the vehicle. Park out of sight." Jozy put a hand up for silence as she made to protest. "We will radio as soon as we have information." Jozy held her eye. "Any information, good or bad. Do you understand?"

She swallowed. "I understand."

"Now." Jozy exchanged looks with the team. "Let's rendezvous with the others and get into position."

Antonia slipped into the back seat of the small blue-and-white police car on legs that felt suddenly numb. Her fingers slipped on the buckle of her seatbelt, and it took a few goes to snick the metal tongue into its sheath. The smell of cheap disinfectant clung to the upholstery.

Get a grip, Antonia, she muttered to herself, in a

voice that she hoped her driver—Alonzo?—didn't hear. He pulled away from the curb with a screech of tires and her body knocked against the scuffed vinyl of the door. Her heart was racing. Her busy eyes had not missed the bulky shapes of bullet proof vests the other policemen and policewoman had been wearing, or the guns riding low on their belts.

Her thoughts circled back to the man who had become the center of this operation, the center of her world. Tyler. The irony was not lost on her: this had been his world when he was a cop. He was a man who had charged into the bleak underworld of crime with the thin comfort of police-issue protective gear covering him, and now he was the one desperately in need of rescue.

She nodded; yes, definitely rescue. She refused to believe he could have been killed. She'd know. She pressed a hand to her chest and felt the shaky intake of breath, the rushed exhalation. She'd know if he was dead, she was sure of it.

The radio on the dashboard crackled to life. She caught some numbers, one and four and five, but the words were too quick, and in a mix of English and creole. She leaned forward and tapped at Alonzo's shoulder as he swerved into a graffiti-stained backlot to park in the shadow of a rusted dumpster. "Alonzo? Can you translate for me?"

The policeman fiddled with the air conditioning

unit until a stream of mold-tainted cold air filled the car. "The teams have arrived at the building," he said. "Some go up..." He mimicked walking up a flight of stairs with his fingers. "Some take the basement. We wait."

"Crap," she muttered. "I hate waiting." She balled her hands into fists and bit into the flesh of her thumb—anything felt better than this unbearable ache of not-knowing.

The minutes passed with all the speed of a glacier. She held out as long as she could then tapped Alonzo on the shoulder again. "Can you radio in and find out what's happening?"

"No, madam. We wait."

She blew out a breath. A colored bird, some sort of prettily plumed parrot, was pecking its way down a flowering tree growing from between cracks in the old pavement, its beak busy among orange blooms. Below it, plastic bags fluttered in the faint breeze, and discarded fruit peel, egg cartons, cigarette stubs littered the dusty street.

The industrial park was a long way from the color and culture of the tourist zone. A bull-shouldered man swaggered down the street, his face shining with sweat. Antonia's eyes dropped to the duffle he held in his hand. *Uncle Leo's Fight Club.* There were definitely no raffia hat stalls or tourists in bikinis in this part of town. She rubbed her hands up her arms, suddenly cold in the noisy blow of air from the dashboard.

She slid her fingers under the silver clasp of the door handle and pulled. Nothing happened. She shot her eyes up to the back of her driver's head. "Why am I locked in?"

He shrugged. "This is a police car, lady. Sometimes our guests are not sitting so happily in our back seat."

Huh. That made sense, even if it made her feel a little like she'd been arrested. "Can I get out? I need some fresh air."

He inclined his head, slid a finger to a hidden button and she heard the mechanism within her door click. She got out of the car and closed the door on his reminder for her to stay close. She rested her hips against the trunk and looked over their surroundings.

The other cars were nowhere in sight. About her, worn *For Lease* signs hung haphazardly in long-empty shopfronts. A trading store stood open, advertising discount cigarettes and mobile phone repairs. Behind the store front, rising seven or eight stories above the street, stood an ugly gray building.

She pictured Jozy and her crew closing in on it, running for cover from pillar to pillar, their walkie-talkies pressed to their lips as they muttered "clear", or "wait,", their hands rigidly signaling *move left, stay low, follow me.*

She'd rather be with them than here, regardless of any danger. This waiting was hideous, she didn't think anything could be worse...but then a round of gunfire tore apart the silence of the dusty street, and she broke into a run.

19

"**W**hy you? Pavlov's the one who's been hunting me down all these years."

Irini pouted, and used the tip of her switchblade to flick a speck of dust off her pantsuit. "Has he?"

Tyler frowned. Yes, he damn well had. Pavlov was the one threatened by the events and meetings Tyler had witnessed. If not, why break his fingers? Why threaten him three years ago on Ballena, why shoot him now and drag him into this hellhole? No. Irini was just playing games—having someone tied up in front of her no doubt appealed to whatever sick fantasies she liked to indulge in.

She slid behind him, leaned in so close he could smell her perfume, feel her breath on the nape of his neck as she spoke. It was like being trapped in a dragon's maw: hot, wet, and unlikely to end well.

"Maybe Pavlov's not the only one with a vested interest in knowing where you are."

She walked her fingers up his arm as she spoke, her long nails rasping over the cuts and scars that covered him from the glass exploding out of the Chihuahua Café's front window.

He'd been keeping tabs on the switchblade, looking for an opportunity to do something. What, he hadn't quite figured out. Seize it with his teeth? His hands were bound tight behind his back and about as useful as one of Antonia's adverbs. But as Irini's words sunk in, his mind stalled. *Maybe Pavlov's not the only one?* He tried to twist his neck, but the cable ties securing him to the chair cut into his skin when he turned so he abandoned the effort. He ran through options. It almost sounded like Irini had wanted him found, not Pavlov. But why?

He'd spent more than a year working his way through the Baltimore chapter of Pavlov's business empire. He'd started as hired muscle, supervising deliveries, monitoring the incoming shipments, but he'd risen up the ranks to trusted driver, chauffeuring Pavlov from A to B and being a human shield for him from car to building, from meeting to meeting. He'd driven Irini around plenty as well, but he'd never got the impression she used her considerable intellect for any purpose other than gratification.

Had he missed something? Was Irini more than Pavlov's mistress?

"If you were so keen to find me, why did that idiot put a bullet in me? A few inches over, and we wouldn't be having this conversation."

Irini rolled her eyes. "That boy, what a moron. I knew you had a set up at the Chihuahua Café, so I did a—"

"How? How did you know?"

"Now, Tyler, you can't expect a girl to give up all her secrets just because you keep asking so nicely. Where was I? That's right. The café. Tommy had the job of bringing you to me, but you arrived hours before he was expecting to see you. I gave him a photo, and when he recognized you, he panicked. That's the trouble with using your customers to do your detail work—they're usually half stoned and fully stupid. He was supposed to bring you to me, not put a bullet in you in the main street of town."

He let go of the *who*, as in who the hell was leaking information to Irini about his whereabouts, and settled on the *why*. "What reason would you have for taking me, if not to give me to Pavlov? I don't get it."

Irini shot a look at the two gunmen patrolling the basement car park. "Do a circuit, will you? Make sure we're still alone." She waited until they'd cleared out of hearing distance. The chain smoker behind him didn't move; clearly, whatever she had to say, she was happy to say in front of him.

She looked Tyler in the eye. "I figured if all those government organizations were so keen to find out what Pavlov was up to, maybe I could be the person they could schmooze to find out more. So I started listening."

Tyler frowned. "Listening how?"

Irini smirked. "You know, honey, you're mighty fine to look at. Mighty fine. But you're not the only good-looking cop I've met. And the other one? Well, he taught me a thing or two. We had a barter thing going."

Tyler tried to keep his face smooth, his anger dulled down. "A barter thing? Like—swapping information?" Holy shit. Had Irini been a snitch, running intel back to some other law enforcement officer the whole time he'd been undercover? Was that who had snitched this time, too? But what cop would have known about today's rendezvous? If he got out of here alive, he was going to personally choke an answer out of Rob Cheng.

She examined her nails. "More like a double agent, darling. Only, the agency holding the greatest claim to my allegiance was the Federal Bureau of Irini. If you see what I'm saying."

He shook his head. "So you decide Pavlov's not treating you well enough and start keeping tabs on him. For who? Who was your contact? Was it someone in Narcotics? And how are you still alive all these years?"

She laughed, enjoying his frustration. He got the feeling he could ask questions until he was blue in the face; she had an agenda of her own.

She leaned in to him, sliding one ivory-clad leg and then the other about him, until she was straddling him. She brought her heavily made up face close to his, so close he could see the lines carving into her upper lip beneath the powder that clung there.

She sniffed and wrinkled her nose. "Dear me, Tyler. You don't smell so good."

He shifted his legs within the confines of the wire lashing him to the chair. "Then do us both a favor and back off."

"Oh, I don't think so. Not yet. You've got something I want." She wriggled on his lap and slid her hand up his good arm, squeezing and kneading his flesh.

He firmed his jaw. "I'm not a dog you can hump, Irini. What's the problem? Pavlov not doing it for you anymore?"

She laughed, a low rumble, and her breath flared over his face, a rank flume from a woman who smoked too much. "You have no idea," she said. "Now hold still, and this won't hurt a bit."

Holy crap. *What* wouldn't hurt? He tried to clear his sleep-deprived, pain-fogged brain. Irini was waving her folding blade about again. "What the hell, Irini? If you're trying to slit my throat, it's going to take a long time with that. I've seen toothpicks that looked more dangerous."

She grinned, and his gaze fastened on the sharp points of her incisors. They suited her—the way a forked tongue suited a snake.

She snapped the blade open, and her left hand pinched at the flesh on his bicep. "Take a breath, handsome," she murmured, and was just raising the blade in her fist when the rapid bark of gunfire sounded from the level above them.

His guts tightened. This was the distraction he needed, now all he needed was some luck.

20

———

*S*he didn't know where she was running to, but she ran anyway, instinct telling her she had to run to the source of the gunfire. If Tyler was in someone's sights, she wasn't about to hide in the back seat of a police car just to be safe. Her safety didn't matter, not when Tyler needed her. Behind her, pounding along the litter-strewn pavement, she could hear Alonzo running in her wake, calling her to come back.

She ignored him and thanked her lucky stars she'd had that New Year's resolution to attend the gym this year more than once a month. She flicked a look over her shoulder as she raced into an alleyway that led to the factory tower. She was no athlete, but fortunately, neither was Alonzo. He was a fifty-something career cop who looked like he was overly fond of his johnny cakes.

As she neared the disused factory, movement in the upper floors caught her eye—police, definitely. Uniformed, disciplined, their movements sharp and sure through the broken windows overlooking the alley as they cleared the floor.

Not up there, then. She spied a ramp heading down into a basement parking garage and made for it, her soft-soled jogging shoes making quiet slap-slap noises. If there was power still attached to the building, it wasn't evident on this floor. Bulbless fixtures hung loose from the ceiling, and no sensor lights flickered to life as she hurried into the dark innards. No exit signs, no directional arrows, no over-head fluorescent lights lit her way.

The deeper she traveled underground, the darker it became, broken only by slits of sunlight at either end of the cavernous garage. She paused, willing her thudding heart rate and racing lungs to calm so she could listen.

Was that voices? Footsteps? The distant crackle of radio?

She was getting close to something—she just wasn't sure what that something was. There'd been no more gunfire, of that she was certain. She didn't think her nerves would have coped with another bout.

For her, growing up in the greater London district, gunfire had been at a remove from normal life. In her home, sure, she'd been totally blasé about it: she binge-watched *NCIS* like the next person and grew up overhearing her parents' decade-long obsession with *The Bill*. And later, at work, her team were sent far and wide into those parts of the world where peace was a dream rather than a reality.

But to hear it and wonder if one of your own was at the receiving end? That was different...and not in a good way.

Ahead of her, columns loomed in the gloom and the faint white of parking garage marks striped the cement floor. Oh, to be back in a world where finding a parking space was the greatest challenge a person could face. She pushed the frivolous thought aside. Keep going, Antonia, she urged herself. Search, look, listen: he's here somewhere, he's just got to be.

She crept forward, column by column. Alonzo was nowhere behind her, she was on her own. Ahead of her, a mutter came to her ears and she crept onward. Yes! Voices, definitely, perhaps on a lower level.

She descended another layer of ramp, rounding a corner to discover a dull glow of artificial light. So. Electricity hummed somewhere in this relic of a building. Shadows competed with pools of light in the deepest layer of the basement, and louder now came the voices: a woman's, a man's. Was it Tyler? Could it be?

She crept closer, her heart in her mouth and rounded a once-white column two feet in width. A tableau spread out before her, one she had not expected. The Royal St Novia and Brisa Police Force appeared to have taken control of the basement. There were criminals, sure, but the two men stood with their guns by their feet and their hands were up in the air, as police officers held them at gunpoint. A stink of something acrid, presumably from the gunfire, hung in the air, but nobody appeared to have been shot.

Then she saw a third gunman, a handsome young man who she would have looked twice at on a busy street. The business end of his gun was pointing at the prisoner tied into the chair. Surely it was Tyler? How many prisoners did drug lords kidnap in one day?

She had to get closer. The light was too dim, the air too smoky, and she was too far away to be sure what was going on. And this damn post in the way wasn't helping.

Her rubber-soled shoes made little noise as she crept forward, but even so, she was heard. A hard hand seized her on the shoulder, and she bit off a shriek as she saw it was a very cranky Detective Lalonde holding her.

"You will not move," Jozy hissed, and pushed her back into the shadow of the cement column. "I mean it. Don't piss me off any more than you already have, Miss Da Silva. Stay still. Stay quiet. There's still a gunman on the loose, this situation is not yet contained."

The detective looked her in the eyes, hard, before abruptly turning on her heel and making her way to the center of the tableau. Her confident voice rang out in the basement, the hollow acoustics a theatrical match to the drama unfolding within. "You, with the gun. You're surrounded. Lower your weapon."

The gunman didn't seem worried about the pissed-off policewoman holding a gun on him. "No chance, lady. If your people come any closer, I put a bullet into the man's ear."

Antonia peered around the pole. One of Lalonde's team held a gun in one hand, and with the other shone a powerful flashlight at the scene of the stand-off.

Tyler! It was definitely Tyler, and he looked alive, if a bit battered and bruised, and—

Her lips pursed. A woman with sleek blonde hair and an even sleeker silk pantsuit was awfully damn close to Tyler, was she—? Yes, she damn well was straddling his lap!

Barely resisting the urge to charge out from behind her cement column, Antonia watched the woman peel her cleavage off Tyler's bandaged chest, then pivot on her heel to raise her hands dramatically in the air. Whoever she was, she didn't seem fazed by the situation in which she found herself center stage, instead taking the time to survey the policemen martialed about the room before locking eyes on Detective Lalonde.

"Officer. There's no need for all this stand off and swagger. We'll come peacefully."

Lalonde's weapon remained steady. "Tell that to your bulldog ramming his gun into Cooper's head."

The women waved a hand airily in the air then turned to the young man behind her. "You heard the police officer, Stan. Drop your weapon."

The man appeared confused by the instruction. "Now? You don't wanna, like, escape? We can use him as a hostage."

"I said drop the gun." Pantsuit woman sounded like she was used to being obeyed without having her commands questioned. She turned back to Jozy when the rasp of the man's gun being kicked across rough cement died away.

"We'll come peacefully, officer," she repeated, and held out her wrists so Jozy could snap her into cuffs. The other police rushed in to cuff the young man, and finally, *finally*, Jozy looked over and gave her a nod.

She ran out from behind the column and made her way over to Tyler.

21

"Fine? You're fine?"

He shrugged. He was a little banged up, and he was mighty pleased to not have a bullet in his head and an anchor tied to his feet and be sinking his way through several hundred feet of deep ocean, but yeah, all things considered, he *was* fine.

"You have the nerve to let me rescue you from America's Most Wanted and I find you being lap-danced by some stiletto-wearing vixen in a pantsuit? I didn't even *shower*, I was so worried about you. I had hot water, clean towels, and pillows which involved actual duck down at my disposal. Did I snuggle in? Did I start giving the handsome bellhop my fluttery eyelash come-hither look? No, dammit. I mobilized a rescue team and got my hot and possibly travel-stained ass here pronto."

Tyler let her rant, just as long as it took for him to wrap his good arm around her waist and haul her in to him. He lowered his head and pressed his lips to hers, feeling the heat of her desperation sink into him, into the shards of pain punishing his chest. He kissed her like a dying man. Like a lonely man. Like a man who thought the only thing left for him was a slow descent into hell, but an angel had arrived to pull him back from the brink, one kiss at a time. When he'd kissed her into a ragged silence, he rested his forehead against hers. "I missed you, too."

Antonia responded by bursting into tears.

"Hey, hey. What's this?" He rubbed his thumb across her cheek, brushing a stripe of dirt from his hand across her face. "Don't cry. Sweetheart. Tell me off again, or something, I can't bear this."

And he couldn't, he realized. Sometime in the past few days, he'd realized his Antonia had a spine of steel hidden under all that frill and flirtation; he'd rather be shot and kidnapped and thrown into a speeding car than have her overwrought with tears over him.

He decided to distract her. "What are you doing here? And how is it our detective friend Ms. Lalonde seems to have taken over?"

Antonia buried her face into his chest so he could barely hear her response. "I had to, Tyler. My god, you were hustled away in a car. I didn't know if you were alive. All I could think of was how competent she'd seemed when she spoke to us on the beach."

He kissed the top of her head. "My avenging angel. Thank you for rescuing me."

She leaned back and looked up at him, eyes narrowed. "There's no need to sound surprised."

He shook his head. "Remind me to never be surprised by anything you do ever again."

A sqwark from a radio nearby had him looking up. Detective Lalonde was directing the uniformed officers out of the building, the three gunmen cuffed and disarmed between them.

"Detective?"

She turned to him. "I'm still debating about whether to put you in handcuffs, Cooper. You can thank your lucky stars you're injured, or I'd have done it by now."

He nodded. She seemed supremely pissed, but that was okay, he could work with that. "Irini needs to be questioned. She's got something, information maybe about Pavlov? About someone in the Balti-more PD she's been working with? She was playing games with me, but there's something there we need to know."

"You running this operation, Cooper?"

He almost grinned. Lalonde was growing on him. "No, ma'am."

"Then keep your trap shut. Alonzo?"

A big dark man was photographing the scene, taping off the chair and guns. No doubt the forensics unit would be here soon to tear the place apart for prints and gun casings. The man looked up.

"When you're done, send me your photos ASAP. I'm taking these two back on the launch to St Novia; we'll run this out of my office."

Alonzo nodded his head in the direction of Irini, handcuffed and standing by an officer wearing the expression of a saint. "What about her?"

"She's coming with us."

Tyler felt his muscles relax, just a little. Finally, some answers might be coming his way. He wrapped his good arm more securely around Antonia and took an unsteady step to follow Lalonde as she headed for the ramp.

"You can lean on me," said Antonia. "I'm stronger than I look."

He grabbed a fistful of her orange blouse between his bloodstained fingers. "Yeah," he said. "I'm starting to work that out."

22

———

ntonia locked herself in the tiny bathroom in the police station and prayed no one needed to use it because she needed a minute.

She needed more than a minute.

She splashed water over her face and stared at herself in the tiny, chipped mirror. Antonia Da Silva, Londoner, confirmed city-dweller, owner of an impressive collection of high-end shoes, and an even more impressive collection of romance disaster stories.

"It's been a wild week," she told her reflection.

"I've had wilder," she could imagine herself giving as a flippant reply, a month from now, when— if—her blood pressure ever returned to normal.

Her hands were shaking, she noticed, as she ran them under the water from the faucet. Her breath was coming in shuddery little gulps, and she had so many tears banked up that her eyeballs felt like they were doing the work of the Hoover dam wall.

She was a mess, and she had to pull herself together. She was stronger than this...she just needed a little time to remind herself of that fact.

She unzipped the bag she'd had strapped across her chest and fished about until she found a comb and mascara. Perhaps if she looked a little more like her badass editor self, she'd start to feel like it. Her fingers brushed against the burner phone Jozy had given her, and an idea struck.

Where had she written the number Ben gave her?

She scrabbled through her satchel until she had the slip in her hand and punched in the numbers. Clicks and digital beeps filled her ear, and then Ben was there.

"Toni. What's up?"

"Tyler's safe," she said, just as the dam wall broke.

"Honey, I'm so pleased. Listen, I've just landed in St. Novia. I've got news, too, and it's good news. Where are you?"

"I'm at the police station," she said thickly. "You don't happen to have my bestie Sabrina with you, by any chance? I think I'm having a mini-breakdown."

"She's at the Manatee Cays, but I can patch you through. Stay on the line, okay?"

"Okay."

"Toni? You're going to be fine."

She hoped he was right.

More digital beeps, and then Sabrina was in her ear, her voice as crisp and close as though she were standing beside her at the bathroom mirror.

"Antonia? My girl, what is going *on*?"

The lump in her throat was hard to shift. "I've got myself caught up in a doozy this time, Sabrina."

"Mmm. You want to tell me how you're feeling? Ben says Tyler's shot, but he's okay, and you've got good people taking care of you."

"That's the short version. The long version I probably don't have time for. The others—Tyler, and Jozy, the detective who's taken charge, and some Eastern European criminal dominatrix called Irini— are waiting for me in an office here. I'm in a police building, Sabrina. A *police building!*"

"You need to do some deep breathing, Toni. Breathe in and out, come on, let's do it together. Let's think calm happy thoughts."

Antonia sucked in a long breath. "Can I think about mojitos?"

"And out," said Sabrina in her ear, her exhalation making a whooshing noise through the phone speaker. "Think about mojitos, and puppies playing at your feet, and winning an International Press award. Think about a sale at your favorite shoe store."

She sucked in another breath. "I do feel a little calmer, Sabrina. This mad phone breathing plan of yours is working."

"I hope so. The college students nearby must think I'm having phone sex with all this huffing and puffing. That, or I've got emphysema."

A laugh gurgled up from somewhere, and she closed her eyes. "You're the best, Sabrina."

"I know. Now dry your eyes and get to that meeting. The sooner this is over, the sooner you can start processing everything that's gone on. And that includes whatever it is that's going to happen now between you and Tyler."

Her and Tyler. That was the question, wasn't it? What were they to each other, anyway? Former lovers? Escapees? Or did they maybe have a chance, finally, of having a future?

23

"This is out of your hands, Tyler."

Tyler frowned at Detective Lalonde, who was seated at her desk in St Novia's police headquarters. "Look, Detective, up until yesterday, I thought I had a fair freaking idea about what was going on. I had info in my head that was two things: proof to help bring about the guilty verdict for Pavlov if the prosecutors in the States ever found enough juice to get him arrested and a death warrant for me, for as long as Pavlov is alive and running the biggest drug empire on the eastern seaboard. And that empire has a long reach, as we all know. But today, in that parking garage, I discovered I am missing some piece of the puzzle, and I need access to Irini to work it out. You've got to let me interview her."

He shot a look back at Antonia, seated by the

door, as quiet as he'd ever seen her. No wonder, they were neck deep in his shitstorm now; if she'd cut and run for the first plane London-bound, he'd not have thought worse of her for it.

Lalonde's chair creaked as she leaned back in it. "I don't *have* to let you do anything, Tyler. On the contrary, the Ballena police have issued a warrant for your arrest after that flyboy stunt you pulled on their airstrip. I'd be willing to bet landing an amphibious plane in a residential area on Brisa after dark would be an offense too, under the rules of the country *I* police. So don't come into my headquarters and start issuing commands. You're not police anymore, here or anywhere."

"Oh, come on, Detective. You and I both know that my aviation fracas is the least of our issues."

She smirked, and he felt a little judder of relief. Detective Lalonde could tie him up in knots with that Ballena warrant, and clearly, she knew it. She was just using it to get his measure. He rethought his approach.

"Jozy. Irini was pussyfooting around some secret agenda she had when I was tied up in that chair. *She* was the one who wanted me taken, not Pavlov himself. It doesn't make sense, and I need to know why. This is my life we're talking about—and I kinda feel like I've given up too much of it to leave these questions unanswered. Please, will you cut me in here? What do you intend to do with Irini?"

Lalonde nodded. "Okay. You've said your piece, now hear me out. Irini is in custody, here at the station. She has too much flotsam to chuck between her and a charge for us to hold her for long. She didn't kidnap you, she didn't shoot you, she didn't get caught holding a gun...you know the score. But I'll share this with you...she doesn't *want* to be released from custody."

He thought this over. Could Irini be in need of police protection? He tried not to let the roar of adrenaline well up. He wasn't in the game anymore —what Irini was up to maybe didn't matter to him— unless, perhaps, Irini was hiding from Pavlov too? "Are you thinking what I'm thinking, Detective?"

She nodded. "Oh, yes. She wants out, but she can't do it without help. She's smart enough to know she won't survive three seconds after she turns on her lover if he's not behind bars made of steel, and I doubt she's got your skills at disappearing from view."

Wow. Freaking *wow*. This could be his chance.

"You've got to let me interview her," he said. Irini would know so, so much about Pavlov's empire. She could be the break every law officer in Baltimore would give his career to interview.

Jozy smiled. "Nice try. But you're not the hotshot here, my friend."

"I *know* her. I know Pavlov. I've got questions you won't even know to ask."

The detective turned away and stared out her window, to where pretty timber boats bobbed among pretty aqua waves. He followed her gaze, wondered what she was thinking. Wondered if she, too, envied the holiday makers, their blithe ignorance of crime and duty and justice.

She drummed her fingers on her desk, ran a nail down the razor-fine iron crease in her sleeve. "I want to work with you, Tyler. You're a credible witness, and between you and Irini, we may have info that's going to look like burnished gold to Interpol, and whichever US government departments are busting their nuts to get Pavlov behind bars. I'm open to the idea of you leading the interview with Irini, but I call the shots. Fight me on this, and I'll work without you. If you want in, you're going to have to start getting a whole lot more cooperative."

He frowned. This was an excellent offer, but he needed more. "I want Antonia out of this. The drop we'd organized to get her some new ID was a bust, she needs papers to get out of St Novia and back to London. I can try contact the courier; he may still be on Brisa, wondering why the Chihuahua Café is covered in crime tape."

Lalonde flicked her eyes over to Antonia, sitting quietly on the far side of the office. He followed her gaze and inspected Antonia's face. Sitting *too* quietly, he realized. Hell, what was afoot now?

"That's not going to happen," said the detective. "For starters, we've retrieved Antonia's belongings from Ballena, including her passport. Travel is not a problem. But Antonia's been working a different angle, and she's on to something."

He looked at Antonia. "What have you done? What angle? You're supposed to be getting out of this mess, not wading further in."

Before she could answer, a knock sounded at the door, and he turned to see a man entering the room. Crap. He hadn't thought he could feel any worse than he already did. He was wrong.

"Ben!" Antonia leapt to her feet and threw her arms around her friend.

For pete's sake, this was hardly a reunion. She might have just handed her hippie, yacht-owning friend a death sentence. Anger swirled in his belly, a sick wad of it. How could she have done this? He watched her give Ben's arm a familiar pat. "I'm sorry to wreck your honeymoon."

"Don't sweat it, Toni. You needed us."

A cough from the detective clearly reminded Antonia she and her buddy Ben weren't at a freaking garden party. Antonia turned back to the group.

"Ben, this is Detective Jozy Lalonde. She's with The Royal St Novia and Brisa Police Force. She's Special Branch, which means she's also the Interpol representative."

Ben leaned over to shake Jozy's hand. "Ben Ryan. IT security. I've worked with Interpol before."

"You have?" Tyler rose to his feet and shook Ben's hand. An IT security expert? Too much was happening, too quickly; he needed to be able to think. The case against Pavlov was growing like a hurricane, and he needed to be one hundred percent able to focus, but all he could think about was the woman he had entangled in his mess of a life, who had now gone out and caught her friends in the same lethal tangle.

"You're sporting a few more bruises than when I saw you last," said Ben.

Tyler rubbed his aching chest. "Yeah." His ribs weren't the problem. Antonia throwing her life away and risking the lives of her friends—that was the problem. He turned to her. "Come with me a second? Outside?"

The detective cleared her throat. "I haven't decided yet whether I'm going to exercise my jurisdictional rights and arrest you. Don't go far."

He shot her a look, linked Antonia's fingers into his, and headed out into the corridor. As soon as the door swung closed behind them, she pulled her hand from his and stood facing him, her eyes narrowed. There was a thin stripe of red on the neckline of her blouse and he ran his finger down it, feeling the fabric shift over the warm skin beneath. His blood stained her clothes. It upset him, he realized. It upset the shit out of him. He didn't want to be the one to stain Antonia's life.

"You didn't tell me you had your passport back."

She shrugged. "When exactly did you want me to start chatting about my travel documents? When we were being hustled out of the parking garage on Brisa in police custody? In the speedboat roaring back over here to St Novia like the hounds of hell were after us? Maybe in the surgery, when the doctor was attending to your bullet wound and bruises?"

He nodded. She was right, this wasn't about her passport at all. "When were you going to tell me you'd gone behind my back and contacted Ben?"

"Yes, I contacted Ben. I had to."

He swore. "No, you didn't. Sharing information is sharing risk, which makes calling your friend indulgent. Your life...his life...don't you get it? I don't want you risking them for me."

Antonia moved in closer. "Indulgent? You think I'm swanning around in the Caribbean indulging myself with a little adventure? I understand the risks, Tyler. So does Ben—I mean, that man is smarter than everyone on this island put together. Do you really think I'm such an airhead that I don't understand how violent your world has been? I *do* understand."

He shook his head. "You're not hearing me. I don't want you involved, not for me. I'm not—"

He bit off the words. He wasn't worth it, he had been about to say, and there it was, the heart of the problem. Saving himself was one thing, if he could do it alone. But saving himself at the expense of others? Antonia? Her friends? Even the prim and proficient Jozy Lalonde? Who was he to them?

"You're not what, Tyler?"

He looked down the corridor, away from her. He wanted to sink himself into all that she offered: fun, heat, solace, just *her*...but how could he?

Her words were soft, when they came. "What are you more afraid of, Tyler? Pavlov? Or letting me into your life? Maybe you need to think about that. I make my own choices about what I'll risk my life for, and I've chosen you. So I'm going back inside that room, and I'm going to do my best to help, with or without your consent. Are you coming?"

She was holding her hand out to him, and he took it, pulling her in to him so her curls ruffled up against his cheek and her hips bumped his. "You're a nuisance, Antonia, you know that?"

She tilted her head back and rested a hand against his cheek. "So I've been told."

He rested his lips against her cheek, nuzzled his

way over until his mouth brushed hers. "I want to argue with you some more, but the truth is, I'm tired."

She linked an arm around him, swiveled in until they were pressed together, fused her lips to his so suddenly he became lost in a barrage of sensation. Her body pushing against his was doing glorious things to his bloodstream, rushing it headlong into his groin so as her hips moved, every sensation felt multiplied a thousandfold. He could feel her breasts against his chest, the soft swell of them there an echo of what they'd shared. A fireball of need filled his head, and he ran rough hands around her, over her, up over the sway in her back, the strong expanse of rib and shoulder blade. He slid his fingers into the hair at the nape of her neck and buried himself in the kiss.

He felt like he could sate himself with her mouth forever. Every need he'd ever felt, every desire he'd ever yearned for, had brought him here, to this moment, with Antonia.

But discipline was what had kept him alive, and so he eased back, pressing a kiss into her curls as he withdrew. He drew a ragged breath, smoothed her hair back from her face. "Let's get this over with, then," he said, and headed back into the office.

24

*D*etective Lalonde was on the phone when they reentered, ordering one of her staff to bring Irini in from the holding cell. She put down the phone and pointed her finger at him. "Let's do this in here, Cooper. You can do the questioning, but you need to keep it professional. I'll be recording this meeting."

"This isn't my first police interview, Detective."

Lalonde nodded. "I know that, but you've got more than a personal stake in this, and you've got a bullet wound in your chest."

He nodded. "Understood."

"Ben and Antonia, in the spirit of cooperation, you can remain, but stay seated over there, and stay quiet, okay?" A knock sounded at the door. "That'll be her. We ready?"

Tyler took in a long slow breath, let it out. Maybe, finally, he was going to be getting some answers.

Irini stepped into the room like she was a celebrity who'd graciously conceded to sign a few autographs for her fans. It irked him. The woman was an operator, with an overinflated idea of her own charm. The sooner this was done, the happier he would be.

Lalonde conducted the necessaries, the warnings, the declaration of the recording. She was thorough, he'd give her that. If this truly was the beginning of an attempt on Pavlov's sovereignty as drug lord, they didn't want to have any loopholes for his lawyers to squirm their way through.

She looked over at him when she was done, gave him the nod.

He cleared his throat. "Please state your name for the record."

"Irini Kostovic."

"Interviewer is Ty—" Shit. He'd not given this a thought when he'd demanded he be the one to interview Irini.

He started again, more slowly. The syllables felt rusty in his mind, dulled by time and disuse. Could he really use his real name? He shook his head. "Interviewer is Tyler Cooper, formally a detective with Baltimore PD, Narcotics Division. Currently living under an assumed identity provided by the US State Department."

He felt more than saw Antonia's reaction. She barely shifted, but he saw from her body language the effect of his words. She'd seen his hesitation, must have guessed his dilemma. His mouth twisted: the gifts of living a false life just kept on giving.

"Irini. What are you doing in the Caribbean? Specifically, why are you here, in St Novia and Brisa?

"I've been looking for you, Tyler."

He frowned at Irini. "What's your interest in me? Are you currying favor with Pavlov, hoping to turn me in to win some brownie points?"

Irini inspected her nails. "Before I answer that, I need some assurance."

He looked up at Detective Lalonde. This was her call, not his. He had no jurisdiction, here or anywhere.

Jozy nodded. "We're going to need a little more information from you, Ms. Kostovic, before we start laying out the red carpet. You know what I mean. You give us Pavlov, all wrapped up in a tidy red bow, then we'll be giving you assurance aplenty. If you're just playing games, we're not giving you anything but a one-way ticket to an accessory to murder charge. Kidnapping. I'll probably think of a few more when I sit down to write up your file."

"I'm giving you Pavlov."

Tyler raised his eyebrows. Was she for real? "For the record, Witness has just agreed to give us information about Anton Pavlov." He could feel the pump of adrenaline kicking in and worked to keep his voice level.

"Why? You've been Pavlov's girlfriend for years. Why turn on him now? Has he dumped you for someone else, is that it?"

Irini narrowed her eyes. "Noone dumps me, Tyler, or Ricky, or whatever your damn name is. I'm getting out, and to get out, I need to take Pavlov out. He doesn't let people leave, as you well know."

Yeah, he sure as shit knew that.

"Why do you want out?"

She rose to her feet, walked in front of the desk to and fro. "You got any cigarettes in here? A girl could use a smoke."

He shook his head. "No smoking. You tell us what we want to hear, you can have a carton. Tell us why you want out."

Irini leaned in close to him. Too close. Then she rested one of her pimped-up fingernails on her own chest and tapped. "I am telling you. This girl got sick of being sent outside. This girl decided she was going to earn herself a little insurance so she could be alpha of her own pack."

"How? What insurance?"

Irini grinned. "I wired that room up like it was a Christmas tree."

Nobody spoke. Tyler looked at Lalonde, who'd stopped scribbling her neat notes. She looked like she'd just discovered Santa Claus was real.

He was the first to break the silence. "You wired Pavlov's inner sanctum? How? Where'd you get the equipment?"

She smiled. "My contact in narcotics gave me lessons. Equipment. In return, I gave him tidbits—let him clear up some low-level street crews—towers in the westside of Baltimore, dockworkers bringing in small-package lots in the containers—nothing that would impact Pavlov's income stream in such a way that might put the wind up him—but enough to keep the cops making arrests, getting some money shots with them on the front page cleaning up the city streets looking like they're winning the battle. Baltimore PD just ate that stuff up."

Lalonde took over the questioning. "So, if the Narcotics Division were getting intel from you, they weren't getting the tapes of what went down in his office. Who was? Where's the data?"

Irini laughed. "Yes, well, now we're getting to the interesting part of the story. I kept enough footage to take Pavlov down. More than enough, I've got him up to his waxed armpits in cocaine, I've even got him planting a bullet in a street seller who he caught using from his own stash."

"You've got Pavlov committing murder on tape?"

She nodded, as though it were no big deal. "Sure."

"And where is this footage now?"

She looked around the room as though she were about to deliver the punchline to a fun joke. "Ricky's got it."

Lalonde frowned. "Who the hell is Ricky?"

He held up a hand. "For the record, Witness is referring to me, Tyler Cooper. Ricky was my assumed name when I was working as an undercover operative in Baltimore, infiltrating the inner circle of the drug empire run by Anton Pavlov."

Lies upon lies. He didn't know what in hell she was playing at, but he was over it. "I hate to disappoint you, Irini, but I've got jackshit. The only reason Pavlov wants me dead is what I've seen—and sadly, I can't just plug a data jack into my head and extract the video footage, much as I'd love to be rid of it."

Irini smirked. "Not out of your brain, no."

"What do you mean?"

"If I may?" Irini stood up and strolled over to his side of the table. "This is why I had you taken in Brisa. I've had my eyes and ears scouting for news of you since the day you disappeared. We knew you weren't dead. Imagine our surprise when we dug up your coffin in Baltimore and no one was in it. Flaco, Kuzman...all the little sycophants in Pavlov's circle know I've been looking for you. They pass info on to me, I put in a good word for them with Pavlov. They thought it was a sign of my devotion—Irini, the mistress, so keen to stay in the big man's favor she's tracking you down as her pet project."

"You dug up his coffin?" Antonia sounded like she was going to be sick. He reached over and squeezed her hand, hard. "But why?"

"Honey, when I want something, I let nothing get in my way. And I want a bit of peace and me-time to enjoy my retirement."

"Your ill-gotten gains, I think you mean," said Tyler.

Irini ran a hand down his bicep, toyed with a scar there. "You ever wonder where you got this?"

"I've got loads of scars." Some of them were even on the outside.

"That scar right there is how we find my data."

He frowned, as the meaning under her words became clear. "Do you mean to tell me you hid some data in my arm? What the hell?"

She shrugged. "What can I say? Science is a marvelous thing. Women have been injecting contraceptive implants into their arms for years. Same process, different implant. I hadn't decided when I was going to make my move, so I needed ways to protect my data. I had two microchips made —one for me, one as a backup that needed to be kept somewhere safe. Somewhere that offered protection."

"And how the hell did my arm get chosen to be your safe place?"

Irini eased a hip onto Lalonde's desk, clearly relishing the attention. "I had, how would you say, blabbed? Yes, blabbed a little too much information to my source in the narcotics division. Pavlov was suspicious. He began talking about a spy in his organization. How could the police have known to raid the suburban house where his operatives cut the drugs? How could they have known the timing for collecting the bags of cash? He began searching everyone, investigating their movements. I injected one microchip into my arm to hide it, and to keep Pavlov's focus away from me I realized he needed to find a mole. So I gave him one."

Her eyes locked on his, and he recognized the truth in her words. She'd known he was an undercover cop, because her lover boy in the narcotics division whose informant she was had told her. She'd been the one to blow his cover.

He felt fury boil up in him like overheated waste oil. He'd blamed one of his own for betraying him, which was still true—whoever the cop was she'd had in her wheelhouse was still guilty of revealing his identity—but the cop hadn't been the one to slip the info to Pavlov; Irini had. To save her own guilty ass.

"So why didn't Pavlov just kill me?"

"He was angry. He had liked you, I think, seen a future for you in the business. Getting reliable helpers who aren't addicted to the product isn't so easy. Once he knew you were a cop, he wanted to know how much you had given away. Perhaps killing you wasn't punishment enough; you know how he liked setting an example."

"He beat the crap out of me, trying to work out how I'd known about the intel you'd fed to the cops. Left me tied to a chair unconscious. Beat the crap out of me again. Broke my fingers. Fun times, Irini, thank you so much."

He heard Antonia gasp beside him, but he was on a roll now. A cable had snapped inside him, one that had been held taut for years binding in his rage, and he forgot he was trying to protect her from the evils of his past, he forgot that he thought she was not equipped to deal with the grim realities of crime's underbelly. Reminding him of the examples Pavlov liked to set had obliterated his control. He'd seen, too well, just how ruthless Pavlov could be.

Irini lifted a shoulder, the silk of her pantsuit lifting as she shrugged off her interest. He felt irrationally angry that she could be lounging about across a desk in a police office, oozing her brand of cloying charm, so casually describing how she'd destroyed his life.

"So what were you doing, Irini, while I was taking the fall so you weren't exposed?"

"I was there," she said. "I saw you. In fact, that was when I had my little, how do you say, brain spark?"

Lalonde cut in. "What was it?"

"I had the second microchip, which was too dangerous to keep now that Pavlov had become so suspicious of everyone around him, and I had an unconscious body, with some finely muscled arms, strapped into a chair in the club. So I injected you with the second data chip."

"Bloody hell," he heard Antonia mutter behind him. She wasn't wrong. He ran a hand over his arm, at the ridge beneath the scar. A callus, he'd thought it, or scar tissue, or a botched job of stitching by a harried doctor at the end of a fourteen-hour shift.

"What was the point?" he demanded. "Pavlov meant to kill me, we both know it. What good would my arm be to you once I was dead?"

She gave him a wink. "Who do you think called 911 and got you rescued?"

He took a deep breath. "You rat on me to Pavlov, knowing it'll end up with me getting killed, then you call the rescue brigade. That is the craziest freaking plan I've ever heard."

"You're alive, aren't you? Safe and well with my microchip snug inside your arm? Besides, you were just my backup plan. I didn't know then that I'd be needing you again."

Lalonde moved around the desk and took over the questioning. "What happened to your plans to leave Pavlov?"

"After the raid, Pavlov switched his base of operations. The raid caused him all sorts of grief; charges were laid, but his lawyers maneuvered their way out of them; he ramped up security, personal and business. Got some experts in to debug his office space regularly, sweep for cameras and so on. I wasn't worried, I had enough data to make him sweat. But then a month or so later, when I was ready to make my break, I tried to read my own microchip."

Lalonde nodded. "Problems?"

"The RFID reader that should have been able to read it, couldn't."

"RFID reader?"

"Radio frequency identification," said Ben, speaking up for the first time. "The microchip shares its data via encrypted signals to an RFID reader. They're not very secure, but you have to be real close to the microchip for them to work. Some tech companies tried to interest their employees in using implanted microchips for signing on and off jobs, food credits at an inhouse canteen, that sort of thing. Too many privacy concerns in my opinion."

Tyler snorted. Irini hadn't given a dime about his privacy concerns. "You got that right. So, Irini, your microchip failed. I assume that's when you thought you'd better go exhume my body and find microchip number two."

Irini nodded. "That is correct. It was a blow, I will concede. You weren't in your budget no-frills coffin, so that's when we realized you must have been taken into witness protection. I've had Pavlov's team looking for you ever since, and my friend from Narcotics. You are my first-class ticket to a new life."

25

"*L*et's find a beach to sit on, just you and me."
Antonia linked her hand into Tyler's as they
hopped out of the police car that had
brought them back to her hotel. Clouds had rolled in
and covered the sky in the time they had been
indoors, and a few rain drops had spattered the dusty
glass of the windshield as they drove.

Tyler looked at the sky. "It's raining, and I just
had three inches of suture stitched into my arm."

Yeah, she'd had the fun of watching it happen
and felt queasy just thinking about it. Watching the
doctor Jozy had located poke about in Tyler's arm
until she found the tiny capsule containing Irini's
microchip had been the last awful moment in a long
twenty-eight hours of awful moments.

That's why she wanted a moment of quiet with

Tyler, just the two of them; a chance to breathe away from everyone, away from the world. Ben was still at the police station, so it was just the two of them, finally. Maybe those glorious ocean waves could sweep away the images swirling through her head. It didn't matter that the sun was hidden, that rain threatened. She wanted to submerge her consciousness in something vast. With Tyler. "There's a little rocky cove to the side of the main beach, just a few minutes' walk from the hotel. It wasn't swamped with tourists this morning; let's go there."

He squeezed her hand. "I might pass out on the beach. Spending the night tied to a chair isn't as fun as it sounds."

"I bet. Just for a little while, I promise, then you can have a sleep in my hotel room while we wait for Ben."

"Okay."

She wasn't sure how to read the resigned note to his voice. That he was bone tired and pushed beyond the limits of endurance, she had no doubt. She'd like to believe he'd given up protesting about her involving her friends in his case, but hey, this was Tyler. He was probably just wary of sparking up another argument about it when he was too tired to think. She turned down the sandy track, pulling him along behind her. They needed to unwind a little, together, loosen the tight wires of tension they'd both been coiled up in over the last few days.

The tiny scrap of beach was as pretty as she remembered it: a few scant feet of sand overhung by palms, waves sliding soft curls of warm water over the shoreline, and mounds of wind-scoured rock bracketing either end. The threat of a sun shower had driven away the other beachgoers, and they had this idyll to themselves.

"How perfect, just us. Let's go in the water, Tyler."

"I'm wounded."

She undid the button of her shorts and encouraged them to shimmy down her legs. She was getting in that ocean, she didn't care what he said. And he was going in with her. "It's just a flesh wound."

Tyler stood his ground. "Easy for you to say. How many bullets have wounded your flesh?"

She stepped out of the pool of fabric at her feet and slid a hand to her blouse. "I think you're chicken."

"Chicken?"

She flipped open a button...and another. She wasn't sure what was driving her to force the issue, but she had so much pent up emotion swirling around, and she'd just had a really great idea how it could be assuaged. Here, on a private little stretch of seashore, under the soothing patter of tropical afternoon rain. "Uh-huh. Cowardy-custard. Lily-livered."

He looked cross, and tired, and a little sulky, which just made her want to push him all the more. She slipped the blouse off her shoulders and stood before him in her underwear. Not quite a bikini, but they were alone, what did it matter?

He groaned. "Bloody hell, Antonia."

She walked up to him, putting a little strut in her step, then stood close, really close, so the cotton of his stained clothing just skimmed her. She placed a hand on his and brought it up to her chest, so his fingers, interlocked with hers, just nudged at her bra strap. "It slides off. Want to help?"

"Antonia." His voice dropped to a rasp as he muttered her name.

She nudged the strap another inch until it hung on the brink of falling. "I didn't quite catch that. Shall I come even closer so you can whisper it in my ear?"

His fingers slid out of hers and both his hands were on her then, sliding, rib to rib over her back. He took in a deep breath, another, the movement of his chest against hers sending goose bumps out from every point of contact.

"Shuck your clothes, Captain. Let's take this reunion into the water so we don't embarrass the seagulls."

She pulled him backwards one step, two, until seawater surged about their feet, cool and cleansing. His hands streaked up her back, fisting in her hair as he brought his mouth down on hers, and the heat that filled her was like a brand, so white hot she could feel it burning through all the worry, all the fear, all the not-damn-knowing that had been keeping her on a knife's edge.

She'd never get enough of this. Never. She kissed him back, putting into it the love she'd been carrying for this man for three long years. Her love for him had been a burden once; when he'd pushed her away she'd had to learn to live with the weight on her heart, and she'd done so.

But now, here, his hands on her flesh, his hot wet mouth fastened on the cords of her neck, her hands sliding between his skin, his clothes, now she could feel that burden burning up along with all the rest. She was flying so close to the heat now, all that remained was him. And her.

"THERE WAS THIS KID. A project kid from the westside, sold drugs floor to floor in the housing towers, maybe fourteen? Fifteen? Couldn't read worth a damn but he could add up his share of the take in a heartbeat. I don't know what his mother called him —she wasn't around—but he was known as Wasp." Tyler drew a finger around his head. "Wore a yellow-

and-black-striped skull cap, about the ugliest thing ever knitted."

Antonia put her arm around his waist, left it there, so their hips bumped as they wandered up the path in the direction of the hotel. He'd not shared this story before—hadn't thought he'd ever want to, but she'd asked him if he'd tell her a little about his life undercover, and this was the story that had come tumbling out.

He slung an arm around her shoulders, hugging her into his side. For a committed loner, he was sure getting used to having Antonia snugged up nice and tight beside him. Maybe she'd do him a favor and stay that way while he collapsed on the hotel bed. He needed to sleep, was desperate for it, but damned if he wanted to be alone. The weakness might have pissed him off once. Not today. Today, he wanted to close his eyes and float off into a dream where Antonia was looking out for him and he could finally, *finally*, go off duty.

"How'd you meet him?"

"Wasp?" He dragged his thoughts back to Baltimore. "The kid was a nuisance, always underfoot. But he was ambitious. School wasn't an option— that's not how you get ahead on the projects. No, he'd figured he wanted more for himself, and that more was coming by way of Pavlov. So when he'd sold out his stash and come in to the club to let the men know he'd need another package delivered, he'd hang around and schmooze."

Antonia smiled. "Schmooze? Like, networking at a cocktail party?"

"Sort of. But Wasp's idea of networking involved getting takeout coffee for the boss, helping the club strippers find their tops after a show, stuff like that."

"You took an interest in him?"

"Black, one sugar. Used to buy me a coffee with his profits—never forgot how I liked it. He'd deliver it with some smartass remark." He'd not thought about Wasp for years—not allowed himself to. The kid had wormed his way through his undercover strategy of not-giving-a-shit and don't-get-personally-involved, which had made the cut, when it came, slice bone deep.

Killed for losing his stash on a cop raid, a raid that had come about from intel Tyler had fed to the downtown narcotics cops. It didn't matter to Pavlov that the raid was organized to appear as a random door-to-door drug bust, the drugs found in a busted dishwasher in a seventh-floor apartment. Pavlov wanted to send a message, loud and clear, to the other sellers.

Tyler had been the first one on scene to see just how Pavlov delivered his warnings. The kid's pants had still been wet where he'd pissed himself before Pavlov's man gunned him down. His black-and-yellow wasp cap sat neatly in place over eyes that could no longer see.

That's what Antonia didn't understand: the responsibility she now bore if anything were to happen to her friend Ben, hell, even to Detective Lalonde. If Pavlov and his crew could put a bullet in a fourteen-year-old kid for misplacing a couple hundred bucks worth of gelcaps, they'd do anything. Anyone. Antonia never needed to feel the guilt of knowing someone's life had been destroyed because she'd brought them into Pavlov's line of sight.

Wasp's dead stare had haunted his dreams for the rest of his time undercover—until they'd been chased out by worse images, worse evidence of just how cheap Pavlov considered any life but his own. He'd not wish those nightmares on anyone, least of all Antonia.

26

———

The room was stuffy, its late-afternoon torpor barely relieved by the rust-stained fan creaking overhead.

"Could you have sprung for a shittier hotel, Toni?" said Ben, as his fingers flew over the keyboard.

Antonia paused, the strip of blood-soaked lint half unpeeled from Tyler's chest. "When you want a cash deal, no questions asked, you get what you get. At least the internet's okay."

Tyler grunted as she tugged the last strands of gauze from his chest.

"The internet's more than okay," said Ben. "Makes me wonder if they're running an online poker business from the hotel laundry. These searches are on the home run."

Antonia saw Tyler frown, and took the opportunity of having him seated on a chair in front of her to lay her hands on his temples and look him in the eye.

"This will *work*, Tyler. Stop worrying."

His lips twisted. "I'll be worrying a lot less, sweetheart, when you've given up on pretending you're Florence Nightingale. I don't need another damn bandage."

She ran her hands up from his temples, smoothed his tangled hair back from his face. He'd slept like a man in a coma for a few hours, showered, but sleep, water, and soap weren't going to cut it on the score mark the bullet had gouged across his chest, or the thin caterpillar of stitches the surgeon had left on his bicep after removing the microchip.

"If you let me put a fresh bandage on, I'll buy you a beer."

He almost smiled. "Yeah, that'll work."

She dropped a kiss on his cheek, his nose, his lips, lingered there until his mouth softened beneath hers. "You ready?" She eased back, waited until his eyes were on hers.

He nodded. "Just do it."

She peeled a clean dressing from the stack of plastic-wrapped packages the doctor had given her, pulled out the twist-top ampoule of antiseptic. "This may sting," she said, and squirted the ink-like substance onto the graze.

"Fuck me," winced Tyler, as she followed it up by

pressing the new dressing onto his chest so it covered the wound. "I'm pretty sure that's earned me two beers."

Ben gave a grunt of satisfaction from over at the desk. "Better make it three, sweetheart. Because Honey's found the Moneyman."

"What?" Tyler stood up suddenly, nudging her back. "Who the hell is Honey? We're supposed to be keeping this investigation under wraps, not blabbing about it all over every chatroom on the internet."

She smoothed a hand down his arm. "Relax. Honey is what Ben calls his laptop. It's weird, I know, he has some sort of fetish for operating systems. It's a geek thing." She tossed the wad of discarded bandages in the trash and moved next to him so they were both standing over Ben's shoulder, looking down onto the computer screen.

A gobble-de-gook of binary code stared up at them, flitting and swarming across the screen like swallows flocking south for the winter.

"Are you making any sense of this, Antonia?" said Tyler.

"Nope."

"It's not just me then. For a second, I wondered how many hallucinogens Irini had pumped into my system, because what I'm seeing makes no sense at all."

"Zeroes and ones," she said. "I hope you've found a bit more than this, Ben."

"You two are philistines."

She snorted. "Says the man who barely owns shoes."

"Hey, reef sandals are *de rigueur* in the islands," said Ben, sounding wounded.

Tyler cut through the banter. "What exactly have you found, Ben?"

"Okay. Antonia gave me a few names: Pavlov, Baltimore, Flaco, Kuzman. My first searches were wide—how do you catch a cautious fish in the ocean, when you only have a hook with no bait?"

Tyler shrugged.

"You don't. Instead of starting with Pavlov, I found Kuzman, then followed him up current until I found the school of fish he likes to swim with. For starters, his name seemed the one most likely to be a real name. Real estate, stocks, political and other donations—turns out, our man Kuzman is quite the philanthropist. I found a Sonny Kuzman, Baltimore upscale address, a much-lauded contributor to the Baltimore Pet Rescue Center. They thank him in their newsletters. And, as it turned out, whoever is in charge of internet security at the animal center knows zip about firewalls. Name, address, social security number, bank account details—it was like slipping a hot knife through lard."

Antonia leaned in, gave Ben's shoulders a quick massage. "You're showing off, hotshot. Cut to the chase. Who's the Moneyman?"

Ben swiveled in his chair and grinned up at them. "Not Moneyman, moneywoman. Ms. Elspeth Laville."

Tyler let out a sigh. "Shit. I've never heard that name."

Ben nodded his head. "Maybe you haven't, but because I truly am a hotshot, I also have a photo of her. You ready?"

Ben swiveled back to the screen and tapped out a sequence of keys. The binary code froze mid-flight, and a grainy image popped up on screen.

Antonia leaned in, even though it wasn't likely she would recognize an underworld figure from Baltimore's drug scene. Tyler went still beside her. She watched his face, the subtle flaring of nostrils, the tensing of his shadowed jaw. Oh yes, he recognized Ms. Elspeth Laville, all right.

"Tyler?"

He spoke, his voice grim. "Yep. Ellie. I never knew her surname. One-time hooker at the club Pavlov runs his operations from. She elbowed her way up the ranks from working the floor to managing the girls. Grew up westside, I'd have said from her accent, the way the spoke. She never crossed my mind as being anything more than a club worker."

Ben had turned back to the screen and began wading through more code. "You don't need a pinstriped suit and a Harvard business degree to be clever, and Ms. Laville is as clever as they come. Luckily, once you have a legal name, some things can't be hidden. Property records, state taxes, bank transactions—even the numbered offshore accounts have names attached to them somewhere. We find the end of her money trail, then we start sniffing our way along it, through whatever corporations and fake transactions she's set up to cover the true source of funds. Sooner or later, we're going to catch us the shiny fish we're really after, Pavlov."

Tyler took a deep breath. "You really think you'll find enough to link her, Pavlov, the money, and the drugs? The whole damn ugly circle?"

He sounded as though he could barely believe the words he'd just uttered. Antonia slipped her arm around his waist and hugged herself into his side. "Believe it, Tyler. You can stop running."

Ben flexed his fingers and eased his way out of the chair he'd been glued to for hours. "Don't pop the corks just yet, Toni. We need to get the data off that microchip Tyler's been incubating. When we have both sources of information, then we'll have the firepower to bring them all down."

Antonia frowned. "Jozy was adamant: the microchip goes to Interpol."

Ben nodded. "That's right. So that's why it's time for us to stop playing caped crusaders and team our resources with the authorities."

Oh. This was going to be the sticking point. She shot a glance over at Tyler. Could he do it? Could he put his trust in the system that had let him down?

The slam of the door as Tyler left the room sounded like a *no*.

27

The creak, creak, creak of the fan punctuated the silence.

Antonia sank onto the bed, her earlier euphoria at the leaps they were making in the case having evaporated. If only Tyler wasn't so damned reticent. She could help him so much better if she understood the whys, the reasons. She looked about the piles of stuff cluttering the room, wondering where she'd thrown her purse when she'd hurried in here with Tyler—gosh, was it just a few hours ago?

How quickly the understanding between them could change.

She spied leopard print in the corner behind the standard lamp and reached down to drag out her purse. Well, she could as quickly turn that under-standing in the right direction again. Cash and cards safely retrieved, she slid her feet back into her sneakers. She'd buy him a beer, insist he talk out his mood with her.

Ben shot her a look. "You going somewhere?"

"You bet I am. He needs to learn to accept our help, Ben, and I'm going to tell him so."

"Maybe you should give him some space."

"Space? He's had five years of space, that's the last thing he needs."

"You're always so sure, Antonia."

She frowned at him. "What do you mean?"

Ben rubbed his hands through his hair. "Shit. I mean, maybe you should give the guy a minute to himself."

She sank back on the bed. Okay, she could work with that. There was a whole lot more she needed to do, anyway, and she had the means sitting right there on the crappy rattan chair in her hotel room.

She toed off her sneakers again and moved past Ben through the french doors out onto the tiny balcony. Tyler's past, his feelings for her, his real name...there was so much she didn't know, and how could she sort it all into an order that made sense, smooth out his hurt edges, if she didn't have his whole story laid out bare before her?

He'd told her snippets. In Jozy's office, when Irini had ticked him off enough to crack through his cold-eyed demeanor, he'd let slip more about his background than she'd heard before. And Wasp!

She rubbed her forehead. How could one man keep so much trauma crated up inside of him? Why couldn't he understand that she was willing to share his burden, in whatever way she could? He kept pushing her away because he thought she couldn't deal with his past, and she was sick of it. It was time to prove he was wrong.

"Ben."

"Hmm?" He was back on his laptop, his attention clearly a long way away from her.

"Can you hack your way into some sort of database and find out Tyler's real name? I need to do some research."

Ben's fingers stilled on the keyboard. "Toni, you know I love you, right?"

She fake-staggered against the french door, nudging its glass into the battered stonework of the wall with a dull bang. "Bloody hell, Ben. If I'd only known earlier, I could have fed Sabrina to the fish back at the Manatee Cays and shimmied my way into her wedding gown."

"As a friend, girlfriend."

She grinned. "Yes, Ben, I know."

"Which is why I'm going to tell you what you don't want to hear."

She frowned. This didn't sound good.

"You asking me to track down merciless drug barons across all fifty states of America, cool. Happy to help. You want me to zip up your frock, de-bug your laptop, sing karaoke with you in a sleazy bar until three in the morning? I'm your guy. But you asking me to breach the privacy of your boyfriend? Dig out his real name when he has gone to such extreme lengths to hide it? You're crossing the line."

"What? I'm not, I'm ju—"

"My line, definitely. These crazy few days have affected your judgement, Antonia."

"Ben! I'm sorry, I di—"

"I haven't finished."

Clearly. Where had her boat-bum-billionaire BFF gone? This Ben didn't look so much like the soft-eyed teddy bear who'd married her childhood friend. He looked like a ruthless genius who could start or solve a worldwide recession with a few well-placed taps onto the keyboard of his beloved laptop.

She shut her mouth and listened.

"You can't tidy up his life, Antonia, with a few flicks of your pen. He's got stuff to deal with, stuff you and I know nothing about, and he's not going to deal with it with you breathing down his neck. He feels betrayed, clearly, by the system, and you and I are wanting him to trust it again. Some things you have to work through on your own."

She breathed in a long slow breath, gazed out

over the glimmer of sea and sand and busy street spread out before her. Was Ben right? Had she been bulldozing her way through Tyler's life like she knew more about it than him? Like she could fix him?

She pressed a hand up to her breastbone. She didn't want him fixed, she wanted him happy, with her. She wanted him to sleep at night without a kit bag packed beside the bed, to enjoy a meal in a café without having to case the joint before he ordered. She wanted him warm, relaxed—and preferably naked—sleeping beside her, with no kamikaze escape looming on the horizon.

She nodded, slowly. She knew Sabrina had married Ben for a reason: the guy gave good advice. The drumroll of epiphany pitter-pattered across her mind: was this the crucial choice she had failed to make in all of her failed relationships? Her long, *long* list of failed relationships. She was too interested in details. She was too, too busy immersing herself into the other person's life, tweaking and schmoozing at the minutia of their lives until they finally brought up their hands and said *no more*.

Ben stood up from the computer screen that had been claiming his attention for the better part of the afternoon and moved past her onto the patio. "We still friends?"

She pursed her lips and gave him the benefit of her most annoyed stare. Ben was right, damn it. She needed to back off and give Tyler some time to deal with the changes of the past few days. A lot of time. As much as it would kill her to do it, she needed to go before she messed up so bad she blew any chance of a relationship with him in the future, when he'd had the time he needed.

She gave Ben a punch in the arm, with a little more force than was strictly necessary. "Yes, my handsome mansplainer. Still friends."

"Great, because we're going for a beer. You're buying."

28

Time, that's what he needed. Five years he'd been out of the game, with all the time in the world to think about what had gone wrong and what he could have done differently. But now he'd been dragged back into the thick of the shitstorm and he had no time to think.

He stabbed his fingers into the keyboard at the internet café, barely paying attention as he answered the string of emails from his office manager. Yes, get the new windscreen for the Cessna. No, hold off on the advertisements in *Islands* magazine—the business was a full-time pilot down with him stashed away here on St Novia—the last thing he needed was more work. Yes, pay the wages ahead of the loan repayment. Crap. Funds were getting tighter the longer he was grounded. They'd be tighter still soon.

If he did what Antonia wanted him to do and returned to the States with Ben, with Lalonde, to see if Pavlov could be brought to trial, his business might not survive. Days, weeks, months—government agencies weren't renowned for their ability to hold hands and play nice. Who knew how long it could take?

And if the microchip data was all some elaborate hoax by Irini to get into protective custody, he'd be back at his old fork in the road: hiding away in witness protection if Cheng got his hands on him, or hidden away on a more permanent basis if Pavlov got his hands on him.

None of those options appealed, and none of those options could include Antonia, either. She'd been upset when he spelled it out, even a fool like he was could see that. Her emotions had been riding a high since they'd left the police station, and she'd wanted him to share the elation, but he'd spent years thinking of emotions as a luxury he couldn't afford. In his world, there was living and there was not living. Black or white. Emotions were colors he wasn't sure he could still see.

She didn't get why he was so reluctant to let her be involved with any plan that involved him. And the truth of the matter was, he didn't want her to get it. Why should she be exposed to the brutal truths haunting his existence? Why should her friends?

They were happy, safe. Why should any of them risk that?

Prostitution rackets, drugs, theft, murder...sure, Antonia knew these things existed, but she'd not seen them, lived through them, wrapped crime scene tape around a fifteen-year-old hooker with a needle stuck in her dead arm and braces still fastened to her teeth. She'd not given CPR to a fellow cop gunned down on a drug bust, then spent weeks washing the taste of blood and regret out of her mouth with bourbon. Worse than all of that was the knowledge that she didn't have addiction and violence poisoning her veins like he did. He was bad blood.

Antonia didn't know; he'd never wanted her to, which was why he'd pushed her away when they first met. He'd wanted her safe, in a carpeted office in London dreaming wild and fantastical thoughts, a long way away from him and the vice that had formed him.

He logged out of the computer and arched his back. He was stiff, and bruised, and the graze on his chest stung like someone had turned a blowtorch on him. He needed a beer like he needed to breathe. He lifted a hand to a waitress hurrying past, bought himself a local beer and took it outside to the dock.

Maybe it was the painkillers the doctor had given him, or lack of sleep. Or maybe it was the adrenaline punch of discovery that Pavlov might, *might*, be vulnerable. Whatever it was, he found his thoughts wandering back to his past.

He'd nearly said his name back there in Lalonde's office when she let him interview Irini—he hadn't thought of his name in years, hadn't allowed himself to.

Daniel Leon. He said it to his beer bottle, as though introducing old friends, and the words felt foreign on his tongue.

Daniel Leon, a kid who'd never known when his next meal would be, or how long he'd be sleeping in a particular bed. He'd not recognized the pressure in his chest as anxiety at the time—that came later, when school counsellors had chipped away at him, and he'd grown up enough to realize that not every kid had spent their early years living with a drug addict mother who'd buy ice before she'd buy her kid a quart of milk. Other kids' lives, when he heard them whine about them, were like listening to science fiction: imagine a parent who nagged you about making your bed, cleaning your teeth, putting the trash out!

He'd grown up not knowing from one day to the next if his mom would still be there when he got home from school, or whether he'd succeed in evading the punching hands of the tough older kids who guarded the doors to the residential towers for whichever drug lord had carved up that part of the city as his or her own.

He'd learned to punch back, and as he grew, the unknown genes who'd fathered him gave him height, and reflexes, and power. That same pressure in his chest that had been worry when he was a little kid with his mom, turned to rage when he was in foster care.

Why shouldn't he have a fancy new smartphone like his foster brother? So he stole one. Why shouldn't he race low-slung cars through the deserted docks of the long empty shipping yards like the wild-eyed youths he looked up to? So he jacked cars on the street, trashed them while he taught himself to wield a four-on-the-floor until he could fishtail round corners, go airborne off a ramp. He'd loved speed, and that weightless sense of being off the ground even then.

Cop-spotter for the guys on retail duty in the towers, shoplifter, dumpster diver, soup kitchen regular, school truant, two stings in juvie—by the time he was sixteen, he'd been ripe with the city's stink of crime and poverty.

Two things had saved him. The first save was the economics teacher at Hank D Smithson High School. He didn't take economics. He snorted—who was he kidding? When he first met Mrs. Lopez, he couldn't have said what subjects he was even enrolled in, because he rarely went and he couldn't have cared less.

But Mrs. Lopez was on duty one day—one of the many days—when Tyler had found himself in detention. He often didn't bother to go, because really, what was the school going to do? Expulsions were saved for the kids caught with guns, or pushing weed on the juniors, or turning tricks in the sports locker room.

But last time he'd gone, there'd been a girl there, with eyes the color of a storm cloud and a laugh that had rolled around the room like thunder until it had rolled right through him and settled like a fist around his groin.

A hard-on in detention. As afternoons went, he'd had worse. So maybe she'd be there again, and he could do more than look and lust this time—maybe he could walk her out, carry her books, or whatever lame-ass thing it was that chicks liked. Maybe he'd even find out her name.

She wasn't there of course. About twenty teenagers lounged in the classroom set aside for detention. The room stank like armpits and burped-up burger breath and old carpet, and the teacher at the front of the room looked about as much fun as a steering wheel lock on a car he wanted to jack.

He shook his head at the memory. Mrs. Lopez saw through him the second he entered that classroom. She'd seen a kid, empty on the inside, full of swag on the outside, and it was his lucky day that she decided to reach out across that empty void of stinking carpet and teenage hormones and try and connect.

First it was the lunch she'd been too busy to eat —could he find a use for a cheese and bologna sandwich and a tub of fruit? He'd been between foster homes at that point, kicked out of one, but not yet tracked down by the authorities to be placed back into care, and the only food he'd eaten that week had been from what he could scrounge from the dumpster outback of the mall. So yeah, he found a use for her spare sandwich.

Then it was the suggestion he join her economics class. So, whatever, he had time, didn't he? He cruised in late, just to show her he wasn't at her beck and call, no matter how damn fine her sandwiches were. He sat on the side and pretended not to listen as she talked about supply and demand, money markets, some dude called Keynes.

But he did listen, and was surprised to realize that he got it. Supply and demand: he'd grown up watching the hustlers in the projects work the game with drugs, stolen goods. Cash came easy for the sellers in the game: the real victories came when they had enough territory to give them power, and enough swag to make them king.

He handed in an assignment and didn't know who was more surprised with the B grade, him or Mrs. Lopez. He handed in another: A minus. With every paper handed in, every look of approval his teacher nodded his way, that awful pressure in his chest he'd lived with his whole life began to melt.

He aced math. He almost flunked English but not quite. He got the prize in economics on his last day, and Mrs. Lopez cried as she hugged him.

His marks were good enough to get him an interview at the Police Academy, and Mrs. Lopez helped him get his juvie record expunged when he turned eighteen. The day he was accepted as a trainee cop in his home city of Baltimore was the day he looked back on as being the second thing that had saved him.

City bylaws, police regulations, a uniform that had to be pressed, tidy, clean—he'd have thought this framework would have chafed, boxed him in like the zoo animals he'd seen on a rare outing with his mom before she died—but he felt the opposite. He felt secure. The pressure in his chest disappeared completely when he joined the force, and he finally understood what the kids had been saying all those years ago when they'd whined about their parents nagging them to make their beds. Parents nagged because they cared. Because they were family. And that's what the Baltimore Police was to him.

Not any longer. Not since the day when he ended up on the run with his fingers broken and his ribs busted and that pressure in his chest back and as big as a frigging hurricane this time. He'd not trusted anyone since and would have said it'd be a cold day in hell before he'd place his blind trust in any official in the US Government.

His thoughts circled back to Antonia, where they had started. Did he really want her to go back to her dreary London office, surrounded by beige carpets within the building and chilly drizzle without?

He had underestimated her, he knew that now. He'd looked on her like a man in a desert might look upon a date palm mirage: he'd been seeing what he needed to see, not what *was*. He'd needed to see that the woman he loved was living a life the opposite to his. He'd seen a woman, free to love as she chose, embrace choices and impulse, free to fling her way headlong into life—all the attributes of life he felt he'd missed out on.

Like a man who'd been flying through storm cloud, he'd been so desperate for a break in the weather when he met Antonia that all he'd seen had been the sunlight. He'd not looked through to the smart, courageous, kickass woman underneath.

Tyler took a last pull of beer, then threw the bottle into the trash and stared out over the busy intersection by the hotel: tourists in their loud shirts, street sellers hawking their woven hats and colored wares.

Maybe that cold day in hell had finally arrived, but, amazingly, he wasn't feeling the chill. He felt the pressure in his chest ease off a touch. He was ready to fall in with Ben's plans, and he had a few ideas of his own that might accelerate their guerrilla attack on Pavlov and his Moneyman/woman Ellie and their whole rotten army.

He looked at his watch. Happy hour at every tourist bar in the country would be kicking off right about now—he'd enjoy a happy hour. A drink of something frivolous with Antonia, perhaps another swim, this time in the moonlight, followed by a perfect, uninterrupted night stretching out before them. On a *mattress*, even.

He smiled. He was beginning to believe he had a future, and that future was looking pretty darned fine. He headed back in the direction of the hotel, to find the person he most wanted to see standing at the center of all his tomorrows.

29

———

$\mathcal{H}$appy hour didn't turn out to be quite so happy.

Antonia had said yes, but she seemed... distracted. She'd said yes to dinner, too, but her distraction hadn't grown any less over the course of a mojito and a platter of swordfish and greens.

The burner phone Jozy had given them buzzed against the timber of the table, and Antonia put down the fork she'd been using to push mango cheesecake about on her plate.

"Hello? Oh, Ben, hi. Hang on, I'll put you on speaker."

Tyler shot a glance around the waterside bar, seeing how far away they were from the other patrons. Despite his newfound feelings of optimism, the last thing they needed was Pavlov and company getting another tip-off, not now when they were on the brink of bringing him down. No one was near them.

Ben's voice was muted by the crappy speaker in the cheap phone, and he leaned forward to listen.

"Okay, I've been in contact with the woman I worked with in the US Government last year."

Antonia looked up at him and whispered, "The woman he worked with is the Vice President."

Of the United States? Jeez. Ben's connections were better than he had thought—way better.

"She's agreed to act as broker. Interpol here on St Novia, meaning Jozy, will take the microchip to her in person. Irini is to remain here at a safe house only Jozy will know the address to."

"What about your info on the Moneyman...well, moneywoman?"

A laugh huffed its way through the tinny speaker. "Yeah, about that. The more I dig, the more I find. I'll be needing to upgrade Honey's storage to cope. I've got a web of transactions emerging, and the great black spider at the center of it has Pavlov's name tattooed all over its hairy ass. Which is where you come in, Tyler."

He'd known it was coming, was finally ready for it. "Say it."

"The warrants have gone out."

"What?" So soon? He hadn't thought the arrests

would start until he got Stateside. The info Ben had shared with the VP must be gold if the authorities had acted so swiftly. He couldn't believe the momentum the storm that had started back in Ballena Airport had gathered.

"Pavlov, Lopez, and two dozen others are being taken tonight. Police in half a dozen cities are making arrests. As soon as they're in custody, you're to come to Washington. Bypass Cheng, bypass anyone downstream of my contact, anyone you know in the Baltimore PD. I'm headed there now to meet face-to-face with my contact. You got any ID you can use? I suspect the name Tyler Cooper will land you in a jail cell until Jozy can wrangle a deal with the aviation authority down there in the Caribbean. If you've got another identity, now's the time to dust him off and get him Stateside."

Tyler looked over at Antonia who was staring at him, brows raised. Yeah—there were a lot of secrets still between them, but for the first time he was letting himself hope those secrets didn't need to be kept to himself.

"I've got ID."

"Great. We'll be staying at the Lincoln Arms in DC. I'll book something roomy, just come straight here."

"I'll find you."

Antonia spoke into the receiver. "We? Is Sabrina with you?"

Ben's tone turned wry. "Well, I am on my honeymoon. My wife likes me to maintain some work/life balance: bringing down a criminal network is work; dipping strawberries in melted chocolate for my wife is life."

Antonia chuckled. "I get the picture."

The sound of muted voices rumbled through the phone, then Ben was back. "Sabrina asks if you've read *The London Times*, yesterday's edition. There's an article on *Bella Magazine* you'll want to read."

"Will do," Antonia said, and ended the call.

She looked pensive, so Tyler reached over and rested a hand over hers. She'd parked her issues with her employer and the board meeting she'd missed while the events of the past few days had consumed their attention, but he knew she'd been devastated about missing it.

He'd make it up to her, if he could. He rubbed a thumb over the back of her hand, tracing a path down over the third finger. A wild-ass thought popped up in his head. What would it feel like, he wondered, to see a band of gold or platinum shining there? *His* band?

He felt a grin welling up, an updraft of relief, and tried to temper it. He wasn't in Washington, not yet— the arrests had yet to be made, and who knew how many diamond-watched lawyers Pavlov had on his payroll. But damnit, he might actually be a free man: free to live wherever he damn liked, free to stop looking over his shoulder every minute.

Free to love anyone he chose.

He leaned across the table and ran his fingers through Antonia's hair, fingers he realized were shaking. Who was he kidding? He'd made his choice three years ago, the second he'd seen Antonia striding along the dusty concourse outside Ballena Airport, a white hat fluttering on her head, a red dress shimmering from neck to knee, and that exotic, honey-hued face filled with fun and mischief. She'd smiled at him, all flirt and cheek, and asked him where she could find a cab into town.

"With me," he'd said, his usual caution knocked flat by the punch of longing.

There was no woman for him but Antonia. And now, after years of believing he had to live his life alone, he'd been given a chance. No, that was wrong —his freedom hadn't been as simply won as a gift— Antonia herself had been pivotal in securing it for him. She'd gone against his wishes—okay, demands —and contacted Ben. She'd shown him that trust was more than a propeller blade that could sever your connection to life; it was also a force that could bring you in to a safe landing.

He owed his freedom to Antonia and her single-minded devotion to freeing him, which was a goal he'd long since stopped hoping for.

"Come for a walk with me," he said, suddenly impatient with the tourists filling up the tables, the waiters clattering past with glassware and trays of tapas. He wanted Antonia to himself, under a swath of star-studded sky, with the murmur of the sea their only music.

She smiled at him, turned a kiss into his hand cupping her face. She nodded towards the beach, where deck chairs lay dotted in the sand, lit up by the bar's strings of fairy lights. "Meet me down there. I'm just going to freshen up."

"You got it."

He threw a few bills onto the table and nodded at the waiter, then made his way over to a deck chair, easing the seat rest back until he was lying down, the stars picked out above him. They looked different from down here on the ground: art rather than science, form rather than function. In the sky, flying at night when the world below was a quilt of neon grids, he could use a sextant on the stars to guide his flight path: Bellatrix and Polaris to the north, Antares to the south.

He didn't need stars to guide his path tonight; he knew exactly where he wanted to go—where, finally, he felt free to go. He closed his eyes, letting Antonia's face fill his thoughts, soothe that age-old ache in his chest. He loved her, and he'd bet his last breath she loved him right back.

Tonight, he was going to tell her.

ANTONIA SMOOTHED her hand over Tyler's chest, the soft folds of his T-shirt warm from the skin beneath despite the breeze drifting in from across the ocean. She ran her fingertips over the ridgeline of bandage that covered his wound. He was asleep on the beach lounge, and no wonder. She felt bone tired herself, and she'd not been shot and beaten.

Just a few inches to the left, and he'd have died. There would have been no more warmth, no more time, no more chances to make something of this— thing—that their relationship had become.

She brushed a hand over his brow, willing his eyes to open. There was so little Tyler had shared with her. So much of who he was, *why* he was, remained a mystery. She'd let the raw drive of her feelings for him overrule her curiosity for too long. She needed answers. She needed Tyler to open up to her, but she wanted him to *want* to share who he was with her.

Ben had spoken a truth today—perhaps truer words than he knew. Her need to know, to smooth, to edit and tidy and catalogue was driving her need to understand Tyler's past, but he'd shut it off from her because he had to. She was causing him pain by insisting he let her in, that he abandon his lone wolf persona and become part of her pack.

Trust, sharing his inner thoughts: they were central to the no-fly zone Tyler had built around himself. And he'd resisted every attempt she'd made to break through it. So much had been taken from him over the past years—his career, his freedom—and now she knew it was time she stopped trying to take away his right to live his life in the way he had chosen.

This was why all her past relationships had failed, because she just kept dig, dig, digging, deeper than they were willing to let her go.

The painfulness of the choice she'd made this afternoon hadn't diminished. She didn't think she'd recover if Tyler were to reject her again, if he were to become like one of those failed romances where the man had finally, driven beyond his endurance, held up his hands and said *no more*. She'd joked in the past about her doomed love life, her failed romances, but those jokes had been made to cover up the hurt beneath, like the tasseled velvet cushions she kept on her sofa back home to distract the eye from the threadbare fabric below. Her heart was feeling just as threadbare.

A soft bleep in her hand focused her attention

back on the burner phone. She'd tried to log on to the London papers while she was in the queue for the ladies' room, but the reception had been too weak to download the files. Perhaps a satellite was directly overhead, because the screen on the phone was filling up with newsprint and sidebar graphics about royal visits and health tips and celebrity love triangles. She scrolled through the features, letting the words flip up and off the screen at speed, until she hit the UK section. And there it was. The headline confirmed her fears: *Bella Magazine Ditches News Team in Mega Makeover.* She read the article, wincing at the statistics: plummeting figures on UK Comscore, rival brands Express and Metro and the Standard the highest performing news brands month after month.

Did she even have a job? Did her staff? She shot a look at Tyler, fast asleep on the chaise longue beside her. He didn't know it, but her decision was made. She might not even have a job to go back to, but go she must, as soon as the arrests were confirmed in the morning and she'd been given the all clear to use her real name to travel.

She owed it to her employer and her colleagues to explain why she hadn't been there for them over the past week. And she owed it to Tyler to give him the time and space he needed to live his life the way he chose.

Tyler looked younger when he slept. She could see the memory of the boy there, the young man who'd overcome so many odds to make something of himself. He deserved this chance to explore his new freedom on his terms, not hers.

She decided to let him sleep there on the beach lounge under the stars. She sank to the sand beside him, leaning against the hard plastic of his chair. It was hard not to let her thoughts travel over the ocean, over the miles of sea and land and time zones to her old life back in London.

News content had been plummeting in reader ratings for years. The modern Londoner wanted their news instantly on live feed on their phone. They wanted color and gloss in their magazines, articles about quinoa and royal christenings rather than researched articles on cross-border politics and nuclear disarmament. She'd do what she could for her team, and for herself. She had contacts, dozens of them, scattered throughout the newsrooms of London and Western Europe. She knew freelancers who loved not being tied to one news desk; maybe she could go freelance herself.

She'd start making calls as soon as she hit London, do up a list of contacts, explain to her boss why she'd been absent for the most important meeting of her career. Maybe she could—

A hand on her back brought her list making to an end.

"Hey."

She spun her head to see a sleepy-eyed Tyler running his hands over his face.

"Sorry. Those painkillers must have had more kick in them than I thought."

She reached up and patted his hand. "You needed the sleep, it's fine."

He rolled to his feet and reached down for a hand to haul her upright. "How about that walk?"

She brushed sand from her shorts and slipped her hand into his. Now was the time; it was pointless delaying it. Somehow, she had to find the strength to let him go—to let him be a free man after all these years.

The sand was cool under her bare feet, its grains so smooth it felt like she was walking on carpet. Tyler pulled her down to the shore, to where seawater lapped in soft curls of foam over the sand, and the music from the restaurant faded into a whisper behind them.

"Antonia."

She waited, but Tyler seemed to have run out of words. Just as the pause had grown to such an unbearable length that she was about to leap into it, he spoke.

"I'm sorry I took off this afternoon."

"No, Tyler. You don't have to be sorry."

"Well, I am." He stopped walking, turned, and grabbed her hand. "I'm pretty much sorry about everything that's happened the last few days, but I'm not sorry you're here."

For a second, Antonia felt her heart leap, her emotions snap and crackle like fireworks at a festival. But then she remembered the vow she'd made. He wasn't sorry now, in the euphoria of knowing the chains of the last five years were about to be unlocked, but he would be. Soon he'd be warning her away.

"I wish it were easier. I wish I didn't have this filthy great sealed section in my past. But my future is with you."

His future? Oh, how she wished that could be true. But she knew herself, better than Ben and Sabrina did, certainly better than Tyler did. She'd pick and chisel and dig away—and she'd ruin it all, the way she always did.

"Antonia, I love you, you know that, right?"

Where had these darned tears come from? She hated crying, hated it. She nodded, tears streaming down her face.

He cocked his head. "You could look a little happier about it, sweetheart."

She couldn't let him go on.

"Tyler." Her voice came out like she had razor

blades in her throat—the sounds all shredded and gritty. "I can't be with you. Not now."

He frowned. "If you mean your job, of course, I know you need to get back to London. Maybe I can join you there after I've been to DC, once this whole case with Pavlov is tied up. Help you, for a change."

She shook her head. "It's not my job. It's me. I've been caught up the last few days, all this drama and action have made me forget who I am—who I *really* am, and…"

She'd run out of words. How could she articulate her feelings? She wanted to be with Tyler like she wanted to live, but now that she had her chance, she felt frozen with fear. Hideous self-knowledge was spinning around and around in her head, like a curse: *you'll wreck this, Antonia, like you always do.*

He'd had enough heartache, more than any man should ever have to bear. She couldn't add to it, the way she undoubtedly would when their relationship came tumbling down.

She said the words that needed to be said. The cut had to be quick and deep, before her courage failed. "I think it's best if you find someplace else to stay tonight. If the arrests have been made and I get the all-clear to travel, I'll be flying out to Gatwick tomorrow morning on the early plane."

HE WATCHED her walk away from him, her silhouette growing smaller with every step. The moon pushed her shadow over the beach towards him, and he felt a terrible yearning to run after the dark shape, to grasp even this intangible remnant of her, if that was all he could have.

Memories were all he had of anyone; why would Antonia be any different? The words he'd never had a chance to say stuck in his throat: Antonia, be mine. Antonia, come close, closer still, way, way closer than that and don't ever, ever leave.

But the words she'd uttered had left him without the will to voice his own.

Hell, what a day. The realization that Pavlov would soon be behind bars had driven pretty much every thought out of his head—every thought but Antonia. But if he couldn't share this moment with her, what use was any of it? The running, the hiding, the burning sense of betrayal that had fueled his will to live the last five years. What did any of that matter now?

He turned up the beach, the cool sand under his feet reminding him that soon, maybe even tomorrow, he could go home to the cottage, to Missy Jane's. If some goon still hadn't got the memo that the game was finally over and caught him there, who the hell cared?

He could sleep tonight in his manager's office at

St Novia airport, maybe, if he could clear the security perimeter. Or he could head back to the bar and find a little comfort from his old friend, cheap whiskey.

He looked up at the moon as though it might have an opinion about which was his best option, then nodded. "Cheap whiskey it is."

30

THREE MONTHS LATER

*A*ntonia swayed with the press of people jammed into the carriage as the underground train hurtled round the bend from Blackfriars to Temple. The London tube in winter peak hour was not for the faint of heart: bitter sleet pounded the ground above, while belowground, overwarm bodies in drenched wool coats created a distinctly unpleasant fog.

She turned her head so her face wasn't quite so near the armpit of a large, harried-looking man whose hand was slung through the chrome handle on the ceiling, and spotted a young man by the window, one of the lucky few who'd scored a seat, reading *Thinkfest*. She danced a little mental jig of triumph; this was her first sighting of the new magazine out in the wild! If she wasn't hemmed in by bodies, she would have scrabbled for her phone and taken a sneaky selfie with the cover in the background.

Creating a monthly print journal from the ashes of her old magazine had not been easy. The income it generated was paltry, too little to offer job security to its contributors, let alone her and the other freelancers who'd clubbed together to start it, but it was a start. And with Charlotte's expert help, she'd managed to launch the magazine with a worldwide exclusive on how a billionaire drug baron had been brought to his knees.

Printing contracts, distribution channels, freelance agreements with her old colleagues keen to pursue news journalism for an independent magazine—the weight of tasks had all but obliterated her in the last few months. Which, she acknowledged, she had wanted. If she was buried in work, she wasn't thinking about Tyler. Wasn't wondering how he was doing, was he happy, did he miss her like she missed him?

She'd left a vital part of herself behind when she flew out of St Novia and Brisa and returned to England. She still didn't know if she'd made the right decision. The email that had pinged into her inbox today, just as she was leaving the temporary office space she'd cadged from a friend, just added to her indecision.

A tinny voice sounded above her head. *Next stop, Embankment. Change here for Circle, Northern and Bakerloo Lines.* Change here. Change here. The two-word phrase echoed around and about in her head. Her worry about her own inability to change was what had made her decide she needed to give Tyler some space. She'd screw it all up by making decisions for him, picking at him about his past, his name, his life before he was Tyler, before he met her.

She slumped a little, stood on one foot to ease the pressure off the aching balls of her feet. So high-heeled fur-trimmed boots weren't an ideal choice for a day at meetings, dragging herself all over the city, lunching with potential advertisers, carting boxes of computer equipment about. They'd looked good when she'd dressed this morning. They'd still be looking good now if they weren't soaked in sleet and mud and beginning to resemble wet bunny rabbits.

Her boots weren't what was getting her down. It was the worry that she'd dressed up her decision to leave Tyler as though she were doing the noble thing, when in reality, she'd been running away. This two-way-street relationship thing was bloody compli-cated—and she'd been worried that she didn't have all the answers.

The train screeched to a giddy halt and people surged around her, some heading out into the plat-form, some pushing deeper in to the hollow tube of the train. Armpit guy breathed a stale waft of Friday lunchtime ale over her, and she winced. *Change here for Bakerloo, District and Northern Lines.*

Those tinny words again, running through her head. *Change here.*

In a split second, she made a decision. She dived for the exit even as the train doors started closing, hauling her laptop bag and coat with her out onto the dirty platform. She *could* change here. She could change into someone who didn't need all the answers. Into someone who could just be happy with what was.

She hurried up the stairs, too impatient to wait for the elevator, heedless of the hundred-odd steps she was having to take. She wanted to reread that email, properly, like someone who intended to do something about it. Last time, she'd skimmed it like a coward and pretended it didn't concern her. And she couldn't read it there in the train; she needed space, clean air, maybe even—and why the hell not, it was Friday after all—a glass of wine.

The street doors loomed ahead of her, and she shot through them. Which direction? She scanned the street, putting to use her extensive knowledge of London's night venues. The sleet had ended, thank heaven, as she'd no umbrella. Riverwards, she thought, to The Potbelly Pig. A snug table by the fire overlooking the river, and she could finally put her own life on the table for review. And she didn't mean to be lenient with her red pen.

AN HOUR LATER, she'd read the email top to bottom and backwards, but still hadn't found the subtext she was looking for. Through the mullioned window of the pub, moonlight shimmered over the Thames like a scene from a fairy tale. As a girl, she would have made up fanciful stories of elven maidens and warrior princes, whose lives would only intersect on moonlit paths. She'd have woven adventure around them, romance—backstories of noble courage and purity of heart. She'd have drawn stars in the sky and nodding bluebells by the foreshore, and frolicsome unicorns plunging into silver-tipped waves.

But that was then. And though her fantasies had changed over the years—and yes, the elven maiden may have gone to university and grown a little less, um, maiden-like—and the warrior prince she'd imagine today would have shorter hair and a greater appreciation for equality between the sexes—the heart of the fantasy remained the same. Her, and someone she could call her own.

She pressed her hand against the sudden pain in her chest. She wanted that someone to be Tyler, but what if she screwed it up?

Your presence is required at a court hearing in the Federation of Brisa and St Novia...

Nope. The email still wasn't giving her the information she needed. Did Tyler want to see her again or not?

A tear splashed down her cheek, and she flicked it away, then stared into the dull red of her wine. Professionally, coming back to London had been the right thing to do. She'd turned a setback into an opportunity, and she was proud of that. Happy even. But personally? No, not so much, and she'd discovered misery made for a lousy life partner.

No magic was coming her way to help her out of the mess she'd made of her love life. She'd walked away from Tyler, even though she'd thought there were good reasons for doing so. No wand could wave him back into her life or teach her she didn't need all the answers. No moon-clad nymphs were tiptoeing towards her from the distant blue yonder to assure her she wouldn't mess it up this time.

Change here. Antonia rubbed the wine off her finger onto a napkin and squared her shoulders. Magic only happened to the heroines who had the courage to fight for their hero even when they couldn't be sure if there was going to be a happy ending.

It was up to her now to create a little magic in her life, to find her courage and set off again on a quest for a hero. Sure, in the past, that quest had led her to kiss a few frogs along the way, try on a few cracked-glass slippers. She was a romantic, and that wasn't a crime.

She drank the last mouthful of wine in her glass, then set it back on the linen-clad tabletop with a snap. Hell no, it wasn't a crime, it was an asset! She was Antonia Da Silva, and she was going to get her man back.

She turned her back on the moon shimmying in through the old pub window and marched back into the snarl of inner-city London. She had plans to make. Planes to book. A hero to catch.

ONE WEEK LATER, the curt words of the email were still driving her nutty with frustration, but at least now she was four thousand miles closer to finding out what they meant.

There'll be a seaplane waiting for you at Ballena Airport to bring you to the island of St Novia. Your attendance is requested at an unofficial hearing. Detective Jozy Lalonde, Assistant Commissioner, Interpol National Central Bureau (NCB), The Royal St. Novia and Brisa Police Force.

She frowned, noting for about the thousandth time that the policewoman's credentials took up more of the message than the actual communication. Would it have overtaxed Jozy to ask how Antonia was doing? After what they'd been through together, you'd think she merited something a little friendlier. She pursed her lips. Not even a hello, or a kind regards, or a smiley-face emoji.

She'd been tempted—true, only for about a millisecond—to lie and say she couldn't come, see if that would shake a few more words out of the prim detective. She was too broke, too busy, too...

Alliteration failed her. The truth of the matter was she'd drop everything and fly halfway around the world on the off chance of running into Tyler in the humid halls of a local police station in Verde-terre, and that damn detective knew it, too. No wonder she'd not bothered to lure her over with pleasantries.

The heat beating up off the smaller runway at Ballena's airport was as recognizable as the blue stripe painted down the fuselage of the amphibious aircraft waiting for her: Tyler's Cessna.

No way. Was he *here?*

But, no. A woman greeted her, who had them airborne and flying west with ruthless efficiency within minutes. And so far, the pilot had evaded every attempt Antonia had made at eliciting information.

She shoved her phone back into her travel bag

and decided to try again. She raised her voice so it could be heard over the propeller. "Who made the booking for the charter flight? Was it the police department? Or your boss?"

The pilot half twisted in her seat, tapped her fingers at the army-green headset clamped to her ears, then turned her attention back to the dials and switches of the cockpit.

"Yeah, I see the earphones," Antonia muttered. "But you could take them off long enough to answer a few questions." Giving up, she looked through the window to the endless seas below. It looked like her future had looked back in London: empty. She closed her eyes, let the rumble and hum of the plane soothe her tired mind.

A bump woke her. The light in the cabin had grown dim, and the propeller's whine had ceased. The plane had landed while she'd dozed, and motored into some sort of hangar. The slop of water under the hull told her they'd not come into the main airstrip on St Novia.

She unclipped her seatbelt and took a moment to study her reflection in her compact mirror. Eyes: brown. Makeup: perfect. Hair: not bad, considering the humidity, the static, the ten hours of flying time. She was good to go. Whatever needed to be said or done at this "unofficial hearing", she was ready to say or do.

Although, what string still needed to be tied, she had no idea. Pavlov was in a holding cell while the authorities drafted the lengthy list of charges Irini's evidence had produced, as were his inner circle of associates. The Moneyman was still at large, but the FBI, the DEA, and every other investigative agency in the Northern Hemisphere with a three-letter acronym had her identity, her picture, her credit card and banking history thanks to Ben's work with Interpol. She'd be trapped in a snare soon enough.

"If you could make your way from the plane, ma'am."

So the pilot *could* speak. She sighed. She'd know soon enough what this was all about. She slid her compact back into her travel bag and made her way out of the plane. The pilot had jumped out ahead of her and was already pulling her battered, jaffa-red case from the cargo hatch.

"You go ahead, ma'am. I just need to do a check on the motor, and I'll be along in a minute or two."

"Okay," she said, reaching down to pull up the handle of her suitcase. She picked her way along the uneven planking of the jetty, the wheels of her case over the wood drowned out by the roar of the propeller spinning to life behind her.

Wait a minute. The wide arch ahead, where galvanized roofing gave way to Caribbean sky, looked familiar. She dropped her case and hurried forward, pausing as jetty gave way to lush emerald-green lawn.

Chickens pecking at worm-rich soil, hibiscus bushes nodding their petalled heads, and a cottage, white and aqua, its wind charm of seashells dancing in the breeze. She was in Esmeralda Bay, at Tyler's house.

She spun seawards as a roar ripped through the silence, and watched, open-mouthed, as the plane she had arrived in tore across the serene waters of the bay and lifted into flight. So much for the pilot being along in a minute. And where were the police officers? Where was Detective Lalonde, who so urgently required her attendance at a hearing?

31

Tyler stood on the beach, his feet in the darker sand where waves swirled in a gentle push of tide. His chest was bare, and dark shorts rode low on his hips. He'd cut his hair, she noticed—the curling ends were gone.

She slipped off the heels she'd worn for the flight over, propped them against her suitcase and walked through the flowering vines crisscrossing the upper slopes of the beach.

She felt a catch in her breath as she walked closer to him, the sting of tears burning a brand on the inside of her eyelids. Being strong in London had been one thing—she had distractions there: a career to rebuild, friends to play with, the biting cold of winter to ice over her miserable heart so she couldn't feel its pathetic calls for comfort.

But here, Tyler standing before her, six foot of warm, barely clothed, steely-jawed manflesh—well, now she was struggling to remember how she'd ever had the strength to leave.

He smiled at her then, and it was as though the sun had slipped a ray of light through a break in clouds. His dear, serious, bad-boy face, alight with... was that happiness?

She stopped a foot away from him, close enough to smell the seawater drying on his shoulders, the soap he'd used at some point earlier in the day. He looked different. It was more than the haircut: he looked relaxed, less like a tightly wound coil. She acknowledged the thought that was zapping uppermost in her mind—he looked heavenly.

"You came," he said.

She pursed her lips, suddenly remembering that she'd been dumped by seaplane and then abandoned. She wasn't about to be distracted by sultry looks and pheromones quite yet. "Where's Jozy? I thought I was being delivered to a police station."

He reached out a hand, stroked a strand of her hair that the wind had found to play with, tucked it behind her ear and lingered there. She pulled her head back slightly before the feel of his fingers grazing her skin could erode her brain's ability to think.

"Jozy's nearby. I thought maybe you and I could have a talk first."

Oh boy, just like that. Now was the time. She had to face up to who she was, who he was, and hope against all hope that she wouldn't screw it up. She was who she was: garrulous, nosy, managing; and he was who he was: aloof, prickly, a survivor who needed time to relearn how to live, now that he was finally free.

"Oh, Tyler." She'd just say it, she thought. "I'm afraid if we have a talk I'll just mess things up."

"Please, Antonia. Trust me."

Trust. There it was, the thorn that had finally pricked her bubble of idealism—the pea in the princess bed, the poison in the apple. Trust had been the crux of the issue between them: she'd trusted Tyler as she'd trusted her friends—without question, without complication.

Tyler hadn't trusted her, and god knows he'd had reason. She wasn't in his shoes—she didn't know what sort of person she would have been if she'd led the life he had lived—and she'd tried to bulldoze her way through it the way she always did. Tyler deserved more. He deserved some peace.

He held out his hand, coaxing her to place her hand in his. She looked at it for a long minute, wanting *so badly* to put her hand in his. Turning away from Tyler had been the hardest thing she'd ever done—heartbreakingly hard.

On a sigh, she slipped her fingers into his. She was here to make magic, wasn't she?

"I want to tell you a story," he said, and tugged on her hand so she was walking with him into the sun.

"What sort of a story?"

He shot a look over at her. "A little bit action, a little bit romance, a little bit fairy tale."

Her resolve wavered some more—she could feel it melting like the polar ice cap under assault from global warming. "My favorite kind. Tell me more."

"There was this guy."

Antonia smiled. Starting a sentence with a passive construction? If the guy he was talking about was *her* guy, she could totally overlook it. "Would I like him?"

He shot her the heartthrob smile she'd seen so rarely. "I'm kinda hoping you would. So, this guy, he's not so great with sharing stuff."

"Like...cookies? Seats on a train? His duvet?"

"All of that and more. And he's taken a few knocks, all of which have taught him that he's been right all along not to share."

She stroked a hand up his arm—she just had to. Those knocks. So brutal, so awful for him to have had to deal with alone.

"But then he meets a girl."

The wind ruffled through her hair as she turned to look up at him. "A girl? Aha, plot complication."

"You've got that right. And our guy, he's totally bowled over by this girl."

"Totally?"

Tyler swung her around so he was facing her, held both her hands in his. "One hundred percent. In fact, the guy loves the girl so much he's too scared to let her into his life."

"Bloody hell, Tyler." Had he just said what she thought he'd just said? She was having trouble separating the fictitious her from the real her. "My head's spinning. Can we cut out the "he" and "she" and switch to you and me?"

"Sure." He took a long breath, and started again. "I want to tell you something. The day this all started, when Pavlov found out I was an undercover cop trying to bring down his empire, something happened to me."

The fingers, the beatings, the fear. And that freak, Irini, injecting secrets into his arm like he was her own personal pin cushion. Yes, terrible things had happened on that day. "I know," she said. "You don't have to rehash it all if you don't want to."

He squeezed her hand. "It's fine, I want to. Looking back, I can see now that despite my upbringing, I still had a core of idealism. You know: if

I worked hard enough, long enough, the good guys would win."

She smiled. She understood that—hadn't that same idealism been the driving tenet of her love life since puberty? If she traveled far enough and wide enough, the love of her life would canter up on a white stallion. She rubbed his hand.

"My idealism was snuffed out that day. And I've not believed in it since then—until I met you."

Antonia felt her heart stall like an airplane that had just lost power.

"There's one more thing."

"Tyler, it's—"

"Hear me out. I've got a lot more I'd like to tell you, if you want to listen, but for now, can I just share one more thing and ask you to be patient about the rest?"

Oh wow. Patient! Of course she could be patient. Well, she could *try*. She took a shuddering breath. "Tell me."

He nodded, took a deep breath and she watched, curious, as dull color flooded his face.

"Are you—?" Surely he wasn't. "Tyler, are you *blushing*?"

He frowned, a Tyler face that she was well familiar with. "Give a guy a break, would you, Antonia? I'm doing this my way."

And she watched, shocked, as he dropped to the

sand on one knee before her, her hands held tightly in his.

"Oh. My. God," she breathed, all rational thought having flounced out of her head.

"Antonia Da Silva."

She could barely recall that those words were her name. Her head was buzzing with little half thoughts like *oh*, and *wow*, and *squeeee*.

He gave her hand a little tug, raised his eyebrow. She gathered her thought processes together with a snap. "Yes?"

"Will you, Antonia Da Silva, marry me, Daniel Leon?"

No amount of daydreaming and wishes on stars had prepared her for this moment. She tried to speak —and failed. Tried to blink—and cried. She did what she'd been wanting to do since she'd first seen Tyler—heck, had he just called himself *Daniel?*— standing there on the beach; she dropped to her knees before him, wrapped her arms around his neck, and kissed him like the hero he was.

SHE'D BEEN SPEECHLESS, and the woman he loved wasn't caught without words very often. Tyler stood back, letting the crowds gather round her, content to just rest his eyes on her after all this time apart.

She'd been even more dumbfounded when the crowd had poured out of his cottage, where he'd had to bribe, threaten, and cajole them to stay while he asked her to marry him.

Missy Jane had been first out the door, muumuu flying, making kissy noises at them before she'd even made it halfway down the beach. He guessed they'd all figured out Antonia was saying yes to his proposal when she launched herself at him and didn't let go. Ben and Sabrina were on their way at a more sedate pace, champagne bottles, platters of cheeses, and an odd assortment of glasses in hand. And Jozy, newest of the inner circle he was proud to recognize as friends, prim as ever, brought up the rear.

He'd phoned Charlotte and Jack in Hawaii, sworn them to secrecy when they'd had to decline his invitation to come out to the island for his surprise engagement party. Charlie had some childhood ailment and was too infectious to travel.

No matter. The person who meant the world to him was here, and that's all that counted. She looked up then and caught his eye. *I love you*, she mouthed at him across the crowded beach.

Yeah. She really did.

LATER, much later, after the champagne had been drunk, and Tyler had talked her out of leaping into his seaplane and flying to Vegas to be married in front of an Elvis impersonator, and their guests had all headed back to their own accommodation, Antonia knelt on the rug they'd laid out on the grass in front of the little white-and-aqua cottage. She looked down at Tyler, who lay back, his head propped on the pillows she'd dragged out from the sofa inside.

She grinned at him. "So, should I call you Daniel, now?"

He closed his eyes for a second. "I don't feel like a Daniel anymore."

"What do you feel like?"

"Like a man whose life started the day he met a brown-eyed woman wearing a wild red dress in the taxi queue at Ballena Airport. I was called Tyler then. I think it's kinda stuck."

She stroked her hand down his face. "Tyler the hero," she murmured.

He snorted. "Not quite."

He was her hero, that she did know. Finally, her dream of a fairy tale romance was coming true.

"You know, that story you told me on the beach wasn't so bad," she said.

"No?"

"But I can think of a few improvements."

Tyler grinned. "Like what?"

"I think you should work a little more on the romance."

"Great idea," he said, pulling her down towards him so she was lying across his chest, her mouth a whisper above his. "Is this working for you?"

She ran her nails down his side, brought them up over the ridges of his ribs, gasped as he flipped her so he was above her, his hands holding her tight against him. He buried his head in her neck and grazed his teeth gently on the skin below her ear.

She grinned. "Work harder."

Loved this book?

Read Charlotte and Jack's prequel story *HERE* (free for subscribers to Stella's newsletter) or visit my website www.stellaquinnauthor.com

Turn the page for more ...

TROPIC STORM

Charlotte Jones paused amid the crowded departure lounge of Los Angeles International Airport. Shining up at her from the display rack at the front of an airport shop was the familiar cover of *Bella* magazine. But was it the latest issue?

She broke into a grin as she pulled the glossy magazine out of its stand. Her last article had made the cover; she hadn't expected that. A dancer slumped on a backstage prop, all heels and legs and bling, her oversize feathers discarded on the floor beside her. Charlotte ran a finger over the dancer's weary face, the loud pop of color from the flamingo pink of the feather. The photographer had nailed it this time.

"You buying that, lady? You wanna library, you're gonna have to go someplace else."

"Relax, I'm buying," she said and placed the magazine down on the counter. She'd have a copy waiting for her when she returned home to London, stuffed into her mailbox and wrapped in a yard of biodegradable plastic, but why wait? She'd never gotten over the thrill of seeing her freelance articles in print, and she had a six-hour flight ahead of her. She'd be able to read the magazine cover to cover.

"A bottle of water too, thanks."

She rifled through the pound notes in her purse until she found her clip of American money, then handed a ten-dollar bill to the rumpled man at the till. Leaving the change on the counter, she headed back into the flow of people and cast a look upward to the screens. The letters clicked over on a departure board, white font over a black background: *Hawaiian Airlines to Honolulu, terminal 5, gate 58.*

A thrum of anticipation joined the jitters in her chest. This was more than a holiday about to start; this was a one-woman retreat, just for her, a journey towards peace, solitude, well-being. She crossed her fingers, pinkie-promised herself that it would work. As much as she loved her job writing opinion pieces in magazines and her hobby-slash-obsession writing for her women's issues blog, she needed to recover before going on assignment again. She closed her eyes and imagined the sunshine, saltwater, and sea breezes soothing her jangled nerves. Hawaii and happiness...she couldn't wait.

The queue to enter the waiting lounge at her gate was snaking down the corridor by the time she made her way through the sprawling airport. Couples leaned on each other, taking selfies to pass the time, and children squealed and bounced with excitement. An elderly woman wearing pearls the size of mothballs was having a heated discussion with a check-in attendant about the size of her carry-on luggage.

Charlotte smiled. People, chatter, hustle and bustle: she'd forgotten how much she used to enjoy the chaos of travel. And today, despite the crowds, she felt good. She felt strong, for the first time in months. Perhaps her psychologist was right and she really would recover. There'd been days when she'd wondered if she'd be trapped by stress forever. How would she work then?

A tinny voice from overhead broke her train of thought. Just as well; now was not the time to be dwelling on what had happened to her in Barwick three months ago.

Passengers on flight HA4 to Honolulu, your plane has been delayed. Please remain near the departure gate and await further instruction.

A collective groan issued from the people queued about her, and she shuffled forward with them through the security check. She'd spent a lot of time in airport lounges over the years. What was an hour or two more?

She slung her leather carryall on to the conveyor belt, showed her passport and ticket to the check-in attendant, and was waved through to the dubious comfort of the holding area. At least there were seats available. She chose a plastic chair by the window and settled in to wait, rolling her shoulders to relax some of the kinks. It had been a long flight over from London, and she was tired.

A toddler nearby broke into a wail, breaking her train of thought. Flashing a look over to the departure screen to check how long she was going to be trapped in a seat next to a young person with lungs the size of Texas, her gaze fell on a dark-suited figure entering the lounge, and all thoughts of kinked muscles fled from her brain.

"Oh my," she muttered.

A handsome man was walking through the security screening area. She studied him covertly over her magazine. Six foot one, she decided, skimming the length of him from his close-cropped, dark-blond hair to his expensively shod feet. His suit was the darkest gray, emphasizing the white of his collar and cuffs, and the body it covered left Charlotte's lips forming an *oh* of admiration. She wondered what color his eyes were, then turned resolutely to her magazine.

She'd never been lucky where men were concerned, no matter what their eye color, so really, what was the point in looking? She flipped through the glossy pages to her article. *Bella* had been her first serious job, back when she'd thought being an investigative reporter in war-torn countries would be a great way to prove to the world that she had made something of herself. Luckily for her, she'd been to school for a time with the magazine's news editor. Antonia still contracted her for the odd article, which helped keep the funds flowing in. And this latest one had been a delight to write. It wasn't her usual piece —she was more at home advising women on ways to hop, skip, and jump over the gender pay gap, or reviewing the latest mindfulness apps bombarding the market—but something about the chorus girls in London's latest stage show had appealed to her. The hard graft behind the glamour, the sweat beneath the sequins...she had found something when she interviewed the dancers which had resonated. The drive to succeed came at a price. For the dancers, it was the injuries, the uncertainty of work ahead, the competition for work within a shrinking industry.

Charlotte knew about paying a price for success. She'd spent the last decade paying it.

The toddler's wail reached a pitch capable of shattering bulletproof glass, and she cast a glance about, wondering if it would be too obvious if she changed seats. Oh, yes! There was one free, and—oh, happy day—it was right next to Mr. Hot Suit. She glanced up at his face, only to encounter him looking back at her with shocked recognition. Oh my god. No, it couldn't be. She dropped her eyes to the magazine she held in her hand and felt heat rushing up through her cheeks.

Jack.

The calm she had been feeling, the happy puff of anticipation about starting her holiday, evaporated. Her hands gripped the *Bella* issue as though it was a shield. Why did it have to be Jack?

She peeled her fingers off the magazine, noting how clammy her palms had become. She had to calm the hell down. Finding herself in the same departure lounge as the man who had smashed her world to smithereens nine years ago...it was too much. Maybe she could have dealt with it calmly if she wasn't already a mess about the fiasco in Barwick. But the fiasco had happened, and she was all out of bravery.

She kept her eyes averted, knowing she was behaving like a big chicken, but unable to help herself. Hopefully, he'd have the decency to stay well away from her. She did not know if she could handle a confrontation with the man she had once been foolish enough to lose her heart to.

Ladies and gentlemen, a voice blared from the speaker above her head, *we are pleased to announce flight HA4 to Honolulu is now ready for boarding.*

Oh, thank heaven. The airline companies fit three hundred people on these planes; with luck, they'd be seated well away from each other. She had an eye mask in her bag and ear plugs. She'd wrap an airline blanket around her head if she had to. She could not face Jack. Not now, not ever.

She slung her bag over her shoulder, checking her belongings were all safely tucked away, then rose to her feet. She marched to the boarding gate, checked her pass, then took off down the long airbridge to the plane. Fast walking was *not* running. Charlotte Jones did *not* run away.

"Well, not often," she admitted to herself as she sank into the plush comfort of her seat. She closed her eyes and willed her heartbeat to settle into a calmer cadence.

Her phone buzzed, and she reached to silence it. The words *Antonia is calling* scrolled over the glass screen. She sighed. Antonia wasn't just the editor of *Bella* magazine—she'd have ended the call if she was, future work prospects be damned—Antonia was also one of her oldest friends and was not the sort of person you could ignore, even from half a world away.

She lifted the phone to her ear and braced herself for the onslaught.

"Charlotte, have you arrived? Tell me everything. Is the water warm? Are the cocktails cold? Wait. Any single guys? You know I've got weeks of holiday owing; I can be there like a shot if there's single guys."

Nothing changed. She smiled. "Toni, I'm nowhere near Hawaii. I'm parked on a tarmac in the States. No cocktail umbrellas in sight."

"Bummer. Call me the instant you get to the hotel, won't you? I'll worry if you don't."

"Yes, matron."

"None of that cheek from you, young lady. But seriously, how are you coping with the crowds? No dramas in the airports? No panicky whatsits?"

She closed her eyes, and a vision of the gray-suited drama called Jack came into view. "Not that sort of drama, no."

There was a pause. Charlotte imagined her friend's brain scrambling through the innuendo of that remark. She chuckled to herself at Toni's next words.

"Tell. Me. Everything."

She let out a breath. Was she ready to talk about

it? She sighed and took the plunge. "You'll never guess the man I just saw at LAX."

"Umm. A Hemsworth? Hugh Grant? Colin Firth?"

"Somebody I actually know."

There was a pause. "I'm struggling here, Charlotte. You live like a nun. Do you even know any men? I can't think of a single one you've given tuppence about since Jack bloody Diamond back when you were a cadet journalist in London and I was backpacking my way through the single men of Europe."

The silence stretched out as Charlotte waited for the penny to drop. Or tuppence, in this case.

"Holy crap. You're not seriously telling me you ran into Jack Diamond?"

"Yep. The rat himself."

"I'm speechless."

Charlotte laughed. "Well, that's a first."

"So, what happened?"

"I ran away."

"Ran away? You? Charlotte the badass women-are-champions blogging queen?"

She could hardly believe it herself. But the heart was a tender thing, and she'd forgotten how tender hers could feel. "It was actually pretty tough seeing him, Toni."

She could hear her friend's nails tapping on a

hard surface. Antonia was at work, no doubt ripping adverbs from some hapless reporter's article.

"Yeah, I bet," Antonia said at last. "Listen, Charlotte, I have to take a call from Barcelona, but we should talk this out. Oh, and you know that draft article you gave me? The one on the Barwick riots?"

Oh yeah, she knew that one all right. She'd written it up in her hospital bed while under the influence of a surfeit of common-sense-dulling drugs. Well, she hadn't so much written it as dictated it into her phone, as her arm had been buried within six inches of plaster. Thousands of words on the women's issues blogger who'd been on her way to a café to interview a woman about a community gardening project but instead found herself in the middle of a riot that swept through the regional city when police shot a man in the street.

She regretted having written it now. She'd been too raw, too deeply affected to be objective in her reporting. Antonia could delete it; that was fine. "Don't worry about the article, I shouldn't have sent it in."

"Don't worry about it? Girlfriend, it is fantastic. I've entered it into the press awards. It's taking center stage in the next issue of *Bella*."

"Antonia—" She drifted to a close. Thinking about that day still had the power to upset her. She'd not be reading the article when it was published.

She heard her friend sigh down her end of the phone. "Charlotte. We don't have to talk about this now; forget I mentioned it, okay? Why don't you skype me when you're settled in Hawaii? I'll invite Sabrina over to my place, and the three of us can bitch about men and bossy editors until you get that sad little sound out of your voice. I don't like hearing it."

Charlotte smiled. Bossy or not, Antonia was as fabulous as a friend could be. "It's a date. And thanks."

She slipped her phone over into airplane mode and dropped it into her bag. She was lucky to have Antonia and Sabrina in her life, and she knew it. Her old school chums had been there for her through the high moments and the low.

The muted hubbub of the filling plane was comfortingly familiar. She turned to her window and gazed across the vacant seat through to the busy airstrip. Only a few more hours until her holiday started. The website for the hotel she had booked promised perfection. Part of the Jewel Resort Group, the Jewel of Oahu was set amid lush Hawaiian gardens, with views spanning a perfect beach and the Pacific Ocean beyond.

She sank into a daydream of bathing in sun-dappled water and lying in the feathered shade of coconut palms. She could think about the project her psychologist had been encouraging her to pursue or maybe read the half dozen books she had included in her luggage. She smiled. Would she read the rom-com first? Or the new thriller that—

"Excuse me."

Charlotte opened her eyes and sat up, reaching out an instinctive hand to smooth her wayward auburn hair. Oh, no. Fate couldn't be so cruel.

"If you wouldn't mind letting me past so I can get to my seat," Jack said.

"Of course," she muttered, rising to her feet. And she'd better get her wits together while she was at it.

She stepped out into the aisle of the plane, her gaze locked on to his. He was even more impressive than she remembered. Her breath caught, and she felt a surge of heat travel through her until even her fingertips tingled. She pressed herself against the seat on the other side of the aisle to widen the gap between the man who had broken her heart and her afflicted senses.

Jack stowed his briefcase and brushed past her in the narrow confines of the airplane corridor. His suit coat dragged at the linen of her dress, and she breathed in his scent, a clean, warm smell overlaid with a whisper of cologne. She gripped her fingers into the worn fabric of the plane seat and forced herself to look away. Any view would be preferable to watching Jack slide past her just inches away.

She waited a beat, then risked a glance sideways.

Jack was seated. She could do this. She could blank him out for the next few hours the way she'd been blanking him out for the last decade. Schooling her features into a neutral expression, she sank once more into her seat, giving him a cool nod.

He raised an eyebrow and held out his hand. "It's been a long time," he said. His American accent reminded her of their differences.

"Has it?" She wanted very badly to ignore that outstretched hand, but pride had her reaching out to shake it. Why give him the satisfaction of learning how flustered she was?

His warm hand closed briefly around hers. Memories of those long fingers and how they felt against her skin crashed through her thoughts. Blanking him out for the last decade hadn't been enough; she should have tried harder. Hypnotism. Therapy. Exorcism. She was saved from having to indulge in further conversation by the arrival of an in-flight steward bearing a tray of drinks.

"We haven't seen you for a while, Mr. Diamond," said the steward.

Jack helped himself to a glass of water. "Work's been keeping me in the States lately, Graeme. How's life in the skies treating you?"

First-name basis with the cabin crew? Jack must be a regular on the flight to Honolulu. She had forgotten he had grown up there. Well, not so much *forgotten* as forced herself to forget. She helped herself to a glass of champagne and nodded her thanks to the steward. Jetlag, fatigue, lack of sleep... her travel was catching up with her, and she took a large sip to steady her jangling nerves. How on earth was she going to survive the next six hours?

If only he'd grown bald and smelly. Or was traveling with a plump wife and screaming toddler triplets in tow and had carrot puree mushed into the front of his suit. Her eyes shot a look over to his left hand before she could prevent them. No ring. Not that she cared. But still, there was no denying it, he was better looking now than the day she had last seen him, when he'd leapt into a taxi and taken off to Heathrow Airport and left her outraged and crying on the curb.

How gullible she had been. How utterly, stupidly foolish to think he had been any different from her parents, from the world. Charlotte closed her eyes against the sting of unshed tears. She would not let this man know how much she still hurt. Pride was all that had kept her going after Jack sauntered out of her life. Her pride and her career. She was damned if she would be losing that too, after all this time.

She could barely remember the girl she had been. An idealist, a dreamer, all enthusiasm and passion and no wisdom. How ironic: she, who'd vowed to forge a career from words and make her living investigating the deeper truths of an issue, had just crawled into a hole of misery when Jack left. She'd not hunted him down and forced him to return. She'd not beaten a path to his door and wedged herself there until he'd explained why a big-buck salary on the far side of the world was more important than her. She'd been too hurt.

Too young, she acknowledged.

She was not that young, foolish girl now. If she weren't feeling so vulnerable after the incident in Barwick, maybe this could have been an opportunity to question the ghosts of her past and finally let them rest. But she *was* vulnerable. This time, she had to put herself first, which meant the last thing she needed was to complicate her much-needed holiday. She would find out where he was headed so she could avoid any further accidental meetings.

Fueling her courage with the last inch of her champagne, she laid a hand on the arm of his chair.

STOWAWAY

CHAPTER ONE ... A SNEAK PEAK

*S*abrina read the words scrolling over the screen of her phone and felt no emotion. *Registration suspended ... compromised patient safety ... administrative tribunal.* Once, she would not have believed that she, Dr. Sabrina Gray, could be accused of incompetence, or have her skills questioned. But now? Here, a little after midnight, in a booze-and-reggae-fueled bar on the disco strip of an island in the Caribbean, she just didn't care. It had been so long since she'd cared about anything but the nightmares.

"Can we buy you a drink, princess?"

Two young men, hardly more than boys, leaned on her table, the rum on their breath even more offensive than their luridly flowered shirts.

"Get lost, boys."

She turned her head, gazed past them to the dance floor where her friend Antonia had disappeared. She wondered if Antonia would notice if she just slipped away. Bars, music, fun...nothing was fun anymore, not even on the sun-kissed holiday island of Ballena. Not for her.

The drunken youths swung into the empty chairs at her table, sure of their welcome. She shot a dark look in the direction of the bouncer, who was engrossed in chatting up a pretty little blonde thing at the doorway who didn't look old enough to gain entry to anything besides a school prom. He'd be no use, clearly. She gave the table a once-over. The warm dregs of cocktails swam under limp umbrellas and toothpicks of fruit. There was nothing here she needed. She snagged her friend's purse from over the back of the chair where Antonia had slung it with gay abandon almost an hour ago, and resigned herself to fighting her way through the throng of sweaty bodies on the dance floor.

Smoke billowed from the DJ pit, garishly lit by rows of colored lights. She leaned back as a scantily clad torso shimmied towards her, dodged a couple possessed by more energy than rhythm, then spotted her friend.

Thank heaven. Despite her tiredness, despite the fog of apathy that traveled everywhere with her these days, she smiled. Antonia was locked in the arms of the pilot she'd met on her first day here in Ballena. That girl could find a silver lining in a hurricane.

A crash sounded behind her, and she spun. A waitress swooped to the floor to gather up shards of broken glassware and Sabrina shuddered, hurriedly averting her eyes. Not tonight, she told herself, plunging deeper into the crowd. She was too fragile to think about sharp edges and soft skin tonight.

She focused on her friend's face instead. She and Antonia had both run away to the Caribbean. Antonia's love life had come unstuck, for about the third time in a year, and she'd decided the only thing that would soothe her bruised heart was a holiday of sunshine and palm trees.

Sabrina didn't expect anything could soothe her own heart, but she'd jumped at the chance to get away from London, from her mother, from the shattering dreams that woke her from sleep night after night.

Coming to Ballena wasn't a holiday for her, she knew that. She'd run away, absconded, escaped. What she hadn't thought through was what miserable company she would be for her fun-loving friend.

She slipped her way between the last few couples dancing between her and her quarry. Luckily Antonia had found something else to focus on other than Sabrina's misery, and nothing focused her friend's attention more than a strong pair of arms in a well-fitting uniform.

Sabrina had discovered she wasn't receptive to her friend's well-meaning attempts to help, because that would mean acknowledging what the problem was, and how could she possibly do that? She wanted to wallow. She *deserved* to wallow.

She flicked a glance at her watch. Midnight was long gone, and the couple of glasses of wine she had indulged in over dinner had combined with the dance music to cause a throb somewhere behind her left temple. She'd give Antonia her purse, then head back to the hotel.

The couple were so engrossed in each other's company, it took them a while to notice her.

"Ahem," she announced loudly in the vicinity of the one ear of her friend which didn't appear to be surgically attached to the pilot's chest.

Startled brown eyes flew open, and Sabrina raised her eyebrows at her friend. "I'm going," she said loudly over the breathy sounds of the current song. "Here's your purse."

"Wait."

Antonia shouted something unintelligible into the pilot's receptive ear before grabbing Sabrina's arm and dragging her over to the relative quiet of the ladies' restroom.

"Is he gorgeous or what?" Antonia said the second the door swung to behind them.

She looked indulgently into the glowing face of her friend and smiled. "Totally gorgeous."

Antonia gazed dreamily into the mirror while she dabbed at the eyeliner melting beneath her eyes, and Sabrina reached behind her friend to smooth a wild strand of her hair back into its high ponytail. She tried to inject a note of enthusiasm in her voice, to share in Antonia's happiness. "Now you've gone and mussed up your hair snuggling into all that buffness."

"So worth it," Antonia said with a grin.

"I hope you're right."

Antonia quirked an eyebrow at her in the mirror. "Well, that's the difference between you and me, Sabrina. I don't mind being wrong every now and then."

Sabrina looked away from Antonia and inspected her reflection critically in the mirror. Tired blue eyes stared back at her, fringed by a thick black ring of eyelashes. Masses of straight black hair fell to her waist, and even after an evening in the smoky, fetid air of the nightclub, her skin retained its pale hue. The Caribbean sun had done little but color her cheeks.

It was the eyes which haunted her. They'd seen

too much. "We both know just how wrong I can be," she said.

Antonia gripped her hand. "Oh, honey. I wasn't talking about your sister. I was just being frivolous about my dismal track record with men. I'm sorry."

Sabrina blinked and mentally cursed herself. Was she trying to spoil her friend's evening?"

"No. I'm the one who's sorry." She shook her head to clear the despondency which clung to her like a shadow. "I'm tired, I think. You know how it goes. Your defenses are always at their lowest when you're having girl-talk in a nightclub ladies' room at one in the morning."

Antonia grinned, pulled a lipstick out of her purse and applied a generous coat of dark plum. "Well, that's a given," she said.

Sabrina watched her friend in the mirror. Antonia had been her confidante since they were freckled first-graders at school. There was very little she couldn't share with her or her other friend Charlotte. She didn't have to hide how she was feeling. "Hadn't you better get back to your pilot friend before some other tourist whisks him off into the distance, leaving a trail of cocktail umbrellas for you to cry over?"

Antonia smiled complacently. "I don't think so. He and I have plans."

"Plans? What sort of plans? Why am I suddenly

feeling nervous?" she demanded, her eyes widening with mock alarm. Antonia was famous for making reckless decisions. She was as reckless and impulsive as Sabrina was dull and... well, whatever she was now. Hollow?

"Relax, Sabrina. We're just going on a little island-hopping adventure on his plane. A day trip. You don't mind, do you?" Antonia's expression grew anxious. "I know we had planned to have this holiday together, but...this guy is special."

She shook her head. "Of course I don't mind. In fact, you should take a few days, see a bit of the islands." She threw an arm around her friend's shoulder in a quick hug. "You two go and enjoy. I've been thinking I might do that diving course we were looking at. It might take my mind off, well. You know."

Antonia gave her arm a squeeze. "I do know. Let's go find Tyler, and we can walk you back to the hotel."

"I think I can manage a hundred feet on my own."

Antonia flashed her a smile. "Okay, then. I'll see you in a couple of days," she said, smacking a boisterous kiss onto Sabrina's cheek before plunging back through the door to throw herself into her pilot's arms.

Sabrina followed at a more sedate pace, using a tissue to wipe the kiss print from her cheek. She couldn't understand her friend's headlong impulses when it came to the opposite sex. She liked male company, sure. She had male friends, colleagues, but she had yet to meet a man who she felt any great stirring of emotion for.

She shrugged her shoulders. It was probably just her. Perhaps she wasn't capable of passion as intense as Antonia obviously was. And maybe it was for the best. She'd made a mess of her relationship with her sister, a fatal mess. She had no business imagining she could make a success of a relationship with a man.

She pushed her way through the double doors to the esplanade. It was warm outside, despite the lateness of the hour, and the air was sharp with salt from the harbor.

A street cleaning machine was bumping and whirring from curb to gutter, a strobe light on its roof sending a whirlpool of reflection across the glass fronts of cafés and souvenir shops lining the esplanade.

Her breath seized, and she felt the tears rising as she remembered that other night, those other strobe lights flickering, flickering ...

Not here, damn it. A sob caught in her chest, and she broke into a run. When would it end? When would she stop reliving that god-awful night?

Time hadn't helped; months had passed, and she

was getting worse, not better. Running away to the other side of the world hadn't helped; the nightmares had packed their heavy baggage and caught a ride on the plane right beside her.

Running to the hotel room in heels along a poorly lit footpath probably wouldn't help either, but at least she'd escape the ghastly flicker of those lights.

She rounded the corner into the bougainvillea-swathed laneway that marked the entrance to the Jewel of Ballena Marina Resort, and a heartbeat later felt her breath being knocked out of her diaphragm. Her body had smacked into a warm, lean, tall someone who was standing in the shadows of the lane.

Read the rest of Stowaway ...

STELLA QUINN'S BOOKS
ROMANCE | ADVENTURE | ESCAPE

What readers have said

"X-factor nailed it. You can start bidding wars with this."

"I want to buy the trilogy – actually, I want you as my new best friend."

"Wonderful voice and loved your humor."

"Really enjoyed these characters."

The Island Escape Series
- can be read in any order -

Romance and drama on sun-dazzled beaches - the heroines are fun and the heroes are heart-throbs, why not escape with them on your own vacation romance?

Prequel novella: And I Always Will (Charlotte & Jack)

Book 1: Tropic Storm (Charlotte & Jack)
Book 2: Stowaway (Sabrina & Ben)
Book 3: Island Fling (Antonia & Tyler)
Christmas novella: Catching Snow (Lisa & Ryan)

The Clementine Springs Series

Small town romance set in Upstate New York - horses and steamboats, country music stars and lakes, why not head escape the crisp mountain air and discover love again?

Spring novella: The Umbrella Diaries (Marianne & Duncan)
Christmas novella: All I Want (Prudence & Adam)
Book 1: *Summer Loving* (Leila & Damon)

Other Books

Keeping Katie: A Gold Coast Retrievers story (Sweet Promise Press)

Australian Rural Romance

The Vet from Snowy River (Harlequin MIRA)
Heartwarming small-town romance

A New Ending (a novella set in Western Qld - FREE for subscribers)

Finding Home (a short story set in the Flinders Ranges)
The Cockatoo Track (a short story set in the Northern Territory)
Looking Back (a short story set in Qld)

To chat, and hear about new releases and library visits, and all things Stella, why not join my reader team! www.stellaquinnauthor.com/subscribe

For books without links here, head on over to my webpage for up-to-date information: www.stellaquinnauthor.com